A Follow Your Heart Novel

Sunsets
&
Dandelion
Kisses

Linda Phillips

I just want to thank God for imagination, and the boatload of it He gave to me. If He can use a donkey to speak, He can use me to write imaginative stories. Thanks, Lord.

Chapter One

F ollow your heart, even if love takes you to the stars in the heavens or down into the depths of the sea. Reach beyond the stars...

Galaxas' head rested in her hands as she stared at the stars, mesmerized, wondering if eyes in the sky are watching the people on Earth. Questions knocked at her mind's door: Are the eyes good or evil? Or both? What is it about the stars? Could that be where love lies? Every night as she stared at the stars, it felt as if the twinkle of the stars wove into tingly strings that swirled right through her heart. And every night, she wrapped her arms around her body and twitched in sync with the stars twinkling in the sky. When reality sunk in, the thought of anyone on Earth ever being interested in her was nothing but hopes scattered in the wind.

～

A pile of DVD cases lay on the floor. A cracking sound filled the air as trembling fingers broke the discs in pieces. Galaxas bit down on her bottom lip as she destroyed her collection of fairy tales, sniffling and wiping the tears before breaking apart the next disc. She stared at the artwork of *Sleeping Beauty* and *Cinderella* before smashing the discs into shards of disappointment. Lips quivering, she spoke out loud in shattered words. "Fairy tales aren't real. Why waste my time imagining a life of love and happiness? Take what you get, and that means settling for a jerk or being lonely. Forever.

"But Sleeping Beauty and Cinderella's life was miserable for a while and look how wonderful everything worked out in the end. Maybe I shouldn't have destroyed the DVDs," she reasoned to herself and threw her hands up. "What does it matter anyway?"

Her nose twitched. "What is that smell? The brownies. Oh no. They're burnt. Just a harbinger of my pathetic life." She jumped up and pulled them out of the stove. The clanging of the pan in the sink resonated throughout her house. She threw a coat on and stomped outside.

A blanket of black silk covered the sky. Did God shake a bottle of glitter over the galaxies? The endless sparkles took Galaxas' breath away. "I wish for you, you, you and you," she said pointing to each star, while repeating the child's rhyme, 'Star Light, Star Bright.' "Hello up there stars. I'm really lonely. Any chance you have someone up there just for me? You know why I ask, don't you? Because I belong up there. I don't belong here."

Her head dropped, timbre low. "Will I ever find someone to love and someone to love me?" She put on a brave demeanor in front of her parents and best friend, but truly she was lonely. What was her choice? Live in seclusion or be ridiculed because of her condition? Wet spots on her coat weren't from raindrops.

But loneliness passed quickly. Fall was in the air. How could she not notice? Her favorite time of the year. The array of colorful leaves crunched under her feet. The air was full of pleasant scents of the fall season. She stared and sniffed at the plethora of colorful leaves covering the ground, exhaling all types of gases from stomata. Pinene, a species of terpene, and a pine scent spread. A noticeable musty smell was present from high-bush cranberry mixed with other natural scents.

Galaxas loved how the Alaska sky in the fall season had a deeper blue color and was always covered with migrating birds flying in a "V" shape. The constant sound of honking followed the "V" formation. She smiled while tilting her head upwards with a hand to block the sun over her three-inch protective sunglasses. The Aurora Borealis would appear very soon with colors that took her breath away. Snowcapped mountains always in her view. A mischievous, chilly breeze of winter burst by, teasing Galaxas. "I'm coming, too. Get ready." The wind gust blew her hair straight out.

It was her routine every evening: A hot cup of cocoa with gobs of whipped cream, a comfy, warm coat and peace and quiet sitting on the porch swing while gazing at the stars. Although, what she wouldn't give for some noisy city sounds. Cars honking, people laughing and carrying on conversations hopping from store to store. Nope. A life of seclusion was what she had to look forward to, and, for the rest of her life.

There was no need to turn the porch light on. She could see fine without it. For reasons she couldn't identify, her body would prickle with fluttery sensations as she stared at the stars.

The porch swing squeaked as it gently swung back and forth. It came to a fast halt. She pushed her head forward, tilted it up and stared in astonishment. One of the stars looked like it was sending a message. It looked like an SOS message trying to get her attention. How was she unaware that the area around her heart had a slight glow? She had no idea about that.

She fell back against the swing, staring into space, mouth dropping inch by inch. *It literally looks as though it is sending a message, and what's even weirder, I feel like it's trying to get my attention.* Being all alone, she usually spoke out loud to herself in an unfulfilling attempt to cover up the loneliness.

She let out a gasp. Lights flickering from the star started forming into something that looked like a flashlight beam shining directly towards her, getting closer and closer. Her heart began to pound and accelerate. Was she imagining it or what? She jumped off the porch swing and backed up towards the front door, listening to the irritating squeak, until the swing came to a stop. The light was now shining on the ground in her front yard heading for the porch. She looked up at the sky. It was still coming from that one star. Hand over her heart, trying to get her frozen feet to move, she finally made it inside and locked the door. Her body leaned against the door while taking rapid breaths. The light shined in underneath the door. Her eyes widened, and in that moment she couldn't breathe.

In the twinkling of an eye, it disappeared. She ran to a window, tilted her head up to look into space. The stars all twinkled normally and not one of them stuck out like the one that shined down.

"Am I losing my mind being out in a wilderness all by myself? Maybe being a recluse is affecting me mentally."

She plopped on the couch. Emotionally exhausted, her body slid down, and her head landed on the pillow. Eyes shut and she was out fast.

Chapter Two

The next day around eleven, waking up in a fog from a long sleep, Galaxas got up from the couch and walked towards the kitchen. She hadn't had a vision in a while, and one just popped up. In the past, when a vision came to her, she couldn't move or speak. This vision was the most intense she had ever experienced.

Galaxas stood frozen in the doorway between the kitchen and living room. In the vision she was being chased by a man, but his face was a blur. He called her a freak, and what scared her the most was his eyes of hate. Real hate. But another figure stood far away on another planet. He whispered and gave her instructions on how to escape.

The vision ended. She shook her head and released deep breaths in and out for a moment, shaky hands grabbing the wall. Starting from her toes, she could feel the prickly bumps develop all the way to her head. She shimmied. There hasn't been a whole lot of visions, just two, but what was concerning is that they both came true.

"Is someone trying to kill me? Why? What have I ever done? I never even see people. Maybe a serial killer trying to escape authorities found his way to my home in the middle of nowhere. When you're losing your mind, you grasp at anything," she reasoned to herself. She plopped on the couch and replayed the vision in her mind, and then laid her head back to help clear her thoughts.

After hours of the same ol' same ol', she worked the rest of the evening on her book as a children's illustrator.

Dark skies set in early in Alaska. Galaxas made a cup of coffee. Zipping up the warm coat, she walked outside carrying the warmth in her hands. The old, squeaky porch swing grinded back and forth, a comforting sound while sipping coffee. When she breathed, it appeared as a misty cloud in the cold air.

Wondering about the vision, she got up and walked around her house. Her eyes could see better and clearer in dark than in the daylight, as though it were a bright, sunshiny day. Some of the boards were dilapidated and an ugly discoloration kept yelling at her to paint the house. But could she afford it? Who would even want to drive this far out for a job?

"Mother and Dad. They'll help. I wonder if it is too late in the season, though," speaking out loud in thought.

Branches snapped on the forest floor behind her. She jumped. It wasn't unusual at all for a moose, grizzly bear or any number of animals to be walking about. But that vision kept flashing back in her mind. *What if the killer is out there? And who was the figure from that planet?*

The cup fell from her hands onto the hard ground. It shattered. The clinking sound of the cup scared her more than the snapping of branches. She ran to the house. Her mom and dad fixed it so that she could lay a thick board across the doorway so that no person or no animal could break in, since she lived in a wilderness environment by herself. She had been called a freak one too many times, and being around people wasn't worth the heartache anymore, so seclusion was her only option.

With sounds of feet shuffling and fast tapping on the floor, she ran door to door and threw a block of wood across for protection.

She dug through the closet, clinking and clanking as she scavenged through her things. She continued searching until she found a gun. Not long ago, a pack of wolves stalked her. She could hear them growl and scratch at the door. They hung around for a couple of days, imprisoning her in her own house. She needed protection. Then her parents drove out and placed bars across all the windows.

Once in a while her boyfriend, Clayton, made it out to her place, but lately he's been a real jerk. Even more than normal. Besides talking with her parents and Clayton, her best friend, Annalee, called a lot and even spent weekends with her. But truthfully, she was lonely and very alone in the wilderness. No one would ever hear her scream.

Galaxas ran to every window and peeked through them. No one. No animal. Feeling relieved, she went to the computer and worked on her own first children's book. Illustrations lay on the desk, done by her at the first thought of writing the fairy tale.

An email notification appeared on the screen. One of the authors wanted to know how she was doing in creating illustrations for her book, mentioning how Galaxas is the most gifted illustrator with whom she had ever worked.

"Good save, Donna." Galaxas giggled at herself. More and more each day she was turning down clients. It was hard enough to find the time to illustrate the workload she already had, not to mention trying to find the time to work on her own book.

Reception in the wilderness was hit or miss. Today was a miss. She hoped an emergency didn't develop. Could she depend on the car starting? Probably not.

Galaxas Anatola Cyrus Gaylord lived on the south coast of Alaska. The cloudiest region of the United States. It is reported to have more cloudy days a year than any other state. The main reason for moving here in the first place. She could relate to vampires needing this degree of cloud coverage, not that she believed they were real, but hey, who knows.

In the beginning of high school, her mother, Nebulane, bought the house because of the hardship Galaxas endured in school. From then on, homeschooling would suffice. She abandoned her own career to homeschool her daughter.

They both had a freakish skin condition and eye disease.

Their skin had a light green/gray tone, and their hair was light green with light gray highlights. Eyes looked like sunrays.

They could get away with the hair color, because nowadays, who doesn't have unnatural hair colors, but the skin tone was never accepted. Thankfully, they could hide it in layers of clothing due to the cold climate. Contact lenses were customized for their eyes, but difficult for Galaxas to endure.

The bright sunlight was blinding to their eyesight. It was physically painful. And even more painful was the ridicule Galaxas got from the other students. After graduating from high school, still homeschooled by her mother, she took online courses and earned a prestigious degree in illustrating. Not wanting to endure ridicule ever again, her mother and father gave her the house close to Seward so that they could move closer to their work.

Her mother was known as a gifted homecare worker. The patients were never alarmed by the skin tone. They had their own problems to deal with and Nebulane was magical in treating their conditions.

Somehow Galaxas' phone rang. She eyed the display. Her mouth puckered and her shoulders slumped. "Should I answer?" She did.

"Hello," she said, disinterest in her voice.

"Hey. I've been trying to call you for days. Are you avoiding me?" Clayton asked in an angry tone.

"You do know I have bad reception out here. If I'm trying to avoid your calls, why would I answer now?"

"Good question. Why would you take the risk of losing the only man in this world who has shown you any interest? Have you looked in the mirror?"

Her lethargic skin tone wanted to turn red. "My name is Galaxas, after all. Maybe the man of my dreams is out there in one of the galaxies, jerk face."

"What did you call me, freak?"

"You know what, I don't need a jerk like you for a boyfriend. Get lost!" She clicked the power button off and threw the phone on the couch, resting on the sofa cushions. He belittled her to the point of being verbally abusive one too many times. How long would it take for him to become physically abusive? She already knew the answer to that question.

Clayton was seething with anger. Spit flicked out of his mouth with each exhale. He gritted his teeth together and fists tightened to the point of losing circulation. When he tried opening them, it was at a slow pace, feeling like arthritis in its final stages.

"She's not dumping me! Is she really that stupid? She should show gratitude that I even agreed to be her boyfriend. Freak! Laughingstock. Oh no. You did not just dump me. No freak dumps me and gets away with it."

Chapter Three

The blushing sky faded away as the sun rose. Galaxas loved all colors the sky painted in Alaska. Working diligently on her illustrations, the phone chimed, alerting her to a new text. She looked warily at it. Hesitantly she opened the text and read:

CLAYTON:

> I'm sorry for how I spoke to you. Would you at least gather my things and bring them to me at Kenai Fjords Park around 1:30 today?

Her mouth rolled. She sat still and thought about it. "Man, I don't want to deal with him. The jerk's ego could never accept being dumped. Especially, by a freak. What should I do? What should I do?"

The phone chimed again.

CLAYTON:

> Please.

GALAXAS:

> Okay.

CLAYTON:

Great.

Either he comes out to get his stuff or she meets him. That seemed to be the lesser of two evils.

Galaxas gathered all his thrill seeker equipment, clothing, and whatnot and piled it in her older SUV, one that had a good 4WD high range system providing better traction. With the rugged terrain of Alaska, she needed it. Her vehicle spat stones and rocks every which way on the dirt road. It would take an hour or more, but soon enough she arrived at Kenai Fjords National Park.

A text popped up.

CLAYTON:

Meet me at our spot.

GALAXAS:

How do you expect me to carry all your stuff?

CLAYTON:

I'll walk back with you. I have a surprise for you.

Like what? Another black eye. Swollen face?

During the drive, she had admitted to herself that maybe he was right. No other guy on this planet would give her the time of day, so what choice did she have? Hope things get better or be alone the rest of her life? What a choice.

Her parents knew nothing about the abuse, not to mention the never-ending verbal abuse.

The air was crisp and clean. It seemed sinful to partake in such a God-given gift Alaska provided. Those thoughts distracted the tension she was feeling. She arrived at their secret spot. No people ever came to this spot that they knew of. Without any reason whatsoever, goosebumps prickled over her skin, and she subconsciously grasped her arms. She turned her head slowly around and scanned the area.

A thump caused her heart to palpitate. A squirrel jumped onto another tree. Her hand pressed forcefully against her heart. She stepped backwards. Eyes of concern stared at the creepy monster tree. Sunrays burst through holes in the dead tree giving it a wicked vibe with evil eyes and pointed teeth. Its frail arm and finger branches shifted in the breeze.

Thoughts came to her mind with questions. *Could he ever kill me? He's abused me in the past but always brought me flowers and gifts regretting his actions. But...this is the first time I actually dumped him.*

The vision popped in her mind. "Could he be the murderer in my vision?" She swallowed hard. A chill ran through her body. She twitched. "Why didn't I see it before?" she whispered to herself.

An eerie silence developed. The birds quit chirping, drumming or making trill sounds, and the buzzing and trills of insects were quieted at an alarming rate.

Trembling, eyes wide as a golf ball, she started to turn and run.

Her loud gasp caused birds to fly out of trees nearby.

He walked out of the trees in front of her. Her heartbeat pounded out of control.

"Were you going to leave?" His voice was concerning. Her eyes kept widening. Goosebumps kept traveling at a fast pace over her body. It was cold, but she was shaking from fear. Crossing her arms and pressing them into her body didn't stop the shaking. Extra-wide eyes watched him. He chuckled as he looked in her eyes.

"I um...I thought maybe I missed you walking towards my car."

"Did you now?"

She nodded her head.

Her breaths were fast now. Shoulders rising up and down. "Are you ready to walk back?" Her words were almost a stutter.

He smiled, but it was a freaky smile, and his amused eyes slanted. Then his sinister smile faded as he walked up close to her.

She couldn't control the trembling. Thump, thump-thump-

thump. Her heart pounded out a tune just like in a horror film before the climax of a murder. He tilted his head and made a disturbing expression. With a quickness, grasp! His hand went to her neck.

"Nobody breaks up with me, freak! Especially a freak!"

Both hands were around her neck now, squeezing, tightening. She grabbed his hands, but he was too strong. It was the evil smile that she couldn't quit looking at.

Oddly, the vision with the figure on a planet came to her thoughts. A smidgen of courage developed. With force and a quickness, her knee pushed into his groin area. He screeched in pain, and his hands automatically let go of her neck as he slumped over, eyes rolling.

Gasping for air, trying to cough, she ran, heart pounding out of her chest, eyes so wide they ached in pain, and bright red hand marks around her neck. She rubbed the area on her neck as she ran. It was a miracle she escaped. Her strength was weak compared to his strength. How she managed to escape the strangulation was baffling to her, because she remembered how scared she was to think straight at the moment.

Coughing and gasping for air accompanied every step she took.

The terrain was so rocky and dangerous in this area. Close by were extremely dangerous cliffs. One slip would be fatal. *He was going to strangle me and throw me over the cliff, I know it*. Tears buried her face.

There was a time she felt love for him. Maybe because he was the only man to give her the time of day, good or bad. There wasn't anyone else to choose. The past few months that love grew to complete disgust. *What a stupid person I am knowing of his abusive nature and agreeing to meet him out here where no one in the world would ever find my body*.

Heart pounding so loudly, she couldn't hear anything else. *Keep running! Keep running! Keep running!* She screamed inside her head. *Don't look back. Just keep running*.

Her running was slowed as she maneuvered around fallen rocks and boulders. She contemplated if she should take the time and look back to see where he was, even though her subconscious said to keep running. Giving in to the temptation, her head turned in his direction, and that is when she saw the look in his eyes. Cold. Evil. Murderous intention filled every crevice of his face. It gave her chills.

She never could outrun him, even when he gave her a head start. *He's going to kill me. I can't outrun him. Maybe I should just stop running and get it over with.* Her lungs burned, and eyes squinting, she needed to stop and catch her breath, but if she does, he'll catch her. *Don't stop,* whispered in her mind.

Too late. She tripped on a rock and down to the ground she fell. She rubbed the burning scrapes on her knees. That is when the customized contacts fell out of her eyes. She tried covering her eyes with her hands, but the light was blinding. She couldn't see anything, and it was quite painful. They automatically scrunched close. This was it and she knew it. Arms behind her, she pushed her body upwards, and the pain caused her head to lower. She closed her eyes for just a second more.

He was becoming physically abusive more and more, always verbally abusive, and yet she always forgave him. But what choice did she have? She was a freak, after all. He belittled her so much that he gave the impression she should be thankful for any attention he provided. Good or bad. Usually bad.

Just thinking about it while waiting for her life to end, she became enraged, face feeling the heat. Anger, repulse and hate consumed her thoughts. *You're not a freak. Don't listen to him.*

"I am not a freak!" she blurted. She puckered her mouth in anger and opened her eyes in his direction. She could hear the loud thump of his feet running close by. He let out a boisterous laugh.

Feeling such hate for him at that moment, intense thoughts took over her mind. *I wish you were dead, disintegrated, embers floating out to space.*

How it happened, she couldn't explain if she tried. Both eyes turned into something that resembled little suns. A bright, scorching light shot out of them and the smell of burning flesh filled her nostrils. She heard screams, popping and crackling, the sound of something disintegrating by fire. Storm clouds rolled in and darkened the sky. She could see now, but opened her eyes slowly, not wanting to see whatever that smell was.

When she finally got the nerve to open her eyes, she saw the look of terror in his face as his body disintegrated into embers that scattered through the air. His face was the last part of his body to dissolve. The only thing left of Clayton was his shoes sitting on the ground where he stood before he had the opportunity to choke the life out of her. Patting her heart she wondered aloud. "Did I do that? Could my thoughts make him disappear, disintegrate him into lifeless particles?"

Winds picked up and the embers of what was once his body blew in every direction. Hands quickly covered her opened mouth. He was gone without a trace.

"Maybe I am a freak? How did I—did my hate for him turn me into a monster just like him? A real freak! I can't even kill a bug, nonetheless a person."

Her knees lowered to the ground, and deep sadness filled her face. Tears were unstoppable. She wanted to die herself at that moment. In physical pain, she limped over to the cliff and stared for minutes. What did she have to live for? She's all alone; a freak; and now a murderer.

Caught off guard, a spacecraft invisible to the naked eye, but not to her eyes, flew past her going faster than the speed of light. The speed of light travels through air and space at a much faster pace than sound, about 273,400 miles per hour.

How is it she didn't know that she had any type of a super-power? Why did it materialize just now?

Shaken from her thoughts, she mouthed, "Think! Think! Think!"

With everything that happened, her body became dizzy, and she was unstable, trying to balance herself, not just from the unstable terrain, but from the shock that engulfed her body. Her head was spinning. The wind picked up and particles of Clayton's disintegrated body flew around her face. Horrified, she screamed. Hands trembling out of control and her eyes squeezed shut, she began smacking her head.

It was just too much. After running a hand through her hair she yelled, "Mom! Help me! Please help me!"

Nothing but an emotional, mental and physical mess, she slurred her words. "I need to see my mother." She took off running, anything to avoid thinking, but the pain caused her to limp as fast as she could possibly manage; more pain as her feet twisted in the rocks while she ran through Clayton's embers still floating around the area.

"Stop it! Stop it, stop it," she yelled out loud grasping her hair in tight, pulling clutches.

Almost calmly, she whispered out loud. "He knew I meant it when I broke up with him. His ego could never accept that. He planned to murder me. My thoughts were self-defense."

She was always self-conscious about her conditions and how people stared in disbelief. Her life flashed before her.

"I don't belong in this world, and I'll never fit in. I'm not meant to be here. Maybe that star or planet was trying to tell me that."

She tried to look up at the sky, but it hurt her eyes way too much. Looking at the stars at night was therapeutic and magical for her. She felt like she was one with the galaxy. Couldn't explain why, but that thought always hit her.

That night sitting on her porch swing gazing at the stars, she spoke to the Lord. Who else could she speak to? Everyone would think she had gone mad. Heck, she even wondered about that.

"Hello Lord. You know I will never fit in here, and you know I never meant for Clayton to actually die, and I didn't even know I had such power to think it. Tell me the truth. I must have dropped from the stars. If only I could be up there with them."

Staring in shock, her eyes followed that same invisible-to-the-human-eye space craft shooting past her cabin.

Her hands clasped onto her head; thoughts spun like she was losing her mind. She popped her head up and sat still. Listening. In the near distance she could hear a hovering sound, and something that mimicked hydraulics. The THUMP of it landing on the ground was easy to identify.

She ran into the house, grabbed the car keys, and with

shaking fingers tried to unlock the SUV. Finally, she was seated in the vehicle.

Her fingers wouldn't stop trembling, and by trying to put the key into the ignition, it kept dropping on the floor. Her eyes grew wide, mouth opening wider and wider, then she forced deep breaths. It wouldn't start. Her forehead kept bumping the steering wheel as she rocked her body back and forth.

"Start you stupid car. I mean it. Drive me to my mom's house. Now!"

She glanced in the direction of the spacecraft and saw a figure standing in front of the forest clearing. She gulped.

The shock was so overwhelming, her head bent down, and eyes closed as if they were glued together. When she tilted her head back up, she was sitting in the car in her mother's driveway.

Chapter Four

Nebulane heard a car motor in the driveway. She jumped off of the couch and looked through the window. Galaxas' forehead was lying on the steering wheel. She just sat there without moving.

Walking up to the car, Nebulane pounded on the window. Galaxas looked up. Her eyes were staring blankly at her like she could see right through her. Her mom pounded on the window again. That snapped her to her senses.

Galaxas stepped out slowly and stood up. Her mom embraced her. "Hello, my dear. I didn't know you were visiting today, or rather, tonight. What a nice surprise."

But Galaxas felt stiff in her arms, immobile. Nebulane backed up and looked down at her eyes. Galaxas just stood staring at her own hands. Her mom gently shook her shoulders.

"Is something wrong?"

Galaxas blew out a sigh. "I don't know. I mean, yes, but I'm not sure. Have you ever had hallucinations without doing drugs?"

"Can't say I have. Come on, let's go in the house and talk."

One arm around her daughter, she urged her feet forward. She escorted her to the couch and closed the door, staring at Galaxas' face.

"Coffee, tea, hot chocolate or what?" Nebulane asked walking backwards towards the kitchen.

With a hand wave, Galaxas replied, "Anything. I don't care."

Nebulane strolled back into the living room carrying a tray with coffee cups. The aroma was intoxicating, even causing Galaxas to sniff the steam rising from the cup.

"You know what's funny, Mom?"

"What's that, Gal?"

"No matter how stressed out or how scared, or even how happy a person is, the smell of coffee seems to make everything feel better."

After patting Galaxas' knee, Nebulane asked, "Would you like to talk about it?"

"I can't make up my mind. You're going to think I'm weird or something. Where's Dad?"

"He's watching sports at Celeste and Kevin's house. Since it's so far away, he's spending the night. I have an early appointment in the morning.

"Gal, you know I would never make assumptions about you like that. So, don't be shy. Just speak your mind."

"Could I stay here tonight, Mom?"

"Of course. I was actually going to visit you today but by the time your father left, it was too late. Men can be needy." Nebulane ended her statement with a huff.

"That's Dad all right, but I wouldn't change one thing about him."

"Nor would I," Nebulane agreed thinking of him with a smile. She gave Galaxas' knee a firm pat. "Now, what's going on?"

Galaxas twiddled her fingers, jumped up from the couch and paced, then she sat back down and twiddled some more. Nebulane could see how hard it was for her to explain, so she remained silent.

Sipping the steaming coffee, Galaxas planned out the words that will probably diagnose her mentally unstable. "Something happened today, Mom. Something really bad."

"Whatever it is, I am here for you, and I will always be here for you. I know my daughter. I love your huge imagination, your kind and gentle heart, and how bold and courageous you can be.

You're as perfect as a person could be. NOTHING, nothing you say will change that."

"Okay, Mom, keep those words in your mind. Here goes. I killed Clayton."

Nebulane choked on her saliva, patting her chest to stop choking. Galaxas leaned back on the couch, crossed her arms, and produced an expression that said "see."

"I'm sorry. That did take me by surprise. Please, continue, please."

"Mom, it's going to take more than a few minutes. It kind of starts at least, if not more, from a year ago."

"We have all night. I'll order pizza so we don't have to cook. Been a long time since you had one, I'd bet," she said forming a cheery smile at Galaxas.

Even being so distressed, Galaxas' mouth watered. "You are so right, Mom. Let's order it."

Pizza ordered, Galaxas hesitantly got to the long explanation. "I know you never liked Clayton, and you were right not to. He verbally and physically abused me for so long." Nebulane choked out a gasp. "Being a freak," Galaxas said straight forward holding her hands up to stop her mother from speaking, "I felt I would never get another chance to be with any guy. He told me that much many times and then many more times. At the beginning, I felt I was in love with him, but now that I think about it, it was probably because he was the only guy who would ever show me any attention.

"Who wouldn't jump at a relationship knowing that? Anyway, we both know people stare at me like I'm a freak, so don't try denying that, Mom."

"All I want to do is listen, Gal, and help any way I can. People are cruel, but there are more kind people in the world than not. Kids and teenagers, well, you've seen the movie *Mean Girls*."

"So...if we go shopping, people won't act like I'm an alien from outer space?" Galaxas asked.

Nebulane had to chuckle, for many reasons that Galaxas wasn't privy to. "There will always be jerks somewhere, but we should give it a go. I have an idea. How about you come to work with me? I never have to hide myself, except my eyes, and that's just so I can see."

"I'll give it some thought, Mom. It would be refreshing to think I could step out of hiding."

"Good." She patted Galaxas' knee again. "Now, what's this all about? A murder?"

"I, um...I, um..."

The doorbell caused them both to jump. "Let me get the pizza. You get paper plates, napkins, and some soda," Nebulane said as she rose from the couch.

They headed in opposite directions. Nebulane forgot to put on a wig, and her facial skin tones were not easy to hide, but she grabbed the money and opened the door. The pizza deliverer stared at her, not scared, but unsure.

"Oh." Realizing he was staring at her, she thought up something fast to say. "We were having a dress rehearsal for a play. That's all." She handed him the money, including a generous tip and whisked the pizza away from his staring eyes. After closing the door, he just stood there for a minute before leaving.

Chapter Five

Nebulane was giggling when Galaxas strolled back into the living room with everything they needed to eat pizza.

"What are you laughing about, Mom?"

"The way that pizza delivery guy stared at me. To be truthful, people still look at me like they're trying to figure out if they will contract some type of disease from me or if I'm just really cool," Nebulane remarked and then snickered. Galaxas snickered likewise.

"Maybe I never asked you before, but how did you come up with the name 'Galaxas'? It's not common in any shape or form."

"One thing at a time. Now, stop trying to avoid talking about it. Just tell me what's going on," her mom said avoiding answering her question regarding her name.

"He was pretty mean to me over the phone. Believe it or not, I had had enough and told him I didn't need him for a boyfriend and called him a jerk. He texted me later and said he was sorry. Would I just meet him at Fjords Park with all his stuff? I weighed the option of him coming to my house or meeting him. Of course, I felt it would be easier to get rid of him if I met up with him.

"Wait. I forgot one important part. I had a vision of a man

chasing me with intentions to murder me, but his face was a blur in the vision."

"Ahhh now I'm scared. I know about your other visions and my mind is already pushing 'forward' past that part," Nebulane confessed.

"I know Mom, but I'm not murdered, obviously, so let me continue. When I walked to our secret spot out in the middle of nowhere, meaning no people are ever out there, fear consumed me, and the vision popped back in my mind. It hit me hard that Clayton is the murderer in my vision, but it was a little too late when I figured it out.

"My feet took off without coaxing, but he jumped out in front of me. Mom, his face was so deranged, almost like he was looking forward to murdering me. Like it was satisfying. Fun. Eating a hot fudge sundae and how fulfilling it is to eat. That deranged.

"He walked up and grabbed my neck and squeezed, but I pushed my knee up into his groin. He fell over in pain. He kept calling me a freak and reminding me how he would be the only guy ever interested in me."

Nebulane bent down to look at her neck. She gasped. Her eyes watered. "You poor, poor darling."

Subconsciously, they both rubbed their neck area back and forth. Galaxas started to explain further what had happened, but she stopped and waited because Nebulane had snapped a picture of her neck with her cellphone. Galaxas assumed in her mind it was in case they needed proof one day.

"I took off running and soon enough tripped. That was it and I knew it. I kept hearing his voice calling me a freak. It made me furious. By the time he got to me, I had pushed myself up and yelled that I am not a freak. When I fell, I lost my contacts and couldn't see well.

"This is the weird part. In my mind, I wished he would disappear, incinerate and float into space. Then I smelled a horrible smell and heard a sizzling sound. The clouds rolled in, and I could see. The last thing I saw was his terrified face disintegrate right before my eyes. I killed him with my thoughts. How? Why? What?"

Nebulane dropped her head in her hands. She sobbed, deep, gut-wrenching sobs.

Galaxas looked at her mother horrified. "Mom. I didn't mean to. I didn't even know I could think him dead. How can this even be possible?" Her body trembled, and she pressed a hand on her stomach. Then she ran to the bathroom.

With everything going on, the slam of the bathroom door caused Nebulane to jump. She could hear her poor daughter. Pushing herself back against the couch, she wiped her eyes.

"How do I tell her?" Nebulane mumbled to herself.

The bathroom door squeaked open. Galaxas walked out still holding a hand over her stomach. Her mouth was wide and turning down.

"Come here and sit down by me," Nebulane insisted. She stroked her hair, and they sat in silence. Neither of them touched the pizza.

"Do you think I'm nuts, Mom?"

"Nope. Not even a little."

Galaxas pushed herself up and turned to look into her mother's saddened eyes. "Are you saying that you believe me?"

"Yes. I believe you."

"How could you? I don't even believe me."

Nebulane blew out a mild trail of breath. "I really believe you. I know my daughter. There has never been a time that I didn't believe you."

"Okay. This is not how I envisioned this conversation to turn out. I'm a murderer, Mom."

She grabbed both of Galaxas' upper arms. "No! You're not a murderer. It was self-defense, and don't you dare talk about yourself like that ever again. Do you understand me?"

"Yes, but I'm still not convinced."

"Did you physically touch him?" Nebulane asked.

"No!"

"Did you know you could think him dead?" Nebulane shook

her head after asking that question, because living a quiet life on Earth it sounded so ridiculous.

"No! Of course not," Galaxas answered fast.

"Well, jury. This is a case of self-defense. This young woman was going to be murdered. She had no idea that a thought could cause his death. Have you reached a verdict Mr. foreperson? Yes, Your Honor. Not guilty." She stared at Galaxas pointedly.

"If I wasn't your daughter, would you still believe that?"

"One hundred percent. You're innocent and you need to believe that for yourself."

"I guess you're right, Mom."

"If you had a gun knowing he was going to murder you, would you have shot him in self-defense?"

Galaxas pondered her question. "I want to say yes, but how could I know that for sure?"

"Nobody could and no one would blame you. Not even a little."

"Well, maybe if they heard the rest of my story they would rethink it," Galaxas said, squishing her head into her shoulders staring at her mother's expression.

"What do you mean? What are you talking about?" Did Nebulane even want to hear the rest of it? She was blowing air out as if she were trying to prevent hyperventilating. "Give me a second to use the bathroom. Why don't you grab a cookie or something and then we'll continue."

Chapter Six

They both returned to the couch and sat down. Both taking deep breaths. Nebulane looked over at Galaxas. "Okay. Please continue."

"Ah, geesh, Mom. This is hard to admit."

"You mean harder than thinking you wished he was dead and it coming true? Harder than that?"

"I saw something, and it terrified me," Galaxas confessed.

"Go ahead, please. You don't need to feel worried about what I may think. I believed you about the murder. To most people, they would think you had a nervous breakdown, but I don't. I believe you. Please, just finish telling me."

"A spacecraft passed by me going so fast. But wait. You know how I love to gaze at the stars each night?"

"Yes, Gal, of course I do."

"A couple nights ago I was mesmerized as usual. Then one star or planet started blinking, and it looked like it was sending an SOS of some sort. In minutes, that light took on the shape of a flashlight shining down. It beamed down to Earth in my front yard, and then it started coming up on my porch. I looked up in the sky and noticed it was that same star. Who wouldn't run, so I ran into the house and locked the door. The light came under my door, and just like that it disappeared. I looked up at that star from a window, but they all looked the same at that point.

"After what happened with Clayton, I was a nervous wreck and didn't think anyone would believe me, so I went home after he disintegrated. That night sitting on the porch, the spacecraft passed by me again and landed in the forest close by. I could hear the sounds it made. When I looked that way, a figure was standing in the clearing. I ran and got my keys, but my hands wouldn't quit shaking. I closed my eyes and banged my head back and forth on the steering wheel and wished my car would drive to your house. When I opened my eyes and looked up, I was sitting in your driveway. Mom, what is happening to me?"

Nebulane rubbed her forehead and then just held it in her hand. Eyes closed. She breathed even heavier as though she was trying to control another hyperventilating-almost incident. With a very serious manner, she sat up and looked into Galaxas' eyes. "Are you certain it was a spacecraft?"

"Yes, Mom. You know our vision at night is like being in the daylight."

"Were you able to identify the figure standing in the clearing?"

"No. I was too freaked out. Why, Mom?"

Nebulane covered her mouth and took a deep breath. "I didn't think they would ever find us."

"What—Who? Who would never find us? Mother! What is going on?"

"Hang on." She grabbed the phone. Galaxas was in freak-out mode. Nebulane held a finger up to shush her. "Mitchell, meet us at the airport. Hurry. It's time."

"Mom! What's going on?"

"We can't talk right now. I have two suitcases in the coat closet. I'll pull my vehicle out of the garage, but you need to back your car up and move it into the garage when I pull out. We don't have time to talk about it right now. I will tell you everything while we drive, and we may need you to use your super skills if it comes down to that."

Galaxas' eyes looked as big as a planet. Her whole face wrinkled. "MOM!"

"There's no time. Just do it, and I'll explain everything in the jeep."

They both took off and accomplished it all in record time.

Nebulane was visibly shaking. Galaxas watched her body tremble, and noticed her mother was too freaked out to speak. Nebulane was constantly looking in the mirrors. Galaxas sat back against the seat and closed her eyes. She prayed fervently.

Chapter Seven

Noticing the scared look on Nebulane's face and how she kept looking at the mirrors, Galaxas wanted to question her mom, but wasn't sure if now was a good time.

"Are you able to tell me what's going on yet?"

"Sorry. I have to pay attention to everything around me."

"Mom, you're looking up in the sky and at the mirrors."

"I know, honey. I know. We're heading to Ted Stevens International Airport in Anchorage. It's a bit of a drive, and your father is going to meet us there. When we are safe and sound on the flight, I promise I'll tell you everything. Everything."

"But—"

"I'm sorry. I just have to pay attention."

A plane zoomed above and Nebulane jumped, and the jeep squealed, gravel spitting here and there. She swerved the jeep and pulled to the side of the road to get her wits about her.

Slapping her chest, trying to catch her breath, she asked,

"You okay, Gal?"

"No Mom, I'm not."

"What you must be thinking. I'll be more careful. We have to keep going. If I feel we are in danger, I will have you use your thoughts to get us to the airport instead of driving. Let's just give it another try."

Galaxas just shook her head without answering.

Deep in thought, Nebulane glanced over to Galaxas several times wondering just how much information she should divulge to her daughter. Not much. It was for her own safety she kept it all a secret anyway. The less she knows, the safer she will be.

"Mom, I have clients waiting for their illustrations. How long will we be gone?"

"I don't know. Honest. Let's just get out of here and sort it all out once we're in the air."

"I'll shut up, but if I can get us anywhere at any time, why can't I just transport us without this time-consuming drive? Where are we going? I have a right to know," Galaxas said fuming.

Nebulane patted Galaxas' knee with trembling fingers. "Of course you do. We have a place in Fort Myers, Florida, at the Buckingham airpark. We have a plane and everything. That's where you attended school until the second year of junior high. Do you remember our place there? The airplanes driving down the roads?"

"What?! I guess not, but now that you mention it, I do remember the kids in school. Then Annalee's family moved to Alaska, and we did, too, soon after. Her dad was stationed there but didn't reenlist. That's when he became a drunk. Annalee said he never had a soldier's heart. It was just a means of income and nothing more."

"Your dad and I both knew that. Poor girl. It's all true.

"Look, I was unaware of your superpower or skill, but it is useless right now and should only be used in dire circumstances, until we figure out how it works."

"So you don't think it is strange that this looney tune thing that happened to me is right out of the *Twilight* Zone? In that case, I'll just use my power to go back home, grab my computer and work stuff and think myself to Florida."

"No! Please don't do that. It's not that simple. We have no idea if someone is watching your place. It would be really bad if they got to you or me."

"Mother, put yourself in my shoes. How am I supposed to sit here and keep my mouth shut with all the questions I have?

Maybe I'm the sane person and you're cracking up. Why would someone be watching my house? None of this is making any sense."

The jeep skidded off the road to a halt, both of them jolting forward and then back against the seat.

"I'm so sorry. I thought a spacecraft just flew by. Maybe I am losing it."

Galaxas rubbed her mother's back. "I'm sorry, Mom. I'll stay quiet and let you focus. I can see how scared you are."

Nebulane let out a sigh. "Thank you. You're right. I just need to focus and get us there in one piece. How about some music?"

"Excellent idea." Galaxas tuned in to a station they both liked. Music does have a way of taming the angry beast. They needed a distraction. Their favorite band was on the radio.

Now at the airport, they parked and grabbed the suitcases. Standing inside the airport, Mitchell waited. When he saw them, he ran and embraced them both. He looked nervously into Galaxas' eyes, not knowing what she knew.

"You okay, kiddo?" he asked.

"As well as can be expected."

"Good." He gently patted her upper arm. "Now, we don't have a lot of time, so here's our tickets and we need to get to our terminal quickly." He made arrangements for some friends to pick up their vehicles and drive them back to their home.

Seated inside the terminal, Galaxas sat staring at the wall. *What is it they both know? How could they keep whatever it is secret from me, and why?*

She looked over at her parents. Nebulane was sifting through a magazine just to pass the time, looking up often and scanning the area around them. Caution beamed from her eyes.

Mitchell held his head between both hands, lost in thought.

Nobody was talkative. Galaxas always wondered why her dad looked so normal compared to them, but just figured it was her mother's side of the family that was blessed with the freakiness.

It was impossible to not feel sadness for how upset Nebulane acted. She was genuinely scared. But why wouldn't she tell Galaxas about whatever she was hiding? Why keep something obviously this important to their wellbeing quiet? The thoughts wouldn't quit buzzing in her mind. It felt like a swarm of bees buzzed their way inside of her head.

"Attention all passengers. The first two rows can board now," spread through the speakers.

Nebulane jumped up and grabbed her suitcase, cautiously pushing Galaxas forward. Her head was in a constant motion of turning. Now seated, Galaxas decided to get some answers.

"Mom, now is as good of a time as any. Tell me what's going on."

Her mom looked all around and turned to the back of her seat. A man looked back at her. "Gal, I'm not trying to avoid explaining, but people are just too close in hearing range. The plane is full. This is too serious to let anyone hear. Besides, the fact we forgot to cover our faces, everyone on the plane is asking questions about us. They will hear our conversation, and we can't afford that. I'm really sorry."

It was true. Everyone kept looking at them. Galaxas slammed back against the seat and closed her eyes. A flight attendant stopped and asked Mitchell a question. He answered quietly.

"It is a skin condition. There is no disease or anything like that anyone has to worry about. You do notice I'm sitting next to them and not the least bit uncomfortable?"

"I see your point, sir. Thank you."

"You bet."

Galaxas kept her eyes closed, but thoughts of how she wished she was home started coming to her mind. She quickly changed her thoughts so that it didn't happen. She just didn't know if she should think or how to think now. How crazy. Earphones automatically went in her ears and music played.

They were in the air. Safe and sound.

The warning sign buzzed and flashed.

Chapter Eight

Nebulane shrieked quietly in terror as an invisible-to-the-naked-eye spacecraft passed by. The turbulence caused by big gusts of wind rocked the plane. Oxygen masks fell from the bin above. Screams of fear were resonating around the plane. The captain's voice came through the sound system.

"Please remain seated and be sure to fasten your seatbelt.

Our plane has just experienced some unusual wind gusts, but we are steady and balanced. Do not worry. The plane is on course and running properly. Please, try to relax. Thank you."

Galaxas had fallen asleep, but all the commotion woke her up. "What's going on?" she asked pulling the earbuds out of her ears.

"A spacecraft just passed us and caused the turbulence. Only I could see it. It's gone."

"Do you think it was the same one I saw? Do we need to be worried?"

"I have no way to know that, and, no, I don't think we need to feel worried. Go back to sleep. We still have three hours of flight."

Mitchell was leaning down to hear the conversation. Galaxas replaced the earbuds and slunk back into the seat, eyes shutting.

Nebulane looked into Mitchell's eyes. He saw the fear. He grabbed her hand and squeezed, trying to assure her that everything would be okay. Except, his nerves trembled inside. What he knew terrified him.

With much caution, Nebulane scanned the airport before they exited it. She used her hand to keep Galaxas behind her. "The taxi is here. Get in it fast," she ordered Galaxas.

Knowing there was no choice, Galaxas just did what she was told. In twenty minutes, they were in the house in the Buckingham airpark. Nebulane ran around the rooms and pulled the blinds down.

Being in the house for the first time in a long time, Galaxas walked around. "How come you never told me that you kept this house?"

"The less you knew, the better."

"And on that note, why would you bring us to the brightest state in the United States? How can our eyesight withstand the bright sunshine?"

"You just answered your own question. If it hurts our eyes, it will also hurt the eyesight of the people searching for us. If you pay attention to the facts, notice they came to Alaska, the cloudiest spot in the country. That is where they would expect to find us."

"So, there are other people just like us?" Galaxas' eyes widened to an oversized position and her mouth dropped.

"We'll get to the explanation in a few minutes. Let's just make sure we're safe and secure before then."

"Mom! It feels like the Daytona 500 is racing through my veins. I'm not talking about 'start your engines.' I'm talking midrace where the speed is so fast, my body is vibrating. I need answers."

"I know you do. Hold on. Mitchell, think you can run out and get us some Chinese takeout?"

"As long as the car starts, and that's a big if." He grabbed a set of keys off a hook and went into the garage.

Inside, they could hear the car start. Nebulane blew a sigh of relief. The garage door opened, and he drove out. She heard a buzzing sound and then a thump signified it had closed. Now she could breathe.

"What about Dad? Shouldn't he be worried that they may find him? Whomever *they* are."

"No. They don't even know about him. He means nothing to them," Nebulane answered.

"Mom, I'm not eating a bite or moving from this spot until you answer my questions."

"Okay. This has to be brought out in the open now. I can see that. Hold onto your seat, girl. It's going to get wild."

The look on Nebulane's face caused shivers to run up and down Galaxas' arms, but it didn't matter. She couldn't stand it any longer. "I'm actually a little worried to find out, but what choice do I have?"

"No, you're right," Nebulane admitted. "Now, there are things you need to know for survival. Give me a second to collect my thoughts." Nebulane debated just how much she should tell her. At least for now. The less she knew, the better. For now.

"Okay. That planet that flickered at you; that's the planet we came from. It is called Betzalel. The meaning of the planet's name is 'in God's shadow'."

Galaxas' head fell down, and her eyes almost popped out. Nebulane had a habit of patting her knee for comfort.

"You see, we are sort of like that flashlight, scanning space for evil beings. A long time ago, something happened where one of our people got mixed up with evil beings and secretly brought them onto our planet. It was all done in secret.

"Pretty soon, the same story as the Garden of Eden, our people were corrupted with evil. An evil so wicked, the scariest horror film couldn't dream it up. A lot of our people got sucked into it. The rest of them escaped to underground hideouts. They —we could make ourselves invisible just by closing our eyes.

"Our planet is dark most of the time. That is why we have eyesight that makes the dark look like sunshine. We do use our eyes like flashlights to scan space. That's what you witnessed.

"How do I tell you this?" She blew air out. "I am queen and ruler of Betzalel. The good and pure armies put me and you in a spacecraft set up to travel to Earth, should it ever come down to that. I didn't want to leave, but they forced me into the spacecraft and blasted us off. They had the codes, and I couldn't figure them out in time to change my course. We were never meant to meet a human. Never meant to be seen by a human. Also, we are not UFO's or UAP's. What people have been encountering has nothing to do with us. That's completely different.

"By the time I made it to Earth, I was weak, and when I landed, the calculations to our planet would automatically dissolve. I have been trying to crack the codes to take me back, but I'm getting nowhere. My spacecraft is hidden, and for now, only I will know of its whereabouts. Don't ask!" she aggressively said holding up her hand.

"The evil armies have taken over our planet. I have to figure out a way to get back and destroy them. You may be the answer. It's just too soon to tell."

Galaxas' eyes bugged out again. "So, you haven't told me everything; have you?"

"No, but all in time. It is important to me and to our planet to keep you alive and keep evil away from you."

"Then, is it fair to say that the figure from the spacecraft was out to capture me?"

"Obviously, I have no way to answer that. I'm taking precautions right now. This will be revealed soon enough, but until the time is right, it is not wise to tell you everything. Trust me."

"Do the people from our planet speak the English language? Man, that felt weird to ask."

"Very similar, sort of like the same, but different. It's hard to explain."

"You know what bothers me the most, Mom? It's how you allowed me to live a life thinking I am a freak. But on 'our planet' I would not be a freak. Don't you think that knowledge would have saved a lot of depression, loneliness, and suicidal thoughts if I had known the truth?" Her eyes squinted tight and a tight pucker to the lips developed, hands not meaning to formed fists.

The statement hit Nebulane hard. She looked down to the floor, and when she looked back up, the revelation of hearing that truth consumed her whole being.

"You're right, Gal. I never even gave that a thought. Fearing what could happen to you was so real and so profound that I never gave a thought to how revealing this could have made your life better. Please forgive my indirect stupidity."

She dropped her heavy forehead in her hand, lost in regret.

Galaxas was still angry, but it was softening to disappointment. Especially by seeing how her mom was devastated by that revelation. Oddly enough, this was information overload and it never registered that her dad wasn't in the ship with them heading to Earth.

The sound of the garage door opening shook them both out of their thoughts. Nebulane ran to the garage entrance and cracked the door open. Her shoulders relaxed. "Let me help you," she said to Mitch.

"Wonderful. As you can see, I stocked up on food while waiting for our order to be finished."

Galaxas strolled out to the garage.

"This bag has your name on it, kiddo," he said with hopeful eyes.

She kissed his cheek and scanned the contents. Her eyes widened and so did her smile. "There must be every sour candy ever created. Thanks, Dad. Oh! My favorite." She pulled out a bag of "Toxic Waste Hazardously Sour" candy. Tongue licking her lips over and over.

"Take a piece, and then let's all help put these groceries away so we can eat the Chinese takeout." The aroma floated through the air. Stomachs growled with delight. They relaxed and spent the rest of the evening watching movies.

A spacecraft scanned the area below, searching, determined. It kept going back and forth on the same route. Inside, sleepy eyes were unaware of its presence.

Chapter Nine

The morning sun burst underneath the blinds, reflecting off the brass rail headboard. Galaxas stretched her arms and yawned. The home was cozy, decked out with soft and luxurious mattresses and blankets. No knickknacks or photographs, except of stars and planets. They were magnificent to look at.

She missed her best friend something fierce. They both received constant ridicule for their looks as children. Instead of making them bitter, they both went in the opposite direction. They cared deeply for hurting souls, people feeling left out and all alone. It wasn't that they were always received by these loners with open arms because that wasn't usually the case. Why even the kids discarded by the "accepted" crowd still rejected her and Annalee.

Annalee lived in an environment of neglect. Her dad worked as little as possible, coming home with the attitude that because he worked, home was a place to sit back, watch television and drink. Don't bug him. He passed away not long ago.

Her mom resented having to take care of her. She would rather be at the bar, laughing with that boisterous, loud laugh. Chores, chores and more chores was the only interaction between them.

When both girls met in art class, before Galaxas was homeschooled, their bond became inseparable. Annalee's parents were more than happy to have her stay almost the whole week at Galaxas' home, except when chores piled up. Yelling after yelling telephone calls embarrassed Annalee too much to bring Galaxas and her parents into that world. She would head home just to end the yelling, for their sake only.

How did they manage to have such a sweet spirit and kind heart after all of that? Both of them. Nebulane and Mitchell made sure these girls knew what love and adoration was, and they felt it. Galaxas' parents' genuine love made them both feel special.

How many injured wildlife did she and Annalee bring to Nebulane? Countless. And how was it they never figured out Nebulane's special gift of healing? It never crossed their minds.

Galaxas strolled out to the living room towards the kitchen, a sinfully, delicious smell floating through the air.

"Good morning," she said with a yawn.

A kiss to the cheek, "Good morning, kiddo. Did you sleep well?" her dad asked.

"Yes, Dad, very well. Where's Mom?"

"She had a hard time getting to sleep. I let her sleep in."

Being in Florida, Galaxas had on a tank top. That is the first time he noticed the hand marks on her neck. He stared as tears formed. She noticed and turned away hoping to avoid the discussion.

"How are you doing with everything?"

"The best I can, Dad. Hello. I'm an actual alien from outer space. You do the math."

He laughed. "Maybe so, but the cutest alien I have ever seen."

"Come on, Dad. I'm a freak."

He took a deep breath, and she could see his face changing colors. He took her hand and said, "Follow me."

Facing a mirror, he said "look." She had on customized eyeglasses so she could see properly. She stared. "Yeah, so?"

"You may have a different color of skin and hair but look how beautiful you are. Don't compare yourself to the people on Earth. Picture yourself with others of your kind, like your mother. Look at your perfect bone structure, your smooth, silky skin, light green hair and gray highlights that shine with radiance. Yesterday, I just saw a girl with dark green hair and blue highlights. Now, that looked freaky. You are not a freak. You are the most beautiful person; besides your mother, I have ever seen. It tears me up to hear you talk so negatively about yourself.

"We're both humans, just from different planets. You see, I have compared you and your mother to Earth humans and wondered how it is you don't see how beautiful you are.

"From now on, I want you to look at the perfection I see. The only thing different about you and your mother is the skin and hair colors. Eyes, too, obviously. But when I look at women that are known as beauties, they don't stand up to your natural beauty. You also have an inward beauty that brings tears to my eyes. For my sake, please, please, never look down on yourself again. Your natural and inward beauty stands out in a crowd."

Speechless at first, a hand covered her mouth and sincere tears dribbled down her cheeks. She turned around and hugged him tightly. "Oh, Dad. I wish I would have had the guts to talk to you like this before. Now that I look at myself, you're right. I'm hot, Dad. Just as hot as those glamour girls. Thanks, Dad."

He rubbed the top of her head. "You are most welcome but know this: Everything I just said is the truth. No bias because I'm your father. It's the whole truth and nothing but the truth, so help me God." He pointed to the heavens as he said it. "Now, I have some mouthwatering waffles waiting to be devoured."

"You won't have to tell me twice," she assured him.

They ate at the kitchen island. Nebulane walked in, still a little weary-eyed. They both looked up and smiled at her. Seeing the tension gone from their faces, she relaxed.

"Did anything happen, because you both seem in good moods?"

"Dad just pointed out how beautiful I am—we are. He made me stand in front of a mirror, and you know what, Mom? He's right. We are beautiful, not a freak in any way."

Nebulane's warm eyes stared at Mitchell. "Now you see why I fell in love with him."

"Oh yeah, I can definitely see that."

He walked over and kissed Nebulane's cheek before handing her a plate of waffles.

"Sorry, Mom, but he does cook better than you."

A chuckle escaped Nebulane. "Tell me. Hey, I have a planet to save, so competing with cooking skills isn't a priority."

"Oh, right. That's the reason, Mom."

Mitchell turned in a flash as he heard a slight slap. Nebulane, in fun, smacked Galaxas' arm and sat down to devour this perfect breakfast. He let out a chuckle.

"I have a great idea," Galaxas said with bright eyes. "How about we get Annalee to fly out here? She has had such a hard life living with an alcoholic mother and no father for years. She has dealt with some real ridicule just like me because she is chubby and dyed her hair different colors. She has a really cute face, and so what if she is overweight. She is still beautiful. You showed me how to see beyond horrible labels by some elitist group of kids. She could run errands for us in the daytime and stuff like that.

"Something else is on my mind. Maybe I can find the courage to get out in the open and just be myself. I think I can stand up for myself, now, and stand proud about my differences. What do you think?"

"Of course, I love this new you, confidence and a genuine goodness about you, but someone could be looking for you," Nebulane said sorrowfully. "I guess I fear that because we are different, not freaks, but beautifully different, it may draw crowds. I'm just not sure it's a good idea to go in public until we know for certain that you and I aren't being hunted."

A beam, only visible to Galaxas and Nebulane's eyes, started shining around their property. Nebulane spotted it. "Follow me, now!"

She grabbed Galaxas' hand and Mitchell followed as they ran into a closet that was customized to hide them.

"Sit still. I'm not a hundred percent certain this mineral we made the closet with will hide us from them. Just don't move."

Nobody moved. They sat still on the bench that was added to

the closet for situations just like this. In thirty minutes, Mitchell poked his head out and looked for any figures. Anything. He ran to the windows and peeked out. He didn't see anything. Slowly, he whispered as he opened the closet door. "I can't see anyone. But I don't have your abilities or skills either."

"Okay, let me take a look." Nebulane walked out cautiously and looked through windows around their house. With shaking hands, she cracked the door open in the garage. Nothing. She made a small opening in the blinds with her fingers and peeked through them. She found nothing. "Come out, Galaxas. I think we're safe."

"Gee, Mom. Will we have to hide like this for the rest of our lives? This really stinks."

"I know. I know. This is all new to me, too. This is the first time it appears someone has found our trail. We never had to hide before. I would like to know just how they picked up on our trail."

It didn't show through her tank top, but a soft glow vibrated around Galaxas' heart. Nobody was paying attention.

"Your Mom's right," Mitchell remarked. "She's gone through a lot to protect you. Allow her the time and space needed to figure this out. But Nebulane, I think Galaxas is absolutely right. We need Annalee. She's like our very own daughter. She's probably in a panic mode wondering where Galaxas is right now. I'll contact her and make arrangements."

Galaxas slammed into him and embraced him. "Thanks, Dad. Thanks so much."

"You're welcome, but I'm being selfish and doing this for all of us. We love her like our own daughter. She lived with us for a year and regretted moving back to help her mom out. I think she'll be just as happy to come here as we will be to have her here."

"Mitchell, I thank God for you every day. Every single day," Nebulane acknowledged.

He put an arm around Nebulane and squeezed her. "Don't think for a moment I don't thank God every day for you two, either. I so do."

Mitchell's fingers clicked on the keyboard. Reservations were made, and Galaxas forwarded all the ticket information to Annalee's email while talking on the phone with her.

~

The next morning Annalee drove to Galaxas' home and sat in the car until she felt no one was around. Galaxas had explained everything that had happened. She ran to the house and unlocked the door with her key. The door squeaked open slowly. Her head poked around the corner, but everything seemed untouched and fine. She shuffled through Galaxas' folders and grabbed everything on the list to be dropped off at the post office and mailed to Florida.

As she locked the door and got into the car, her body was covered with goosebumps. She didn't understand why, but it frightened her. She scanned the area but could see nothing or no one to cause concern. A figure watched her from the bushes. Full of excitement to be going to Florida, music blasted from the radio, and she threw her head all around to the beat.

The figure in the bushes tilted his head watching her.

"Now Galaxas and I can work together on our first children's books. We are the best illustrators to enter the publishing world. We'll become famous and rich." She bobbed up and down to the music all the way home.

Her mother drove her to the airport, but scoffed as Annalee exited the car. She wouldn't even say goodbye, but rather, she tried to guilt Annalee for leaving her to fend for herself.

Annalee handed her mother a wad of cash. Her mom's eyes popped wide open, and she sifted through it and smiled.

"Try to use it for bills, Mother, not booze. Bye, Mom."

When Annalee looked back into the car, her mother was staring at the money with a big smile, cars beeping, noise filling the air, not even noticing that Annalee walked away. Her mom turned her head and cursed at the annoying people beeping at her. If she hadn't expected it, Annalee would have broken down at the rejection she felt, but it was a normal part of her life. No expectations of a change were hopeful.

On the plane, a wind gust caused the plane to wobble and interrupt everyone's attention. Oxygen masks fell from the bins above. Passengers screamed and clutched each other's hands. The plane balanced out and the poor captain's voice was a quiver trying to reassure the passengers that all is back on track. To please not worry.

Annalee looked out the window. The bright sunrays blinded her eyes. She scratched her head wondering where that gust of wind came from. Nothing seemed strange or out of the ordinary, so she leaned her head back, earplugs in to block all the noise from the airplane's engine, and closed her eyes until a flight attendant announced over the speakers that they will be landing shortly.

The announcement came. Hands rubbing together and an excited smile, supplies were packed up quickly.

Exiting the plane, a figure stood hidden at the pickup terminal and watched the activity. As Annalee looked for Mitchell's car, her body prickled from toes to head. Her eyes squinted. "It's hot out here, so why did I get a cold chill? Maybe it's the excitement." Her eyes glanced around nervously. And then she saw Mitchell looking like a clown waving at her from a car. She laughed. They hugged and got inside the car and pulled away from the curb to leave. Darn if her body didn't develop with goosebumps as she looked around.

The invisible figure of somebody watched every move and was gone in a split second.

Noticing her shiver, Mitchell turned the air conditioner temperature up.

Chapter Ten

Galaxas heard the clinking of bangle bracelets. Her best friend, Annalee, had arrived. She always sounded like a gypsy wearing so much clanging jewelry. The bedroom door swung open, and she ran to the living room.

Hugs, kisses, endless chatter, and tension disappeared. Galaxas helped to carry the suitcases to the guest room. "Mom is making lunch. I think its egg salad sandwiches, chips and veggies."

"Oh good. I'm starving," Annalee admitted.

"Hey, look at you. You've lost a lot of weight," Galaxas said turning her around, back and forth.

"Yeah. Well, if I ever want a boyfriend, figured I better give it a try."

"Just stop it! You were beautiful then and beautiful now."

Annalee noticed the hand marks on her neck. "Hey, what happened to your neck?"

Galaxas swallowed a few times and blood seemed to drain from her face. She had forgotten that Annalee didn't know very much. "You're not going to believe me if I tell you, so I need to speak with Mom to see how much I can explain to you. It's a safety thing, I'm told." She rubbed her neck.

Annalee pushed her head back and squinted her eyes. "I don't know how to respond to that, but you know me, I have to know everything. I just have to. I will find out what happened, Gal."

They giggled as Galaxas pulled her to the kitchen.

"Our troublemaker has arrived, Mom. She needs answers."

Nebulane blew out a sigh. "Could we please just eat lunch in peace first? Please?"

"Sure, just until we eat. But that's all. I will pester the living daylights out of you, safety issue or not. Just know that," Annalee remarked swiping her hands together.

Nebulane shook her head and set plates on the island counter.

During lunch, Annalee ate a fourth of what she usually ate. Mitchell looked at her with questions. She glanced at him annoyed. "I'm trying to lose weight. Is that a crime?"

"No, dear. You look great. Hey, you're not going to color your hair blonde or anything like that, are you?" he asked.

She tapped her lips with a finger. "Hmmm, think I could pull that off?"

Galaxas looked at her affectionately. "Of course you could, silly. You do whatever makes you happy. If anyone deserves happiness, you do."

"Thanks, girl."

After cleanup, Galaxas spoke to her mother in private. "Mom, I'm not going to keep her in the dark like I was. It could jeopardize her safety right now. She needs to know the little bit that I know."

"All right. Ease her into it," Nebulane replied hesitantly.

"Will do. Over and out," she ended saying with a salute.

Having Annalee around was like medication to her. They went into her room, turned on some music, and she filled Annalee in about everything, beginning with what happened with Clayton.

Annalee sat frozen on the bed, but her expression was bright. She wanted to know more and more. Questions blurted out before Galaxas could finish a sentence.

"Oh, Galaxas. I can't believe he tried to strangle you. I mean, what's scary is that I can picture him doing just that. There was always an uncomfortable feeling about him. How did you meet him anyways? I must have forgotten."

"He was lost in the forest when he found my house, in bad shape, so I nursed him back to health. It took him some time to get used to my freakiness, which I no longer believe about myself. Forget my skin tone. Just look at my features. I'm beautiful." She pushed her face up close to Annalee.

They both burst out laughing. "If memory serves me correct, I told you that you were beautiful and not a freak. You let that jerk brainwash you. But seriously, you can think something in your mind and make it happen?"

"Yes, it's true," Galaxas replied.

"Do it. Make yourself appear next to the window."

"No! Mom said I have to leave it alone until I can figure out how to use the power properly. For instance, what if you get on my nerves and I wish you to go back to your home, and poof, you're gone."

"Hey!"

"That would never happen, you goof."

"You know what thought just hit me, Gal?"

"No, I don't have the power to read minds."

Annalee busted up laughing before she made her remark. "My best friend is an alien from outer space."

They both fell over in a laughing fit.

"And my new favorite television show is *My Favorite Martian*," Annalee said choking with laughter. She busted out in hysterics. They both fell on the bed laughing harder.

"Now my obsession with being an astrophile makes sense," Galaxas said as she pondered.

"I forget. What is an astrophile?" Annalee asked.

"A person fond of star lore."

"This just hit me. I'm going to have to tell Pastor Who Dunnit that a color needs to be added to the *Jesus Loves the Little Children* song," Galaxas said while laughing. "You know, Red, "green," and yellow, black and white..."

"Oh, that's funny. How did you come up with his nickname, Gal?" Annalee inquired.

"Well, his last name is 'Dunnit,' so when he talks about a character in the Bible, I always yell out, "Tell us, Pastor Who Dunnit, who done it. You've heard me say it a million times."

"A million, huh? You're such a dork, Gal. I forgot about that."

"Yeah, well, once I decided to live in seclusion, going to church was out of the question. Even people in the congregation stared at me."

"To their defense, when you see someone who sticks out in a crowd, good or bad, don't you stare?"

"I hate it when you make sense, Annalee." She gave her a playful shove.

Galaxas sat up and got quiet. Her face was serious, almost sad.

Wondering what to say, Annalee hesitantly asked, "Is something the matter?"

"When Mom told me all of this, it hit me that if I had known I wasn't some freak, maybe I wouldn't have felt that way all these years. You know the devastation of how I thought I was a freak and what it did to me. I almost hated her at that moment."

Annalee laid a hand on her shoulder. Galaxas glanced up at her with sad eyes. Then Annalee commented, "I understand that totally. It would have been helpful to understand why you are so different, to the point of being ridiculed like you had a disease, but your mom felt it was necessary to keep you safe. Whether or not you believe her, you have no way of understanding the fear she felt for you. At this point, it's best to move forward, not backward."

"Wise one. You're right, Annalee. But you know what else I was thinking about? We never really discussed the topic of being in love because I always felt it was impossible for me. But you know what?"

"No, what?" Annalee was dying to know.

"Maybe there is love beyond the stars. I have always felt tingles when I stared up into the sky, like romance twinkled through the galaxy waiting for me. Maybe I'll get the chance to know what love really feels like now."

She plopped a hand on Annalee's arm. "Do you think it is possible I will meet someone from my planet?"

Annalee gasped and pointed.

"What? What are you pointing at?"

She looked downward and a soft glow mildly vibrated around her heart. Her terrified eyes rubbed her heart area. With extra-wide eyes, she rubbed her chest area. She shot Annalee a fearful look and then looked back down as it faded away.

"Okay, I'm officially freaked out," Annalee said.

"You and me both," Galaxas agreed.

"Here's an idea. I think our minds could use a break, and I need a distraction before I completely freak out. Let's work on our books and illustrations. I need to get them out to the authors before they freak out. Have you been keeping up with the workload? I dread looking at my email," rubbing her heart area in worry Galaxas suggested.

"Well, what else would I have been doing? But I like your plan. I'll grab some coffee and be right back," Annalee replied.

Leaves and sticks crunched just outside of Galaxas' window. She jumped up and peeked out. Next, she scanned the area, but if someone was there, they were gone now. All she saw was shadows of trees and the house. The sound came back, but up above. She crossed her arms and pressed her hands firmly on her arms and looked up at a tree. Squirrels chased each other up and down the tree. It caused a smile to form. She never saw the figure of a person fading away.

Chapter Eleven

"**W**ow! We sure got a lot of work done."

"Yeah," Galaxas replied. "Donna loves the illustrations. On to the next author. Will we ever find time to work on our own books?"

"Right? Maybe we should stop accepting new clients for a little while so we can work on them. What do you say?" Annalee asked.

"When you're right, you're right. How else can we get anything done?" Galaxas answered in agreement.

Nebulane hurled their door open. "In the closet. Now!"

Annalee followed Galaxas. She watched her and Nebulane's hands tremble. Mitchell placed a hand on each one of their hands to calm them down.

"Somebody is definitely looking for us," Nebulane whispered.

"Why Mom? Why do they still need to find us?"

Nebulane, not in the mood to talk or reveal the truth, shrugged her shoulders.

"Let me take a look, except that really makes no sense. How about we go together, Nebulane? I can't use my eyes the way you can," Mitchell suggested.

"That does make perfect sense, Mitch."

They did a search, but nothing was found. "It's looking like we will have to move from this place. They're—whomever they are—onto us. Come on out girls."

"This is getting tiresome," Galaxas groaned.

"Someone is definitely looking for me. We need to pack up and get out of here," Nebulane added in a worried tone.

"Come on. I haven't even visited a Florida beach. From the ice cold to warm and sunny, how could you do this to me?" Annalee argued.

Nebulane tapped her head. "That gives me a wonderful idea. Since they aren't after you and have no idea who you are, we'll let you stay here while we go to another home. With you and Mitchell staying here, we can find out if someone is really looking for us.

"We have another place in the mountains, and I guess we'll fly. We have an old jalopy in the garage for transportation."

"Or just use transcontinental Galaxas," Annalee remarked humorously.

"Annalee, this is serious." Nebulane puckered her mouth.

"Mitchell, you'll have to stay here and keep watch of everything. They could walk right through these doors, and you would never see them. We'll take with us anything that would refer to us just in case."

"But…"

"Mitchell, we've discussed this. You knew there was a possibility this could happen. It won't be forever. Just until we are certain whoever is out there leaves this place alone. Please understand. Besides, I'd feel better for Annalee if you were here with her."

"I suppose you're right. Let's get on with it. I'd rather be separated from you for a short while instead of forever."

"Mother, what if it's a member from your royal guard looking for us?"

"Or what if it's someone from the evil army? We can't take that chance," Nebulane noted. "None of you understand what I'm talking about. This isn't an attempt to keep you all in the dark. This is like dealing with Satan himself. That much evilness."

Not another word was said. What she said summed it all up and gave them all a better perspective. They gathered all their personal belongings and anything that would connect to them, should a person from their planet be brave enough to come inside and look around. Tears and hugs, they were ready.

Nebulane and Galaxas stood in the foyer holding luggage.

There was silence among them. What would happen if the evil army found them? What would happen if the evil army associated Mitchell and Annalee with Nebulane? All these questions and more circulated through their minds and no one was brave enough to ask the questions.

At the airport, a few teardrops fell, but there was no time to discuss anything else. They needed to get out of here and now. Hugs, kisses, the announcement traveled through the speakers: "Please board."

"Wow, Mom. This place is sort of...old. I mean, it's clean but really old."

"Your dad and I make good money, but not enough money to afford luxurious homes in each state."

"We have a place in more states?"

"No, that was an exaggeration. Just the three areas. Now, let's take a look around to be sure we're safe."

A thud of the luggage and book materials landed on the floor.

They searched the inside and outside. Back to seclusion. They walked back inside and Galaxas heard the tapping of paws. She looked just in time to see a mouse scamper into a hole.

"You sure it's safe here? This place looks like it could collapse at any moment."

"It may look hideous on the outside, but the foundation is secure. We made sure of it."

"Hey Mom. Is life on our planet similar to Earth?"

"God has been very gracious to us. Of course it is different being mostly dark, but we do get indirect sunlight. We are able to grow crops and we even have trees and plenty of water sources. It's beautiful in its own way. It is sort of like looking at a black and white picture, but the colors are there; just deeply faded."

"And just how will I ever see our planet?"

A hand rested on her shoulder. With a serious face Nebulane answered. "It will happen. I have to go back. Just waiting for our battle plan to be finalized. Once in a great while, someone from our planet sends me a message to update me on the conditions. You saw how they did that with your own eyes."

"Except for one very important thing: the message was for me; not you. I know someone is trying to get my attention, but who?" Galaxas asked in thought.

Nebulane dropped to the couch. Face unreadable. As she stared blankly, her thoughts came out of her mouth unknowingly. "You don't know that. It's most likely the message was for me, but you were the one to see it."

"For some reason, I don't believe you, Mom. You've been hiding a lot from me. I am a grown woman. Why can't you acknowledge that?"

Nebulane didn't mean to let out such a loud sigh. "This is just as hard for me as it is for you. I want to tell you everything. You heard the line 'if I tell you, I will have to kill you'."

Galaxas raised an eyebrow at that remark.

"Hold on. Not going to kill you or anything like that, but until I am certain you aren't in danger, I have to be selective in what I can tell you whether you're an adult or not. I'm sorry. I don't enjoy this anymore than you do."

"Do you think the man I am supposed to marry is on our planet right now?"

"Yes, very possible. He could even be looking for you," she said in a trance-like state.

"Do you know what you just said?"

"Can't say that I do."

"Mom. You said my mate may be looking for me. Maybe that code was for me from him."

"Oh, drat! I was just lost in thought."

"Well?"

"How can I explain this? Let's see." She rubbed her face. "On our planet our mates are automatically fit for us at birth. When the time is right, the male will know and begin to search for you. I tried to ignore it and not have to discuss it with you until it was time. When it is time, you'll know and won't have to guess. That's the way it is on our planet, and I wish not to discuss it ANYMORE."

"How? How did you ignore it? Mom, I want to know, so you better tell me the truth, or our relationship could turn bad."

Nebulane's shocked face stared in disbelief.

"I have a right to know, Mom."

"Yes, you do," she sighed. "My fear is, what if your mate turned evil? I could not possibly let you go with him. His evilness will corrupt you and turn you into one of them. Can't you see how difficult this is for me? And for our planet, if that is true?"

"Of course I do. But how does the male know who their mate is?" Galaxas was determined to get answers.

"Unlike Earth, our true love shows in a physical manner."

"Hhhhhhh!" She slapped a hand to her mouth. The glow around her heart is maybe a consequence of this, she couldn't help but wonder. "Mother, you're driving me crazy. What happens physically?"

Both hands covered Nebulane's head as it lowered, and she paced back and forth. "I don't know what to do. It never occurred to me that this would even happen," she said out loud talking more to herself than to Galaxas. She avoided the whole truth, because if it was time for her mate, a glow would start flashing around her heart. And even more concerning, Galaxas would turn twenty-five at the end of the year. That is usually the age love is revealed on their planet. As far as she knew, that hadn't happened yet. Until then, this would stay in her secret chambers. The news would only cause Galaxas frustration in wanting to meet him.

"When it happens, I can't allow you to meet him until I know for certain he wasn't corrupted."

"Wait a minute, Mom. If our mate is determined at birth, how did you end up with Dad?"

"Pbbbbbt," rolled off Nebulane's lips. "Look, we'll discuss that in a minute. We have to figure out what to do about who may be searching for me."

"Or for me," Galaxas blurted out.

"It seems unavoidable, Mom. Maybe we should set up a trap and get to the bottom of this."

"So...you're okay with turning evil? Because it will happen without your knowledge. I actually thought I could be near it and not be influenced, but I was wrong. One day you'll meet the man who had the guts to pull me away and send me here."

Rubbing her arms she added. "It creeps in like a virus. You don't see or feel it coming, and BAM, it gets you. The effect is slow at first, so you don't notice the transformation. But then it possesses your soul and no one around you is able to get it out of you.

"My dear friend was strongminded and able to stop it before it took over my soul. Now do you see my hesitation?"

"Yes, I really do. But again, how do we avoid it?"

"We can't. We can just prolong the meeting. I've been working on a way to seek out the truth. I think I can detect a condition now, but I just need to be sure for your sake. You're my world. I could never live with knowing I allowed evil to take over you."

"Gosh, Mom. As sweet as that statement is, I need to know how to shield myself from the evil."

"You're right. Let's go grab some supplies and food and when we get back, we'll discuss it. Cover up as best you can and wear dark sunglasses."

Galaxas almost responded with "duh" but decided to keep quiet.

Chapter Twelve

B ack in Florida, Mitchell and Annalee, not realizing it, expressed solemn faces after dropping off Nebulane and Galaxas. They walked backwards and slipped onto the couch and recliner. Still no words came out of their mouths. They had a blank stare. It was sad not knowing how long they would be apart.

A...choo! Annalee's sneeze startled them both.

"What in the world. You scared me, but I think I needed it to snap me out of this dull feeling inside of me," Mitchell commented.

"It really did work, not that I could help sneezing."

"Let's just get to work and pass the time away," he suggested.

They both went to separate rooms and the mouse clicked. The clicking of the keyboard worked tirelessly. Annalee walked out to the kitchen for some water. Mitchell had the same idea.

Both of them opening and closing their fingers grabbed a bottle of water. Fingers needing a rest.

"Maybe I'll find a snack," Annalee mentioned out loud. "Got any berries or fruit?"

"Yeah, just open one of the drawers and you'll find something. Hey, hand me the chips, please."

She frowned but handed them to him. "You keep chips in the refrigerator?"

"Yeah. They seem to stay crisper."

"Huh?" she reacted with a crinkled face.

"I'm beat, but I got a lot of work done," he said as he crunched on a chip.

"Me, as well. I submitted Galaxas' and my illustrations and began working on another author's request. I'll get us caught up. At least Galaxas and I have similar art ideas, so it usually goes through without a hitch," she commented happily.

"I noticed that. Have you always been interested in drawing and art like Galaxas?"

"Always. We became best friends since nobody else wanted anything to do with us. Then we had such similar ideas that we decided to open our business together after college."

"Did you take online courses, too?" Mitchell asked as he stared out the window while crunching on chips.

"Well, I'm offended. I worked on my laptop that YOU bought me right next to Galaxas every day."

He slapped his forehead. "How could I have forgotten that? Of course I remember."

"Break time. Let's watch something on television for a few minutes. I need a break," she sighed.

He laid his head against the recliner and crossed his legs. "I like your thinking."

For about half an hour they watched the television. A creaking sound caught their attention, and they looked in that direction. The kitchen door creaked open slowly and then closed. Their eyes were huge. They couldn't move a muscle. Then they saw a piece of rug flip over and the screech of a table chair being moved.

They were too frightened to move. The sound of footsteps was now audible. Doors squeaking open and papers being shuffled. The computer mouse made clicking noises. Mitchell and Annalee stared into each other's bugged out eyes.

Following the mild tapping of footsteps with their hearing and eyes, the kitchen rug flipped back over, and the door squeaked open; then closed.

Holding their breath and finally able to deflate it, they

wiggled their bodies around to get circulation moving. Annalee heard Mitchell's neck crack and looked at him with worry.

"Ahh, that feels better," he said.

"Was that a ghost?" Annalee asked as she trembled slightly.

"I think it was someone from their planet. Don't ask me how or why, but I think they can all become invisible to us."

"That was just weird. Spooky." Her body shimmied.

"I'm going to see if I can get in touch with Nebulane and let her know what just happened," he acknowledged.

"That's a good idea."

Nebulane's phone rang and rang. Finally, she managed to dig it out of the purse. "Hello, hello."

"Neb, you guys okay?"

"Yes, we're fine. Everything okay there?"

"Actually, no. Someone invisibly just walked through our house. It freaked us both out."

"Did anything happen? I mean, are you both okay?"

"Nothing happened and we're both okay. We just couldn't physically move for a while. It is spooky to think someone can walk right in our house and we can't see them."

"This goes to show that I'm right. They found us. I need to figure out a plan. Gotta go, Mitch. Love you so much."

"Neb! Wait! I...love...you...too." But she was no longer on the phone.

He looked lost when he turned and looked at Annalee. "I have no idea what's going to happen. What this means for them."

She placed a hand on his arm. "Don't go thinking the worst. Just don't go there. It's going to work out. You'll see."

"Yes. We have to stay focused. You're right. It will work out."

"Galaxas, it's time we live normally and just be prepared for anything. At least Mitchell and Annalee will be safe, but we need to discuss how to handle meeting people from our planet and figure out how to tell if they're evil or not."

"Do I have a choice? I don't know how it will affect me being around evil."

Nebulane held her hands up shaking her head. "Who knows?

I do know you can try to escape, but all in time. We just need to figure out who is searching for me and why."

"Good grief, Mom. They could be searching for me. This sounds like a movie. Maybe I'm dreaming it."

"If only," Nebulane replied in a far-off stare.

Chapter Thirteen

So far so good. Nebulane and Galaxas took many walks. It was cool enough outside so that they could wear sweat-shirts, and Galaxas could add more layers to hopefully prevent her mom from seeing the glow around her heart. It would freak her out more. *Could this possibly be what she was talking about that something physical happens to our bodies when the time is approaching to find our loved one?* Something she fought in her mind, because she wanted love, but not if he was evil.

"It's kind of a sweet idea that when we are old enough and ready for love, it shows physically. That's actually sweet. Mom, is love on our planet romantic like it can be here?"

"Very much. Maybe even more so. Since both seek each other and no one else, the love bond is so romantic. If he is good, you will always be in deep love."

"And if he's evil?"

"As long as you remain pure and good, you can escape. God gave us discernment to abstain from evil. If you are strong enough, spiritually, mentally and physically, you can escape."

"It's just scary to wonder if my true love is evil or good."

Nebulane patted her shoulder. "I understand and I'm so sorry this is undetermined for you at this point."

"Now that I think about it, an arranged marriage doesn't sound very romantic," Galaxas questioned.

"Ah, see, that's where you're wrong. We don't know who God has picked for us until it is time. We go through life dating, wondering if he's the one, and sometimes hoping he's the one. It's as real and normal as relationships here on Earth. We have absolutely no clue who that person will be. So you see, there is a mystery to it."

"What if we don't like the person we're supposed to be with?" Galaxas asked fearfully.

"That couldn't and has never happened. What could change is if that person is converted into evil, like many have done on our planet. Then God releases you from that bond."

"Extraordinary. But regardless of that insightful information, we need to discuss our plan for when we do meet. I need to know how to discern his character," Galaxas added.

Hands formed in prayer, Galaxas prayed. "Please Lord. Help me to know whether he is good or bad right off the bat. Give us a foolproof escape plan that includes Dad and Annalee. Thank you, Lord."

"You, my dear, just gave me an idea. A good one," Nebulane commented with excitement.

"Let's hear it."

"See this?" She pulled a pendant in the shape of a sun from under her shirt. "I will dig out the one I have saved for you. It's in a secret spot. If a person ends up corrupted, the pendant no longer works for them. Being here for so long, I forgot all about it.

"For those of us who remained pure, it is a defense weapon to use against the evil. It can disintegrate them into oblivion. If you are pure, when you hold the sun in your hand it will glow bright, like sunrays.

"When we get back to Florida, I'll get it for you. The man you are to wed should have one and it should glow. If he is evil, he cannot touch the pendant. It is like poison," Nebulane explained.

"What if they found a way to deceive us? You know, created a pendant to imitate the one we wear and push a button to get it to glow?" Galaxas asked.

"You're right. I never thought about that. Let's keep praying about it."

"I'm a little freaked out about all of this. I should be joyous and looking forward to meeting my mate, but honestly, I'm a little frightened, Mom. By everything."

"Hey, don't give up and let's try to expect a good outcome," she replied and with a warmness rubbing Galaxas' back.

"Yeah, sure. That will be easy. Not!"

∽

"When will they be back, Mitchell? It seems like it's been forever since we've seen them?" Annalee inquired.

"Don't I know it. It so happens that I mentioned this very subject to Nebulane just today. I believe we have thrown whoever is looking for them off the path. It just makes sense for them to come back here since the visitors haven't been stalking out our place. That we can tell, anyway. You haven't seen or heard someone invisible walking around, have you? Isn't that just weird to say?"

"Yeah, it is, but nope. I haven't seen or heard anything weird. But what you said makes total sense. It is a terrifying thought to know someone could be watching us right in the same room. They could kill us in our sleep. Did you ever think of that?" she said looking around the room.

He heard a tapping and looked over at her. She was biting her fingernails.

"If they wanted to hurt us, they should have done that by now. Nebulane agreed with me and is giving it a lot of thought. I'm hoping to get her answer by tomorrow."

"Good." She rubbed her hands together. "I have a surprise for Galaxas. I finished our work so that we can give all our attention to writing and illustrating our own books."

"Really? Did the authors like the illustrations?" he asked.

"No. They loved them."

"Good job. I'm so proud of you, Annalee."

"Wow! I never heard those words before." Her head drooped.

"You deserve to hear them. I'm sorry you never had a good family life. Except, you will always have that with us. Just stay with us and quit worrying about going back to your mother. She brings you down, Anna. You are a daughter to us. We love you just like a daughter."

"If I didn't think you were feeling sorry for me, I might consider it, but I can't take advantage of the only mom and dad I have ever known. I don't want you to get tired of me being around," she confessed.

"Do you know what you're saying? Even when you get on our nerves, we have always wanted you with us."

Pointing to herself, wide lips forming downward, "Me get on your nerves?!"

"Yeah you. Like we never get on your nerves."

She folded her arms. "Good point." Nose up in the air.

"You being part of our family has never changed and will never change. All families get aggravated with each other. That's normal. We did not want you to leave the last time. You left without our consent. Were you happy staying with your mother?"

"No, never. I just didn't want to wear out my welcome. If Galaxas didn't live so far away from our office, I would have lived in her house. Now I see that we can work from home just as easily as going to the office. In the near future, that's what we'll do."

"Annalee, we don't ever want you to leave. You're our daughter and it hurts to think you don't feel that way."

"Okay Dad. You win. Do you think Galaxas will ever move back to her house in Alaska?"

"First of all, no. I would never let her stay that far away ever again. Secondly, I have a feeling all our lives will change now that someone from their planet is looking for them," Mitchell answered with a questionable look.

"That's funny. I was thinking the same thing."

≈

Mitchell woke up and smelled bacon cooking. "She's making breakfast."

He got dressed and walked to the kitchen. Nebulane jumped out and embraced him.

"My dear, how long have you been here?"

"Early this morning. I didn't want to wake you," Nebulane answered cheerfully.

"It is so good to be with you again. Where's Gal?" he asked.

"Sleeping. We thought about what you said and decided it made sense. Here we are. Ta da!"

"So, I guess they never found you in North Carolina?" he noted.

"No. To be safe, we figured it best to come back and really throw them off the trail. This newfound skill of Galaxas has come in handy. They can't seem to follow us that way. Eventually, yes, they will, but it's a great backup plan. I just need to figure out how it really works."

"Neb, I'm so worried that it will happen. I'll never see you again, or Galaxas."

"Please don't fret over something that hasn't happened. Let's embrace life together while we can, Mitch."

He squeezed her hand. "Yes, let's do that."

She sat in thought. A giggle escaped. "I'll never forget the first time I met you. I was lost here on Earth, in another world, scared and untrusting. You found me on one of your excavations and saved my life. You took me in, gave me food and shelter, and never asked for a thing. How could I not fall in love with you?"

"I wondered how you two met," Galaxas' voice trailed from the hallway. Her head poked around the corner. Mitchell ran up and grabbed her, swinging her around. "I always knew you were an amazing person, Dad." She still didn't put her mother's words together about her dad not being with them as they came to Earth. It was information overload.

He placed a hand on her cheek. "How could I not be? I have the three most wonderful women in the world."

"Speaking of three, where is our other daughter?" Nebulane asked.

Sniffles were heard in the hallway. Galaxas ran and pulled Annalee out. Wiping her tears, she said, "I'm starting to feel like your real daughter. I don't know why I'm crying," she replied feeling embarrassed.

"Because you know we all love you, sis," Galaxas replied.

Annalee broke out in a tearful smile. Nebulane and Mitchell walked up and all four embraced.

"Okay. Enough of this mushy stuff. Let's eat," Annalee said still embarrassed.

After breakfast Galaxas and Annalee went to a bedroom. Seeing the backed-up workload completed brought much joy to Galaxas. She hugged and thanked Annalee. They grabbed their children's books and began writing.

Not giving any thought, Annalee opened the heavy curtains to bring in some light. Galaxas brought up an arm to cover her eyes.

"Annalee! What are you trying to do to me?"

"Sorry. While you were gone, I instinctively opened the curtains for natural light. I'll close them." Galaxas was able to relax and return to her work.

"You know, you're like a vampire. You can't be in sunlight."

"Oh, okay. Get back to work," Galaxas said in jest.

"What story did you come up with anyway?" Galaxas inquired.

"My Best Friend the Alien."

"Really?" Galaxas asked.

"Yeah. Look at my illustrations."

"It looks just like me. That's really sweet. Thank you," Galaxas remarked touched.

"And are you sticking with your original story?" Annalee asked of her.

"Yes. I mean, it's almost done anyway. I titled it 'Ember Pines,' but I already have plans for a second book: 'My best Friend the Human.' Take a look at my illustrations. I was excited and already started them."

"How funny. That looks just like me," Annalee remarked.

"Hey, I have another surprise for you. I'm going to color my hair with natural colors. My appointment is tomorrow."

"No kidding. How much weight have you lost? You're getting skinny."

"Thirty pounds. I really feel better. More energy."

~

Annalee walked into the house after her hair appointment.

Galaxas heard the commotion in the living room and her bedroom door flung open, and paper rattled as it hit the floor. "What's going on?"

Mitchell and Nebulane moved out of the way and Annalee stood perfectly still waiting for Galaxas' response. She slapped a hand across her mouth. "Is that you, Annalee?"

"In the flesh."

"You look amazing. The hair colors look so natural on you."

"My natural hair color is a dark auburn, so we went with that and added golden highlights. Guess what? On the way to my car a cute guy stopped and took down my phone number. First time ever!"

Galaxas grabbed her arm and pulled her to the bedroom. "Come on, I want all the details." She was excited for her friend.

The springs squeaked as they both jumped on the bed, sitting on their knees. Galaxas' face was bright with a wide smile. "So, what's his name and what does he look like?"

"His name is Gordon. He is almost six feet, from the best I can tell. He's thin, but in good shape. Muscles easily identified. He has brown hair, blue eyes and the most masculine jawline you ever saw. His voice is a little on the deep side."

"So, did he just walk up to you or how did it happen?" Galaxas inquired.

"I dropped my keys. I didn't even notice him because I've always been shy, expecting rejection from guys. Same ol' same ol'. He spoke up and said something like 'Please allow me.' Then we just started talking. He is a senior at Florida Gulf Coast University. I guess his major in forensics will lead him to more schooling. Not sure where he will continue his education."

Annalee's phone rang. She looked at the display. It was Gordon. "Huh! It's him."

"Remember, you're beautiful, special and intelligent. Have confidence when talking to him. Answer it!"

Galaxas backed out of the room as Annalee answered, "Hello.

She plopped on the couch excited. "I'm so happy for her," Galaxas said to her dad. But a sadness developed.

"What is it, kiddo?" Mitchell asked, placing a hand on her knee.

"Don't get me wrong. I am so happy for her. But I want that, too."

He didn't see it, but Nebulane shuddered inside thinking she saw the glow, but denial shook it right out of her mind. Galaxas' heart had a mild glow around it. "It's going to happen," he said, almost with sadness. "My fear is that your circumstances will take you away and I'll never see you again. But, for your sake, I wish you to feel the love just like your mother and I have."

"Perhaps, but having to leave you, well, that part stinks," Galaxas added. They all just watched television without speaking for the rest of the evening.

Chapter Fourteen

Galaxas tossed and turned. In her sleep she moaned. Not fully alert, she jumped up in the bed and sat still replaying the dream in her mind. Flinging the blanket off, she ran to Annalee's room. Her parents' bedroom was on the other side of the house, and they didn't hear the fast-paced run. As the door swung open and smacked into the wall, it woke Annalee up in a fret.

"What's wrong? Is there a fire? Are aliens here to destroy our planet?"

Shaking her head in amusement Galaxas replied, "No, nothing like that. But you do sort of look like an alien yourself, miss rat's nest times two."

Annalee glanced at the clock. The red glow of the numbers showed it was 2:30 am. Pointing her hand to the clock, she said, "Any idea what time it is?"

"I'm sorry. I needed to tell you before I forget the dream."

Now curious, Annalee leaned forward. "Go on, then. Let's hear it."

"I met her."

"Her? I thought you were going to meet him. You know, your mate."

"Ember Pines, that's who. Annalee, she is so amazing, so beautiful, even though her golden hair looks messy and clumps together at times. It has real gold streaks throughout it. It wasn't just her appearance. Goodness, humbleness and kindness radiated through her eyes.

"But something bad happened. Something that's not in my book. In my dream, she was grown up. Annalee! It's like she is real."

"Hhhh! That just gave me goosebumps. Look, Gal." She held her arm out.

"Me, too. See." Galaxas held her arm out.

"So, back to the story. Something bad happened. She woke up in an unfamiliar place and had lost her memory. The place was somewhere on a ranch. Oddly enough, it looked an awful lot like my home in Seward. Anyhow, a man came home one evening and saw a glow coming from a bush. He walked up carefully, head poking out in front of him. His nerves were reacting at the speed of light. There was a curious, lovely, and natural fragrance that lingered around that spot.

"She lied curled up in a ball with a gown that appeared too big for her tiny body, torn and covered in a sparkly dust, sand and burr-like weeds. His heart pounded and his furrowed brow gave place to the questions in his mind.

"He stepped on a branch, and it crackled under his boots. It caused her to stir, so he touched her shoulder. She pushed herself up to a sitting position, hesitantly, scanning the area. When her eyes met his, she sighed with fear while backing up against a shrub. Her extra-wide eyes made me sad. The reaction was heartbreaking.

"How did she get here? Who is he? Is he going to hurt me? All those questions were apparent from her expression. That's when she saw me. I looked at her with empathy. Her pleading eyes broke my heart. I had the same questions as she did. Her begging eyes followed me as I faded away.

"Annalee. There was something so special about her and she was real. I'm guessing a victim of some malicious attempt to hurt her. If only I could describe how amazing she was. But why? Something said she was important, needed, loved but abandoned. Royalty, perhaps? It kind of reminded me of my circumstances, except she knew nothing of who she was or what happened. That much I could tell and even felt.

"I couldn't let that dream fade without telling someone."

"Good golly Miss Molly. That was a fascinating dream. And to feel like you were actually there and met the protagonist of your children's story. Kind of weird, but so amazing.

"Thank you for sharing. I'm really glad you shared this dream. Mystery. Suspense. Romance, no doubt, and probably b-e-t-r-a-y-a-l." Annalee savored "betrayal" with building anticipation. Picturing it in her mind.

"Now you've got my curious juices flowing. Maybe, just maybe, there is an adult version of Ember Pines coming in the not-too-distant future," Annalee remarked pondering her thoughts out loud.

Galaxas' face lit up at her statement.

Annalee clapped her hands. "Now get out of here. I need my beauty sleep." She gave Galaxas a gentle shove.

Chapter Fifteen

S till lost in the dream from the night before, Galaxas continued writing the children's version of Ember Pines. It was coming together wonderfully. All that was left were some more illustrations. After meeting her in a dream, it made the illustrations more significant to her.

But something clicked in her memory. *In my children's story Ember met her true love, one that was arranged just like mine, but she didn't know it at the time. Same circumstances, except she was too young for it to play out in my children's book.* "Hmmm."

This time she felt vibrations from her heart. Her head bent down, and the eyeglasses almost exploded from her face. The glow was ten times brighter than ever before. She took excited breaths. Her body and mind were yelling that something is going on here.

"What's happening? I can't get over this weird feeling that keeps bringing my mind to think this is good, not a bad thing." Her shoulders slumped. Would her mother ever share the secrets of their world with her or keep her in the dark forever, for her own good?

She broke out in a cold sweat. Physical trembling shook her whole body, but it wasn't from a sickness. Not that she knew of anyway. A virus makes a person ill. This feeling was excitement. Galaxas paced around the room. If her mother knew about any of this, it may just send her to the looney bin. She just can't handle anything else.

But what about Galaxas? How much more could she endure? This was wearing her down, obviously physically and mentally.

"Who could I talk to? Annalee is just as lost as I am. She would have no answers. I can't let anyone know about this, and I can't expose Annalee to anymore craziness."

She packed on clothing to cover the heart area so none of her family could see what was going on with it. While the rest of them watched a recording on the television, she sat outside on the porch swing without their knowledge. They thought she was in her room working on the book.

Cold sweats increased. Droplets fell from her forehead.

Moisture developed on the neck and underarm area of her shirt. It wasn't from being hot or ill. It just happened.

"Ick. I don't like this," flapping her arms up and down. Her mouth dipped down.

Trembling grew stronger. How could she hide this new physical development from her family? Maybe she should tell them she came down with a virus, but do people from her planet get sick? Her mother never got sick.

To make things worse, she really had no idea if this physical development was because it was time to meet her dream guy or some weird thing that happens to people like her. Maybe she really is sick.

The butterflies flitting around in her stomach were so strong. If it has to do with a guy, then she was willing to meet him. How could she go on like this? It's virtually impossible at this point. Something has to happen before her heart bursts through her chest.

"Maybe he'll be really good. And maybe our lives together can save our planet. And maybe we will be so in love that it would be a crime to keep us apart.

"What if he's ugly? What if he thinks I'm ugly?"

Her head was spinning with questions. To avoid thinking any further about it, she worked on the book all day. She even convinced Annalee to bring lunch and afternoon tea to her. The illustrations were coming to life. Almost physically. It was so strange to look at, as though the illustrations were alive.

Annalee popped into her room erupting with excitement.

"Guess what?"

"What?" Galaxas said swinging her hands with the same excitement.

"I have a date with Gordon tonight for dinner." She hopped up and down. Galaxas jumped up and joined hands.

"Girl, I'm so happy for you. What time? Oh no!"

"What? What?"

"Is he picking you up here?"

Her shoulders slumped. "Really? You alien goof. Of course not. I told him I would meet him at the restaurant."

"Do you think you'll be able to eat?"

"I'm sure going to try, but most likely I'll get a doggie bag."

"No time to waste. Let's see what you'll wear." Galaxas grabbed her hand and pulled her to the bedroom.

"Oh, geez. Most of my clothes are for when I was a hippopotamus."

"Well! I happen to think hippopotamuses are adorable, and so were you when you were overweight," Galaxas reacted with sentiment.

"You, I believe. It's all those mean girls and guys who showed me otherwise."

"I obviously can't come with you, but you need to go shopping and pick out something that matches the style of the restaurant. You know, classy, casual, or fast food," Galaxas directed her.

With a thumbs up, Annalee was gone.

Penetrating thoughts seeped through Galaxas' mind. "Maybe I should sit outside alone tonight. Obviously, I should fix myself up, too, if my dream man happens to be looking for me tonight. Nothing too childish, not too sexy, but an outfit that stands out. Something he'll never forget. I know that snug, but not too snug, short, but not too short, casual emerald green dress. Annalee said I look stunning in it.

"She should get a dress like that. I'll text her." She stopped in thought momentarily realizing she was talking to herself again. She hadn't done that since Clayton's death. A smile formed. It felt good to realize she didn't have to carry on a conversation with herself.

The text chimed that it was sent. Annalee's reply came next.

"Great minds think alike. Already bought it. Thanks."

After a shower and getting dressed, Annalee knocked on Galaxas' door. She was physically but mildly trembling.

"Come on in." She took one look at Annalee and her colored pencil clinked and clinked to a stop on the floor. Her chair screeched as she jumped up. Hands turned Annalee around for observation.

"All I can say is wow!"

"I have never worn anything like this. Be honest. Is it too much? Do I look hideous? I bought another outfit just in case," Annalee asked uncertain.

"If you change it, I'll punch you right in the face."

Annalee's head jumped back. "I wasn't expecting that reaction."

"It's hard, I know. After the ridicule we both received all our lives, it's understandable, but you need to walk out of here confidently. You look so beautiful. Believe me. I would never let you walk out of here if you weren't a showstopper, Annalee."

"My stomach is queasy, Gal. I don't know if I can go through with this date."

"Take my advice. You're intelligent and beautiful. Keep those thoughts at all times and talk about positive things, like your writing, illustrating, books, music, etc. Try to stay away from past ridicule, home life, things that will bring the mood down. If he's the right guy, later those things will come out and need to come out. Just let the first date be fun. Just have fun."

"Okay. Thanks for the advice. How did you get so wise?" Annalee asked.

"*Frasier*," Galaxas giggled, "and reading, blah, blah, blah."

"Gotcha."

Now that she was gone, Galaxas jumped in the shower, fixed herself up and laid the dress out for later. No way was she going to give her parents anything to question. Tingles ran down her spine at the anticipation of a possible meeting of her dream man.

"Am I making all of this up in my head because I want to be in a relationship so badly? I sound like a thirteen-year-old child. I don't know what's real or make believe anymore."

She held her heavy head in her hand and closed her eyes. A cold sweat developed again and this time she noticed the trembles on her body after reopening her eyes.

Deep breaths kept coming out of her mouth in an attempt to calm herself down. "That's it. I have to talk with Mom. What if I really have a disease?"

The door opened quietly. She walked softly down the hallway, stopping and starting. Feeling silly and then concerned. Her parents were talking, so now was as good of a time as any to eavesdrop.

"Nebulane, please calm down before you have a heart attack," Mitchell insisted. "Everything is going to work out. We'll keep her safe. I don't know how to help you calm down. Your hand is trembling like I've never seen before."

"You can't help me. I am so fearful for my child that I can't quit shaking. Until I know what's going on, I will not be okay. I'm sorry for what this is doing to you. To all of you," she acknowledged.

Those words caused Galaxas to turn around and go back to her room. How could she possibly tell Nebulane what physical changes her body is making? Cold sweat droplets fell on her arm. But all of a sudden, bursts of light flashed through her shirt from the heart area.

To survive, she had to shut down her mental thoughts. Cold sweat kept pouring down her shirt. It looked like she was caught in a rainstorm. Dizziness claimed her and she fell onto the bed and did not move.

Chapter Sixteen

T he porch swing rocked back and forth that evening. Stars glittered happy thoughts. Galaxas had butterflies in her stomach as she searched the sky. She kept looking at her cellphone realizing it was now 10 o'clock. Her head tilted down so she could examine the area of her heart. No glow whatsoever.

"Am I really sitting out here expecting to meet this guy who is supposed to become my husband? How utterly insane this sounds. Maybe my mother and I really do have a skin condition and perhaps it's causing her to lose her mind and make all this stuff up. But wouldn't my father tell me? And, what about that light signal I saw up in space? Did I make that up? Was it all some delusional episode that I disintegrated Clayton with my eyes? Was he even real?"

The insects and frogs played a melody for her. She laid her head back and just sat motionless. When she sat back up, the cellphone shined the time on the clock to be 11 o'clock. Slow steps, head drooping, Galaxas crawled back into the window of her room. She changed into pj's and went out to the kitchen for a glass of water, shaking her head at how psychotic she felt.

"Thought you were asleep."

"No, Dad. Just came to get some water. I was hoping Annalee

would be back by now, but that must be a good sign. I'm ready for bed now."

"You almost have a sound of disappointment in your tone."

"Oh, do I?" She faked a yawn. "Just tired. That's all." She kissed his cheek. "Night, Dad."

"Night, kiddo."

She sat at the window in the dark, searching, hoping. A light spotted, her heart beat faster. She pushed herself up closer to the window and followed the light. Then she slid back and relaxed. Annalee was home. But curiosity about the date gave her a new energy.

She jumped up and ran to Annalee's room and turned the light on, anxious to hear how the date went. She literally plopped her body on the bed waiting for her. On the desk were illustrations. She leaned over and grabbed one. Her eyes blurred. It was an illustration of Annalee and her in a warm embrace, and of Annalee with wacky hair colors. She rubbed the picture affectionately with her finger.

"Waiting up for me, Mom?" Annalee asked.

"Yes, young lady. Do you know what time it is?" Galaxas laughed and so did Annalee.

"I see you found my illustrations."

Galaxas held the page over her heart. "It's precious. So precious to me."

"To me as well," Annalee commented emotionally.

Handing her the page, Annalee placed it back on the desk.

"Well?" Galaxas said pointedly.

"Okay, you snooper. I'll tell you all of it. I had a nice time. We spoke easily and I kept replaying in my mind what you instructed me not to say, and you were right.

"He's charming, good looking and intelligent. Being my first opportunity to feel good about myself, I kept myself calm and collected, not wanting him to think I was desperate for attention, even though I was. You understand."

"Certainly. Of course," Galaxas replied.

"We had a good conversation, and he complimented my

attire. He looked so good. But you want to know if he kissed me; right?"

"Duh!" Galaxas said with her hands flying up.

"Just a very soft kiss to the lips as we departed. He did say he'd call me and perhaps we could go out next week. There were no butterflies or hornets," Annalee noted with a giggle. "There was complete caution on my part, prohibiting myself to look upon him as a potential relationship because of my past. I don't want to react in a foolish manner.

"I saw him look at other attractive girls and they looked back. Guys and girls were always stopping by the table. He is quite popular. Quite likeable."

"Yeah, but did you like him?" Galaxas asked sincerely.

"Of course, but there wasn't any spark, like I desperately hoped for. Maybe I still imagine myself as a fat chick and subconsciously don't expect it to be too good."

"You're preaching to the choir," Galaxas sighed. I'm proud of you for keeping your head together. He may or may not be the one for you. Time will tell."

Annalee's eyes popped open. "Gal, are you sick?"

"No. Why do you ask?"

Her eyes looked like they would pop out of the sockets. "You are sweating like a pig. That is an old saying, in case you get offended. And you're trembling really badly. Hhhh! Did you see that? Light bursts just came out of your heart." Annalee slapped a hand to her heart and produced a shocked face.

"Annalee, I don't know what's happening to me and you can't tell Mom. She's on the verge of a collapse. Do you really believe any of the stories we told you? I'm starting to think my mom and I are clinically insane. My heart feels physical pain. A heaviness that scares me.

"I also feel an urgency about wanting to meet my dream man, if he even exists. Those thoughts won't leave no matter how hard I try to ignore them. I just don't understand. That could be a story Mom made up because she's going crazy."

"So, now you think everything has been a huge ruse or psychotic episode?" Annalee asked in a disappointed timbre.

Galaxas held her hands out. "You tell me."

"Not one teensy weensy bit do I believe either of you are insane. Yes, I believe everything you told me. I met Clayton and always thought he had marbles loose."

"Shoo," Galaxas replied wiping her forehead. "I even began to wonder if I made him up."

"Sorry to disappoint you, but you're not crazy. Everything has happened so fast that your mental capability is having a hard time keeping up. Maybe you need more memory storage." Annalee chuckled. "You know what I think?"

"Evidently I don't, unless that's another superpower I have and don't know about it."

"If you're not sick, then maybe according to your planet's customs, this is that physical evidence that your mate is looking for you, Gal."

"Or Mom made it all up."

"Did you see a spaceship go by or not? And did you see a figure standing in the clearing right afterwards?" Annalee was serious.

"Unless I was having hallucinations, yes, I did."

"I may have a solution. Without telling your parents, I think it would be wise for you to meet this guy, if he really exists," Annalee remarked with a tiny amount of excitement in her voice.

"Okay wise one, how?"

"That light beam could be a sign. Since we don't know how it works, how about you sit outside at night, and I will keep your parents from knowing the truth. Maybe the light from your heart is a signal for him to find you. I mean, how the heck do I know, but for the sake of your sanity, let's give it a try. Look at you. I just hope it's not some sickness from your planet. What if you need medicine or something that only comes from your planet? You have to end all of this, Gal."

"This sounds totally cuckoo, but you're right. Look at how hard my heart is beating."

"Oh-my-gosh. Does it hurt?"

"No. It's actually an excited feeling. I can't explain, because how the heck do I know?" Galaxas dropped her head.

"If something doesn't happen in two weeks, I'm going to your mother."

"Promise you won't say anything until then," Galaxas begged.

Annalee extended her hand and Galaxas shook it. "It's a deal, McSpeal." Her bangle bracelets jingled.

Galaxas formed a one-sided grin at her choice of words.

～

The next evening, they sat outside. "Anna, what if he lost interest in trying to find me? My heart lost its glow."

She wiggled her hands around. "Gal, I know nothing of your planet's culture. There is no answer I can give you except to never give up hoping. Never."

"That's what I thought you'd say, but you're right. I won't give up."

"By the way, how many times have I told you to use my full name? I don't like being called Ann or Anna."

After slapping a hand against her mouth, Galaxas made the "oops" expression. "Wait a minute. Why is it okay for you to call me 'Gal'?"

"Hmmf. Because it's not as boring as Ann or Anna."

"I happen to think Ann or Anna is a pretty name," Galaxas responded. Annalee waved her off.

～

Day two, three, four, and fourteen passed by. Annalee walked into her room and found Galaxas sitting at the desk with her head lying on her hands. She forced her to go outside for fresh air and promised Galaxas that she would cover for her in case anyone walking by noticed her and asked questions about her appearance.

Galaxas sat on the porch swing with a face that depicted the very essence of disappointment. She wasn't a gloomy, doomsday type of person regardless of the lonely life she had lived. At the very moment, sunrays burst through the sky and snuck under the porch ceiling that caressed her arm with warmth. It gave her a brighter outlook. For her sake all these years, her personality always reverted back to being perky.

Annalee peeked through the window and walked out to the porch. "How about you cover up and we take a walk. Here," she said handing over a long-sleeved shirt, "This material is made to keep us cool in hot climates. Put on a cap and those three-inch sunglasses and let's get some fresh air."

"Really? You think it's safe?"

"Very safe. We'll tell people you have a disease-free skin and eye condition, should anyone ask."

"That sounds like a wonderful idea. Let me change and off we go," Annalee replied.

After a lot of coaxing and begging, Nebulane gave in.

"It's quite beautiful out today. The temperature must be in the low 70's. There is nothing like the great outdoors to lighten a mood," Galaxas mentioned.

"Hey, just ask the good doctor for advice and you'll be happy," Annalee said smugly.

"By doctor, I'm assuming you're referring to yourself?"

"The one and only." Annalee smiled and winked.

"Does Mom look worse to you?"

"Not like mentally losing it but worry. Yes, she seems more worried," Annalee agreed.

"Neither of us have any idea if the story about your mate is true, but if they have the capability to hunt you down, then why is it taking so dang long?"

"First off, we don't know if Mom made that story up because of how sad I was feeling in my circumstances, knowing here on Earth I will never find someone who isn't freaked out by my appearance. I will have to spend my life alone. But she said when the time is right, he would start searching for me. She just didn't explain how or when. I don't know what else to say," Galaxas explained with frustration.

"I would never betray our friendship, but two weeks is up.

LINDA PHILLIPS

I'm worried about your health. You haven't noticed me watching you, but your symptoms are getting way worse. Gal, I won't sit back and watch you die."

"Apart from these symptoms, I feel fine."

"Do you know for a fact that it isn't an illness?" Annalee asked.

Galaxas hung her head. "No, I don't really know." Galaxas froze in mid step.

"What's the matter? Gal?" She shook her shoulder.

"Look at my heart. Is it glowing?"

"Yikes! Like the sun," Annalee replied with wide eyes.

"We better get back and fast. I don't want anyone to see it. Let's act like we're jogging."

"I dig it," Annalee remarked.

"You what it?" Galaxas said with a scrunched face.

"Oh, never mind. It's time to talk with your mom."

"Shhh, listen. Do you hear something?" Galaxas asked.

"No, nothing."

"Maybe it was just my imagination. Come on, Anna. A deal is a deal. But if Mom is too weirded out, let's go day by day. I don't want to see her in an asylum."

Annalee smirked at her for only using part of her name, again. "That sounds fair. Okay."

When they got to the driveway, Galaxas spotted her mother sitting on the porch swing. A hand held Annalee back.

"Hold on. Take some deep breaths and walk up casually. Don't let on what you know until we can figure out her state of mind," Galaxas instructed.

"That makes a lot of sense."

The glow around Galaxas' heart area faded and didn't show through her clothing at the moment.

"Hello, Mother. I'm a grown woman and I don't need you checking up on me." She was trying to act normal and not let on how she was worried about Nebulane's mental health.

"I, um...I...I'm sorry. I'm just worried for your safety."

"Look," Galaxas said twirling around, "all in one piece. Come on inside, Mom. I'm taking a shower. There is more sweat on me than an athlete."

Guilt taking hold of her face, Nebulane just nodded her head and went inside with them. Galaxas jumped in the shower, threw on a cute short set and sat around until it got dark, looking out the window like she was a detective at a stakeout. Outside, the skies were dark now. She paced in her room, then went out to dinner, constantly watching her mother's face.

Nebulane looked curious at Galaxas and asked, "Are you on a sugar high, because your words are coming out fast and jittery."

"That's it. No more sugar for me for a while. I can't even eat this divine dinner you prepared. I think I'll go work on my illustrations for a while." She glanced at Annalee with a direct stare, hoping her physical ailments weren't exposed.

"Oh, yeah, good idea. I meant to tell you that there is probably an hour's worth of emails waiting for your response. We have many illustration requests, with Donna begging," Annalee responded with fast thinking. And it was true.

"Oooh, I better get to it then." She skipped off. "No interruptions," trailed from her lips. The door clunked as it closed. She just needed to think of the next step. She heard something weird on their walk and couldn't help but wonder about it.

"Do you mind if I close the blinds?" Annalee asked Nebulane.

"Go right ahead. Normally they would have been closed hours ago. Guess I was preoccupied," saying it while staring blankly at the wall.

Annalee felt a nervous jilt surge through her veins before pulling the blinds down. She never saw Nebulane this lost in thought before and also how odd she had been acting.

"I think I'll go work on my book," Annalee said in passing.

"All right, dear."

The dark sky twinkled with stars.

A soft tapping increased the jitters Galaxas felt. "Is that you, Annalee?"

"Yes."

She unlocked the door and held a finger up, then motioned her forward with a hand.

"Is she any better?" Galaxas asked.

"No, worse."

I need some air and alone time. Please try to keep Mom from looking for me." Galaxas took a deep breath and crossed her fingers. Out the window she went. It was 8:00 p.m. She rocked quietly on the porch swing. The television volume was loud enough for her to hear. 9 o'clock passed. The porch swing slowed to a stop. 10 o'clock.

Her nervous system had slowed down to normal. Shoulders slightly slumping, thoughts poured through her mind. Just past 10:00 o'clock, she grabbed her phone and stood up. A frustrated sigh blew out of her mouth. It doesn't matter anymore. She can't live like this and needs answers. It was time to talk with her mom. There will never be a good time, and maybe for her own life, she has to discuss all of it. She took a step and felt an odd sensation, then froze like an ice cube.

"Hello."

Her heart picked up speed, she gulped and turned slowly. Fingers beginning to shake, she looked into eyes that looked like mini suns, just like hers. They both stood there unmoving. There stood this big, gorgeous man who had the same skin and hair color as she did. He held one dandelion. Her phone chimed. She ignored it.

With great caution, he extended his hand with the dandelion. "I brought this for you." His voice was sexy, deep, and gentle.

She swallowed as tingles soared through her veins. Her chest rose slowly up and down. His voice melted her insides. She swallowed hard. She didn't know what to do, so she stood there staring. The feelings inside her wanted to be near him.

"I saw men giving flowers to girls and thought you may like one." He didn't know or understand Earth customs, only from what he had observed. Looking at the dandelion, she broke out in a snicker. It was so darn charming.

With shaky hands she took it. "Thank you. Who...who are you?"

"I have been searching for you. My name is Troid. My heart

guided me here to you. Every time I found you, you disappeared, and I had to start searching again. You won't disappear, will you?"

"How am I supposed to believe you?" she asked.

"Can you see the glow around my heart?"

She nodded.

"On our planet, it means you and I are meant to be together. Our heart only glows when we are near or next to the person we will love for life." As if she were cold, she wrapped her arms around her chest and rubbed her arms. Why is this tingling sensation so powerful?

"You may not understand this, being on Earth your whole life, but you are the light of my heart, my heart's fire, Galaxas." He gently took her hand and moved it to his heart. A force field of frissons exploded in her body.

"Do you feel the warmth, the fire?" Both of his hands pushed her out at arms' length. Combining both of their hearts, the glow took on colors of a sunset. Stuttering at this phenomenon, he asked, "Do you see how you light up my heart? You are the light of my heart. And together, just look at this glow. In all my years, I have never witnessed this amount of a glow and these colors between anyone but us. Wow! We must have a heavenly love like no other."

The words melted her. Not only did she feel the warmth, almost too hot to touch, but she saw the evidence of their hearts glow like a sunset. Being on Earth and never experiencing anything like this or able to understand what he was saying, she couldn't help but think: *He just met me. How could he say something like that? Talk about a unique pickup line. What am I supposed to think? Oh, gosh. I'm so drawn to him that I don't want whatever is happening to stop.*

His words were inspiring. It was sweet and affectionate. Romantic.

"How do you know my name? I didn't know yours. And, how could you say those things to someone you just met?"

"Our people told me your name. They know of you and Queen Nebulane. In our world, once we know who our mate is, that is just how we feel. I can't help how I feel for you, whether you understand it or not. Could we sit and talk?"

Actually, Galaxas felt every bit of what he was saying, but she was too confused to admit it.

"Are you evil? I need to see your sun pendant," she demanded.

A genuine smile formed. He pulled it out and the beams were bright, so bright she panicked.

"Put it away. Hurry before my mother sees this light.

"Now, how do I know it is real and that you're truly part of the good army?" She stared with a seriousness.

"Let's compare your pendant with mine," she demanded again. The pendants were made of the same material and completely identical in shape and color. Still uneasy, what choice does she have? And all this tingling inside felt too wonderful to stop now.

"Please, have a seat," she said.

His footsteps were heavy but confident, the deck boards sounding like they would collapse with each step he took. Soft but strong. She sat down next to him and almost asked for a defibrillator as she gulped.

Heart thumping, she said, "My mother doesn't know you're here. She will freak out and send you away or send our family away. She escaped the evil. Are you with them, corrupted like them or what?"

"We have some real secretive hiding spots on our planet. We also have a huge army awaiting the queen to give us the go ahead and attack. Take back our planet. They are strong and evil, so we don't mix with them. But we have the hand of God on our side. Timing is everything, so we will wait on God's direction. Queen Nebulane created the hideout a long time ago that only a few people knew about. That is where we have been hiding.

"As you can tell, our technology is far ahead of Earths, but God gave us different goals. Our planet's name means 'in God's shadow'. We keep watch, but one of our own betrayed us, is how we got in this mess.

"As far as us," his index finger pointed to himself and then to her, "even though our true love is ordained at birth, we can refuse to be with that person, but we'll never find love again. It's kind of sad. Please don't refuse me, Galaxas. Can't you feel how much I love you already? Living here on this planet, of course I expect you to question my proclamation. On our planet, when the time is right it happens immediately. We know and feel the love that quickly."

He placed her hand on his heart. She started to pull away, but the warmth was irresistible. His chest felt like steel. His hand was strong but gentle. His scent had to be a mixture of galaxies. It was so enticing and tingly. He was everything and so much, much more than she ever anticipated. Was it this easy to fall in love?

"Do you feel the sparks between us?"

She nodded.

He pointed up at the stars. "You and I are made out of those stars. Our hearts twinkle in unison with their warmth."

A smile developed on her charming face.

"You and I will take overruling our country. We were meant to be together."

Mouth blowing up, she sputtered and pointed to herself. "Me? Rule?"

"Your mother didn't tell you? I see. Yes, that is the plan."

Her phone chimed. She looked at the text. "I need to respond."

The reply said, "I'm fine. He's here! I am so in love. What's better than gorgeous? Because he's that gorgeous."

The reply had a smiley face with tears of happiness from Annalee.

"I can't let my mother see you. We'll have to meet again but not here. It's possible that you found a way to get around being truthful with me about being corrupted. I need more proof. I'll meet you tomorrow evening at the Buckingham Community Center after dark. I am bringing my best friend with me. You'll be able to find me. It's just down Buckingham Road."

Disappointed, he managed a smile. "Sure, if you like. I'm bringing my best friend, too."

He stood, extended his hand for her to accept. She did and he pulled her up next to him. His hand gently moved hair from her eyes. She quivered. "Galaxas, I really do love you. You are more beautiful than I ever imagined. I know this sounds crazy to you, since you grew up on a different planet, but I'm being honest."

He gently removed the dandelion from her hand and pressed it on her nose, then both cheeks, and lastly, on her lips. She grasped onto his arms as best she could. She was nothing but a bowl of jello.

Then he did the unthinkable. His lips touched her cheek, and he held her up because she almost slid to the ground. Unexplainable. Her sincere smile caused him to brush his hand across her cheek.

"Until tomorrow. I want to walk in our sunset forever and give you dandelion kisses." The glow from their hearts had transformed into the colors of a sunset once again. Of all the people on his planet, this was a first.

He handed her the dandelion and was gone in a flash. Her breaths were almost hyperventilating. She took deep breaths to steady herself. Holding the dandelion like it would break in two, she climbed back in the window. Quickly, she threw on her pajamas.

Annalee heard Galaxas' bedroom door squeak open. She jumped off the bed and slowly opened her door. Galaxas stood there motionless holding the dandelion.

"Get in here. Hurry up. Tell me everything," Annalee said with bursting excitement. "Why do you have yellow stains on your face?"

Very carefully, Galaxas laid the dandelion on the nightstand and robotically touched her face. Her arms hugged herself tightly. "You'll get to meet him tomorrow. We're meeting him and his best friend at the Buckingham Community Center tomorrow evening. The yellow spots are from dandelion kisses."

They held hands and bounced up and down.

"Is he good?" Annalee asked.

"Yes. Well, I think. He showed me the identical pendant.

He's so beautiful. Annalee, I honestly thought I was going to pass out from the electricity flowing through my body. It can't be explained. Is it silly for me to admit that I love him? I really love him already."

"Wow! Look at my arms. Hurry." Annalee pulled the sleeve up.

"That's what my insides look like right now," Galaxas confided.

"What does he look like, Gal?"

"Of course, there is no one on Earth to compare to, but he is about six foot five or taller. He is extremely muscular, big and strong, but not sickening. It's natural. His hair hangs down past his chin about one to two inches. Annalee, he's gentle, romantic, kind and patient. He thinks I'm beautiful, not a freak. His name is Troid."

"I love that name," Annalee said pulling her hands together under her chin.

"Get this, he told me he loved me. He placed my hand over his heart and told me to feel the love. I felt it. It was so romantic. I can't help but feel he is good and not corrupted. There is no sign of evil at all, Annalee."

"What about your mom? Will you tell her?"

"Not until I'm sure." That statement changed Galaxas' mien.

"Oh, wow, this is exciting," Annalee remarked holding her hands together next to her sunshiny face.

"You have been out on a few more dates with Gordon. How do you feel about him now?" Galaxas asked Annalee.

"Not sure. I'm sensing a little control vibe from him. He acts like 'oops' and tries to cover it up."

"Get out fast! Warning, warning! Another Clayton," Galaxas replied flailing her arms around like the robot of *Lost in Space*.

"Don't think so, but I'm taking precautions," Annalee replied staring at the wall. They both headed to bed. Galaxas stared at the ceiling for a while before passing out.

Chapter Seventeen

After a night of tossing and turning, pillow flattened from fluffing it so much, Galaxas turned on the radio and sat cross- legged on the bed. Grand Funk blasted through the speakers, and words to the song brought a connection. She searched the internet for the lyrics. Her door flew open so fast, her hair blew out.

She opened Annalee's door and jumped on her bed. Shaking her, she said, "Wake up! Wake up! Look at these lyrics."

Annalee's half open eyes tried to seek clarity. She pushed her body up enough to see Galaxas and removed a wide strip of hair from covering her eyes. Sleepy eyes glanced over at the clock. "It's early but not too early. What is it, Gal?" A tone that said, couldn't whatever it is wait.

"Read these lyrics but replace 'girl' with 'boy'."

Impatiently she grabbed the phone and sighed. Then she read it, mostly so that Galaxas would go away and let her get back to sleep.

I'm in love with the girl (boy) that I'm talking about
I'm in love with the girl (boy) I can't live without
I'm in love but I sure picked a bad time
To be in love
To be in love

"That's nice." Annalee dropped the phone and closed her eyes.

"Annalee!" Galaxas shook her. "That's nice? That's all?"

"What do you want me to say? I love the song."

Holding hands over her heart, a serious face, Galaxas commented, "It's how I feel about Troid. You have to admit it's a bad time to be in love. Think how Mom and Dad will react."

"Got it. Yes, the song makes sense. It must have been written solely for you." There was a teensy amount of sarcasm in her voice.

Galaxas slapped Annalee's arm in fun. "I can't help it. He's in my thoughts constantly. Get this: we're going to rule our planet together."

"So, he's a prince? King?" Annalee asked as her face brightened.

Fingers rubbing her jaw, Galaxas responded. "I don't really know. After what Mom told me, does that mean I'm a princess or a queen?"

Annalee was wide awake now. "We need clarification." She jumped up, grabbed a robe and pulled Galaxas with her.

They both stood not knowing how to ask the questions running through their minds. Nebulane looked up from reading a book while crunching on toast. Her face showed she was trying to analyze their thoughts.

"Let's hear it, girls," she said in hesitancy.

"Mom, am I princess?" Galaxas' forehead crimped.

"Have to say, I didn't see that coming. On our planet we really don't identify someone as a princess. You automatically would take over my role when I stepped down. I guess if you compare it to Earth, then yes, you are."

Galaxas and Annalee shared a Shawn and Gus fist bump like they did on the television series *Psych*, one of their favorite shows.

"Does that also mean the guy I marry has to be royal?"

"No. He will be from a well-standing, Godly family. Probably the highest rank leading our armies," Nebulane answered.

"By any chance does a guy come to your mind?" Galaxas

asked with a hopeful visage. Who you think would be chosen for me?"

"Unfortunately, I left before anything like that was revealed. I always had suspicions of my most royal guard's son. Zareb was my most loyal royal guard. I always wondered if maybe his son would be the one."

"What was his son's name?" Galaxas asked with tingles running through her body.

"I can't remember."

⁓

Galaxas was lost in thought. The feeling inside was more pleasurable than she ever could foresee. Her head lay in her hand, eyes staring into oblivion.

Annalee walked up. "Follow your heart, even if love takes you to the stars in the heavens or down into the depths of the sea." She softly touched Galaxas' shoulder. "Reach beyond the stars, Gal."

"Right now, I don't know if that's good or bad advice, because my heart is taking me to the stars."

"We'll figure it out. Don't fret." Annalee patted her shoulder.

The girls worked up a plan to leave later that night. Annalee stood in the hallway and yelled to Galaxas. "Galaxas, will you ride with me to get some fries and a soda?"

She cracked her door open just enough to be heard. "Kind of busy."

"You need a break," Annalee lied. "The break will help clear your thoughts. Tell me that's not true?"

"All right, you nag. Give me a minute." Galaxas' words were a front to keep Nebulane from knowing the truth. She dressed in the cutest outfit, and they walked out to the living room together.

"Is that a new outfit, Annalee? It's adorable," Galaxas asked.

"Why, yes, it is, Gal. I see you're wearing the outfit I bought you. Really cute on you, too."

"So, I take it you girls are heading out for some fries?" Nebulane ascertained.

"Yes, Mom. Is there anything we can bring back for you?"

"No thank you."

"When is Mitchell coming back?" Annalee asked sincerely.

"Hopefully by the end of the month. He has found some amazing things on the dig. He said it is one of the best expeditions yet," Nebulane replied.

"Gosh, I miss him," Galaxas acknowledged.

"Me, too," Nebulane and Annalee responded together.

"We'll be back in a little while. Bye, Mom," Galaxas yelled walking out.

"Yeah, bye, Mom," Annalee repeated. Nebulane teared up about Annalee's response. They really did love her like a daughter.

"Okay, girls."

Inside the car, Galaxas became quiet. Annalee glanced over at her.

"You're nervous; aren't you?"

Galaxas held up her arm. Annalee could see her hand shake.

"Listen. I'll say the name 'Grand Funk' and that will alert you to a warning. You grab my hand and transport us out of there if you feel threatened," Annalee said with a double take at the absurdity of her remark.

"Transport us? That sounds insane. How will you know if he is dangerous? There's no way you could tell," Galaxas riposted.

"Okay, then you yell 'Grand Funk' and grab my hand. Isn't 'Grand Funk' the coolest name ever?" Annalee asked whimsically.

"I'm in total agreement. Coolest name ever."

The car turned slowly into the Buckingham Community Center parking lot.

"You better park across the road. The playground is closed, and we don't want any police officers stopping in," Galaxas informed her.

"Wise thinking, Princess Galaxas."

Galaxas waved her hand out to show how ridiculous that sounded.

"Any sign of him?" Annalee asked.

Galaxas' powerful vision scanned the area. "Nope. Not yet."

Annalee grabbed her arm and pulled her across the street. They stayed close to each other and found a park bench to sit on. They jabbered to help alleviate the climbing nerves.

"Maybe he's lost. After all, he's not from around here," Annalee said.

Galaxas shook her head. "Or maybe..."

"Hello." His melting voice came from behind them. Instant tingling covered her body.

They both turned towards his voice. Annalee looking around to see him, but without the powerful vision Galaxas had, it was impossible. She jabbed Galaxas with her elbow. "Get him to come into the light."

"Would you mind stepping into the light so I can introduce you to my friend."

He didn't answer but just moved out of the darkness. Annalee almost collapsed. Galaxas fell into a trance at the sight of him.

Using a hand to cover one side of her mouth, "Gal, you're not kidding. I can't think of a word that would justify how gorgeous he is," Annalee whispered in her ear.

Coming back down to earth, she replied, "He can hear you," she said with a swing of her head.

"Troid, please meet Annalee."

He smiled and shook her hand. She was speechless, hands flimsy in his. "Oh, my," she sighed. He licked his lips and held in a chuckle.

"Raiden, please come and meet my Galaxas and her friend."

He stepped out and Annalee gasped and then tripped. Raiden hurried to her side and gently helped to stand her up.

Troid looked at Galaxas amused. "She's a mess," Galaxas replied with an affectionate laugh.

"It's so nice to finally meet you. My, but you are incredibly beautiful," Raiden said shaking Galaxas' hand. And you, as well," he said shaking Annalee's hand."

Being so flabbergasted, all Annalee could do was smile and nod her head.

"Shall we sit down?" Troid inquired of Galaxas.

"Annalee, why don't you and Raiden sit on that bench, and we'll sit right next to you."

Galaxas couldn't remember a time when she saw Annalee at a loss for words.

"She thinks you're gorgeous, and from her reaction, I can tell she thinks the same of Raiden. She's used to the difference in our appearances from hanging around me all these years."

With their skin tone, you couldn't tell he blushed, but his shy smile and fidgeting was point enough.

"So, have you given much thought to our meeting yesterday?" he asked Galaxas.

"The problem is that I don't know how to think. I'm completely ignorant of our planet, from living here on Earth all this time. My mother is terrified you may be evil and here to capture us."

"Certainly, I can understand her fears and even justify the precautions she has taken to keep you safe. She's an admirable woman. The stories I heard about her ruling is inspiring, courageous, and sincere. I look so forward to meeting her, but yet, a little intimidated."

"No kidding. To me, she's just Mom. I guess she had to adapt to this lifestyle and not bring attention to herself."

He took her hand and held it between his. "Galaxas, if I wanted to capture you, we would have brought an army. We would have completed the task."

"See, my mind keeps playing games. It's telling me that maybe this is all an act to get us to trust you and bring us back to the planet. Then you will use subterfuge to convert us to the evil side. See how my dumb mind works."

He cracked a smile. "There is nothing dumb about you, and I guess you have every right to wonder. I won't push you into anything. Trust is just as important to me. Maybe on this planet it is hard to understand how two people could be this deeply in love at first sight, like us."

She could see his heart palpitations, wondering if that was a Betzalel thing. Watching him with warm eyes and a toasty heart, with the most genuine, handsome, loving face she ever saw, he finished his proclamation.

"Galaxas, you are everything I wished for and more. My heart leaps with excitement being with you. I truly, with all my heart, love you. Just the thought of not spending my life with you breaks my heart. Life will be meaningless. Please, don't reject me."

His bright glowing light around the heart reflected on the playground equipment until he made the last statement. It caught Galaxas' attention and she couldn't help but stare as the glow began to dull. As sweetly and affectionately as possible, she held his hand and squeezed it. "I'd be a liar if I said I didn't feel the same way. I feel it, too."

Both of their hearts shot out a glow so powerful, it caused Annalee and Raiden to take notice.

"Wow!" Raiden exclaimed. "All my life, I have never witnessed such a strong love bond. It almost makes me senti-mental, even bringing tears to my eyes."

"You're saying that the way their heart glows indicates they are deeply in love?" Annalee asked.

"This isn't the first time I've witnessed it, but this is the first time I have seen such power, such a deep love bond, one that affects my soul. And to be honest, they have a glow I have never witnessed before. Their hearts have the glow of a sunset. Don't you agree?"

"Now that you mention it, yes. It's absolutely stunning, and a little overwhelming. This is better than any love story I've ever read or watched," Annalee confessed.

"Believe it or not, I've had fun not being in a relationship, but after seeing them, I want what they have," he admitted while watching Troid and Galaxas.

"Oh! So, you haven't found yours yet? Does it have to be

someone from your planet?" She tried her best not to be so obvious.

"Most likely. Unless the girl for me has been corrupted.

Then it changes and God gives me, or any of us, another chance to find love."

Annalee's face brightened up.

"And you? Did you find yours?" he asked Annalee.

"It's different here. We don't have a physical event that directs us to that person. We just hope the person we marry will bring that type of love. Cherished love. And, no, I have not found him."

"Not understanding how you do things here on Earth, all I can do is ask, but I hope you will want to spend time with me while we're here."

Could he read her mind? She swallowed hard. "It would be my pleasure. Any idea how long you will be here?"

"None. It all depends on those two," he said pointing.

Annalee glanced over at Galaxas just as Troid cupped her face and pulled her slowly to him. He kissed her gently, then a whole lot of warmth took over. Her hands went around his neck, and they kissed with intentions of not wanting to stop. Annalee's body tickled with intensity, as if a bed covering of goose-down feathers was brushing her body without the cover.

Checking the time on her cellphone, Annalee cleared her throat. Galaxas broke away from the magnetic pull of Troid's lips and sheepishly looked for Annalee.

"As much as I hate to leave, Galaxas, your mother is probably in panic mode. We should leave before she suspects anything."

"Oops. I lost track of time," Galaxas confessed.

"No kidding," Annalee commented satirically. Galaxas stuck her tongue out.

"Do you have some sort of mind-controlling power or magnetic grasp?" Galaxas asked Troid.

"Not the last time I looked. I was wondering the same thing about you," Troid admitted.

She stood up and he followed. He reached for her arm. "Galaxas, I'm not ready for you to leave. Do you have to go?"

"Yes. Annalee is right. I have to be completely certain before you can meet my mother, and Mom is probably freaking out." She glanced at her cellphone. "Yup, three texts and two calls. I gotta go."

"When will I see you again?" Troid's voice was strong and unsure.

"By any chance do you have cellphones?"

"We have communication devices. He held his sleeve up. See that button, it does it all."

"Do I give you my phone number or do you give me yours?"

"Put your phone up and I'll scan it. Then I can get in touch with you." She did and it buzzed as it scanned. He exhaled a relieved sigh.

"Let me figure out how and when we can get together. You can contact me tomorrow, but I just can't allow my mom to know. I'll figure out a way."

He pulled her in tight, stared into her eyes and kissed her with a prayer in his heart. He just can't lose her now.

Raiden planted a soft kiss on Annalee's cheek. "Wherever he goes, I go, so I'll see you then." If she were ice cream, she would be melting into a runny liquid form.

In the car Galaxas sent a text to her mom apologizing for missing her texts and calls and that they sat out on a park bench talking without their phones.

"Now what?" Annalee asked.

Galaxas shook her head back and forth. "I don't know what to do. Mom will get suspicious fast. I can't keep this hidden from her for very long."

"Gal, why not tell her. He seems legit to me."

"What if it's a trick? So far, I'm giving in way too easily. Maybe he cast a spell on me."

"Oh no he didn't. He has your heart. That boy has the deepest kind of love for you, Gal."

"You don't think it could be a trick? How can we feel this much love this fast? It just doesn't seem normal." Galaxas stared at the car panel lost in thought.

"Not to me. It looks sincere. This isn't a Hollywood film,

Gal. On your planet, this is how it's done. I mean, sheesh, how could you let that hunk of wonderful guy go? You're nuts if you do.

"Soooo, how was that incredible kiss? Did you feel sparks?" Annalee asked as her body twitched.

Galaxas thought momentarily. "No, no sparks."

"Aah, drat."

Galaxas smiled wide. "I felt a wildfire."

"'You dirty rat'," Annalee said imitating James Cagney. How many times did she sit through one of his films with Mitchell? "I mean, you looked like you were under his spell."

"Whatever it was, there isn't a firehose strong enough to extinguish the fire I felt."

"Ooh-la-la and woo-hoo" Annalee gently punched her arm.

"Seems to me you fell head over heels for Raiden."

"Over and over and over. Did you not notice how gorgeous he was?" Annalee asked.

"How could I not? But my heart was detoured right to Troid. I couldn't see anything but him."

"What is your honest opinion of him?" Annalee asked.

Before she could answer, a weird message came over her phone display. "I really love you."

"How could I forget to ask him if he is Zareb's son?"

Galaxas typed back not knowing if the message went through.

Her heart started glowing like the morning sun. His reply was "Yes."

"Huh-huh-huh-huh!" She patted her heart at a fast pace. It felt like a force field of tingles enveloped her.

"Before I get us in an accident, what's going on?" Annalee demanded to know loudly.

"His father's name is Zareb."

"Look, Gal. Look at my arm."

"Mine, too." Galaxas twitched.

Neither of them spoke the rest of the way home.

Chapter Eighteen

The phone chimed. Galaxas rubbed her eyes, blinked and grabbed the phone.

"Good morning my love."

She smiled and replied. "Good morning."

Chime.

"Tell Annalee good morning from Raiden, please."

"Sure thing."

Stumbling out of bed, she pounded softly on Annalee's door.

"Whatttttt," Annalee responded annoyed.

"Can I come in?"

"When have you ever knocked anyways?"

A "whooo!" sound traveled underneath the crack in the door. Galaxas threw the door open. "You're just not a morning person, are you?"

"No, I'm not, and proud of it," Annalee responded.

"Well, I won't bother you about the message from Raiden then."

Annalee jumped up like lightning. "Oh yes you will."

"I don't feel like getting my head snapped off." Galaxas turned to walk off.

"If you don't start talking it may be a punch in the nose."

They both broke out in laughter.

"He just said to tell you good morning."

"Aw, that's so sweet." Annalee fell back on the pillow and smiled.

"I have an idea. Hide all the printer paper and this evening after dinner and we'll have to make an office supply run. You insist I ride with you," Galaxas said rubbing her hands together.

"Brilliant. You're good at deception."

Galaxas slumped her shoulders. "That doesn't sound nice. I don't like deceiving my mother. This whole thing seems so childish, like we're in high school."

"Tonight, we tell Mom, Gal. And you are an adult and should be able to do things without your mother having to know everything, but this situation is different and requires her interference."

"Let me go back to my room and make plans. Keep tonight open," Galaxas told Annalee.

Late morning, Galaxas sat down with Nebulane and showed her what she was working on and included the illustrations.

"This is such a charming story and it's different from all the other fairy tales. These illustrations are outstanding. I'm so proud of you."

"Thanks, Mom."

"How about my other daughter? Is her story and illustrations done? I'd like to see them."

She hopped up. "I'll go get her."

"You want to see my work, I presume?" Annalee asked.

Nebulane patted the sofa cushion. Annalee complied and handed her the pages. As hard as it was for her to sit quietly, foot tapping the soft rug, she managed.

"This is so delightful, and your illustrations are outstanding as well. I love the story between you and Galaxas."

"I think it was fate we found each other. We both received endless criticism in school, and it brought us together like sisters. It was a two-way street. She helped me survive and I helped her. And I'll never take for granted how special you and Mitchell made me feel. Thank you, from the bottom of my heart."

"You're welcome, but only if you call me mom and Mitchell

dad. No more of this using our first names." Nebulane smiled sincerely.

Galaxas wrapped an arm around Annalee's shoulder and said, "Well?"

"It will take some practice, but I will darn sure try.

"On another note, I've been doing some new exercises. Does my butt look toned?" Annalee turned around and stuck her butt up. She wasn't good with sentimental talk, never receiving affection her whole life, so she always used humor to compensate for the uneasiness.

Galaxas shoved her onto the couch. "Dork girl."

They all had a much-needed laugh-in.

"Mother, is it possible they use the same language on your planet as the language here?" Annalee enquired.

"Believe it or not, Annalee, yes, mostly, but somewhat different. The whole planet uses one language."

"That's kind of weird. I guess movies stereotype aliens, so that's all I've had to go by," Galaxas remarked in thought.

"You know, I still can't get over the fact that 'my family'," Annalee said with pride, "are real to goodness aliens."

Another laugh-in.

After dinner, Galaxas stuffed an outfit and shoes into a tote bag. An adorable, snug-fitting pair of jeans and a soft, blush color shirt. She tossed the bag out the window. Time to execute their plan.

She opened the bedroom door and yelled out, "Annalee, we're out of paper. Can you run to the store and pick some up?"

"Only if you ride along with me."

"Okay. I could use a break," Galaxas snapped back fast before she lost her nerve.

"Mother, anything you need while we're out?" Galaxas asked.

"Again? It seems you're always going somewhere in the evenings, even though it's still light out. Cover up well, Gal."

"I will. Mom, it's difficult for us to be trapped and in seclusion. What young adult wants to stay home?"

She nodded her head. "Right. I understand. Get out of here you two."

They drove to the office supply store and stocked up on office supplies. When they got back in the car, Galaxas was looking down with her forehead wrinkling.

"What's going on in there?" Annalee asked, tapping Galaxas' head.

"Do you think Troid really thinks I'm beautiful or blinded by our preordained bond?"

"Will you believe me if I tell you the truth?"

"Good question." Galaxas looked seriously in her eyes. "Okay, but just be honest. That's all I ask."

"No, you're not beautiful," Annalee said with a furious face.

Eyes as big as a snowball, Galaxas responded. "You don't have to be that honest."

"I wasn't finished. Beautiful is not strong enough of a word. It always infuriated me growing up listening to you whine. If your skin and hair tone were our colors, you would have the biggest model contract in the world. And, if your eyes weren't like miniature suns."

"Oh yeah! I felt the same thing about you," Galaxas said with puckered lips while crossing her arms. "Just because you were thirty to forty pounds overweight, it did not take away from your beauty. You're beautiful, too."

They laughed at each other and Galaxas changed clothes.

"Well, it's dusk, so we should be going. By the way, you look so good in that outfit," Annalee commented.

"So do you with that toned butt and those snug pants. Hey, I have a wild idea. You want to take a walk on the wild side?" Galaxas' face lighted up.

Annalee's mouth stretched wide. "How wild?"

A whimsical, feisty expression covered Galaxas' face. With eyebrows moving up and down, she said. "Hold my hand."

At the speed of a snail, Annalee complied. Before she knew it, they were sitting on a park bench at the Buckingham Community Park.

"Hhhh! That was so weird, but so much fun! Do it again. Do it again," Annalee begged.

"Not now. They're going to be here any time. Oh Good.

There is a ballgame going on, so let's find a bench away from the noise and lights."

They jabbered while waiting. The guys walked out of the woods right in front of them, startling Galaxas. Her breathing moved at a rapid pace. Troid ran to her and put both hands on her arms.

"I'm sorry. We didn't mean to startle you."

She patted her chest. "No, no that wasn't it. I just had a flashback of a really horrific incident from a short while back

where someone walked out of the trees like you just did."

"Do you want to talk about it?"

"No, not now."

Annalee watched Galaxas. She understood what it was all about, and her eyes softened for her friend. Correction, sister. She was really liking this new family thing.

If that wasn't enough, a crack and crunch above them added to the franticness. Troid looked up and yelled, "Raiden!"

Raiden looked up just as a large branch began to tumble down on them. Both men held their hands up high. The branch landed on them as though it was as light as a feather. They tossed it back into the trees.

"Call me impressed. Do you guys have super-human strength?" Annalee asked in shock.

Raiden responded. "Not that we're aware of."

"Are all the men on our planet that strong?" Galaxas asked.

"To us it is natural, and yes, I guess we all are. Aren't the men on this planet the same?" Troid asked Galaxas.

She let out a snort. "Ah, no. I mean, there are some strong men, but nothing like that."

"What about *Rambo*?" Annalee asked.

Galaxas sneered at Annalee. "Really?"

Annalee just made some quirky expressions and giggled.

They both pulled the women up. "Come on. Let's find a safer spot," Troid insisted.

Both couples held hands. Annalee's heart was pounding like a jackhammer.

"If you don't have sunlight on your planet, what do you eat?

Plants and vegetables need sunlight," Annalee's inquisitive mind wanted to know.

"We get enough sunlight, about three hours a day, but indirect. On Earth a lot of plants and vegetables are grown in what you call a greenhouse. I did some research and found that scientists here are experimenting with artificial light and being successful. So, to answer your question, yes, we do eat vegetables and fruit and plenty of protein sources," Raiden answered.

Just then Annalee's phone chimed. She read the text and an eyebrow raised.

"Something interesting?" Raiden asked.

"A guy I've been dating wants to go out tomorrow to dinner and dancing."

Raiden looked disappointed.

Troid whispered to Galaxas. "I don't see how it is possible, but is there a very mild glow to Raiden's heart?"

She cautiously bent over and made a quiet gasp. "Is it possible?"

He shrugged his shoulders. "Unless…" He stopped to think before continuing. Galaxas hanging on his every word. "…the girl ordained for him became corrupted."

Galaxas' mouth dropped. "Could she survive on our planet?"

He patted her hand. "I don't mean this in an arrogant way, but our technology and intelligence are superior. I don't know. Maybe God needed it this way. Look how you've adapted to this world. Why can't we build glasses for her to see just like you have done here?"

Her mouth puckered in amusement. "By jove, I think you've got it."

"Huh?"

"Slang, but what I meant is that you have a good point," Galaxas replied.

They both looked over and Annalee and Raiden were embraced in a soft and sweet kiss.

Galaxas noticed Raiden's heart was flashing mildly and a thought hit her.

"I know! It reminds me of an imprinting, you know, like with Jacob on one of the *Twilight* movies."

Troid's shoulders slumped, and he replied, "Huh?"

"Never mind. Boy do you have a lot to learn," she smirked in fun.

This time he didn't mumble it, but Troid's face showed his thought of "huh"?

After a wonderful, glorious night, the women departed.

Annalee couldn't get over how strange it felt to transport in body form. They walked into the house with bags of office supplies.

"Did you get lost or something?" Nebulane asked almost angrily.

Galaxas answered her mother. Before they got home, she had changed back into the original clothes she wore. "No, just enjoying the freedom of getting out."

They walked to the bedrooms and changed into pajamas. A soft knock sounded on Galaxas' door.

"Yes."

"Can I come in?" Annalee whispered.

"Of course."

Annalee closed the door. She had a smile on her face. Galaxas knew it well. "Gal, is my heart glowing?"

She laughed. "Just what are you saying?"

"Extra, extra, read all about it. I'm in love and you can't stop it," Annalee said as she fell over onto a pillow laughing.

"Guess what?" Galaxas said.

"What?"

"Troid and I saw Raiden's heart glow, but it was mild."

"How can that be?"

"He reminded me that if his girl on our planet became corrupted, he has another chance to find love. Don't blow that chance, Annalee."

"Huh? Just what, pray tell, am I supposed to do about it?"

Galaxas twisted her mouth, tilted her head up and an index finger tapped her cheek. "What do you feel about him?"

"Ohhh, man, I feel gooood."

"Is it possible to say love at first sight?" Galaxas questioned her.

"Like major, yeah."

"There, you have it. Troid also pointed out that our planet is superior in technology and intelligence. If I can adapt here, you surely can adapt there."

"Me...go to your planet and live?"

"Yup, well after we take it back, I guess. Too soon to make plans."

"Then I will stick out like a sore thumb like you do here. I will be ridiculed just like you are here. After sharing the ridicule with you here on Earth, I don't think I could bear it anymore," Annalee admitted.

"Listen. You are the best friend of the someday queen herself. You've heard the line, 'Off with her head.' Problem solved."

Annalee pushed Galaxas over on the bed and they fell back in a laughing bout. "You can't even kill a bug."

"How true is that?"

Annalee snapped her fingers. "Darn! I forgot that I made a date with Gordon for tomorrow. It will be the last one. I'm going to suggest dinner and a movie instead of dancing."

"Phooey. I guess one night apart from these guys should be good for us. But, tomorrow, we tell Mom, Annalee."

Annalee crossed fingers on both hands. Then she hummed the Beethoven's 'Symphony No.5' tune. Dun Dun Dun Dunnnnn!

Annalee was in a trance-like state thinking about what Galaxas told her. She wanted to believe it so badly, but the past haunted her. The one thing she couldn't deny was how strongly she wanted Galaxas to be right. Her hands pulled her arms together and she squeezed her eyes closed.

She needed more clarification, so she snuck into Galaxas' bedroom. Galaxas was standing in the window staring at the stars. She was so lost in thought, she didn't even hear Annalee come in.

Annalee said softly, "Follow your heart, even if love takes you to the stars in the heavens or down into the depths of the sea. Reach beyond the stars, Gal."

She twisted her mouth back and forth. "Okay, you win. To the stars. I always felt a connection with the stars. Now I know why."

Chapter Nineteen

Galaxas rubbed her stomach and paced in one direction, while Annalee paced in a different direction.

"Enough of this. We're adults, not teenagers. We need to act like an adult and walk in there and get it over with," Annalee insisted.

"You're right. How can I rule a planet and be such a scaredy cat?" Annalee made a meow sound. Galaxas shook her head. "I need to take control. Let's just do this."

Nebulane was emptying the dishwasher.

"Mom, I need to speak with you," Galaxas stuttered.

Paying attention to the task at hand, Nebulane replied. "In a minute."

The girls walked to the living room and sat on the couch. Nebulane walked in drying her hands on a hand towel. "What's up, girls?"

Galaxas jumped up off the couch and paced. Annalee did the same, and like in the bedroom, in different directions.

"Whoa! Sounds serious," Nebulane said humorously.

"I haven't said anything, Mom," Galaxas said wiggling her nervous hands.

Very calmly, she replied, "Girls, whatever it is, I'm sure I can handle it."

A pucker to the mouth and a forwardness, Galaxas spewed it out, "I met him."

"Met who?"

"The guy from our planet."

"Say what!"

"We've been meeting them these past few nights."

"Them?"

"Yes, Troid and Raiden. He's my love, Mom."

As she tried to speak, it was as though a scream was caught in Nebulane's throat. Then an explosion. "How could you do this to me? To our planet? You could be jeopardizing its existence. You shouldn't have done this without me."

"And what, Mom? Let them capture the queen herself. If you remember, I will be ruling our planet. Give me some credit for trying to protect you and do the necessary thing. Could you have been able to identify them as evil or not? I did everything you said to do."

Nebulane now paced, staring at the floor, hand running through the hair on top of her head. "I would like to think that my experience would have guided me, so I would have to say yes."

"Well then, you would be wrong. If they're faking it, they are really good at it."

"Now what, now what, now what?" Nebulane couldn't think, couldn't stop pacing.

"Meet them and see for yourself. Troid was right. Now that they know of our whereabouts, if they were evil, why not bring an army and capture us. Don't worry, I also suggested that they could be planning to trick us into believing they are good and take us back to our planet just to trick us into becoming corrupted. Well, I don't believe they are evil. And Troid's father is Zareb."

That information stopped Nebulane from pacing. "What?"

"It's true."

"This changes things. I just don't know how to process this new information."

"How about this: You meet them tomorrow and we go from there? We can sit really close to each other and in a second grab hands for me to transport us out of there. But, Mom, they knew you were here all along and didn't attempt to do anything about it.

"That's not all, Mom. Troid and I think Raiden imprinted on Annalee."

"Imprinted?" Nebulane asked with a questionable look.

"Well, you know, like the glowing of his heart."

"She's not our people. It's not possible."

"Oh yes, it is. Troid and I saw with our own eyes. What about you? Dad isn't from our planet." It still didn't register to Galaxas that she was born before they left their planet.

That revelation caused Nebulane to choke on her own saliva.

"That's different."

"How, Mom?"

"I don't know," Nebulane replied all hyper and uncertain. "It's probably best if I go in my room to rest and give this some good thought. I should probably call your father, too."

"Annalee has a date tonight with Gordon."

"Good. This will give us time to think it through," Nebulane said while thinking.

Nebulane sat on the chaise lounge and prayed for a miracle and answers. Galaxas could hear her telling Mitchell to calm down in their bedroom.

The clicking of heels caught Galaxas' attention. She turned her head in that direction. "You look smashing, Anna."

Annalee shot bullets with her eyes. "Thanks, but I'm thinking of canceling."

"No. This is a good distraction and gives us an opportunity to figure things out until we meet the guys tomorrow."

Sounding like Eeyore from *Winnie the Pooh* movies, Annalee said, "Okay." She really didn't want to go.

After dinner, Annalee and Gordon drove to the movies in his car. She felt a chill, and thrilling goosebumps covered her skin, but she couldn't identify why she felt that way. She shook it off and decided it was best to tell Gordon how she felt and that she wouldn't be seeing him after this evening. They parked. As he turned to step out, she grabbed his arm.

"Wait. I need to talk with you about something."

His head turned back in her direction. His eyes stared her down trying to analyze her expression. He pulled his leg back inside and closed the door.

"Please, speak."

She took a deep breath and exhaled. What was the big deal? It's not like they were a couple. With his popularity, he'd find someone else in no time.

"I won't be seeing you after tonight."

"And why not? Did I approve of this change?" he said with an icy glare.

Her face wrinkled. "Approve? Sorry, but you don't have a right to approve or disapprove."

"How do you figure?" he asked with an intimidating tone.

"Because we're not a couple. And, because I met someone I want to possibly spend my life with."

"Do you know what this could do to my reputation? No girl has ever broken it off with me." His face turned the color of anger. He gritted his teeth and breathed heavily.

"I don't care about your stupid reputation or you." She put her hand on the door handle and began to twist it. With force he grabbed her arm and pulled her from the door handle.

"You will not break it off with me until I think it's time.

Then I'll break it off with you." Once again with intimidating tones and facial expressions.

She twisted out of his grip. "I'm leaving."

"Oh no you're not." His grip was so tight she flinched in pain.

Like right out of a Sci-Fi novel, the driver's door was pulled off its hinges. Raiden and Troid stood there. Raiden dropped the door. "Get your hands off of her or I'll tear your arm off."

Annalee's eyes were in a permanent wide-eyed stare, and she was speechless. Gordon was too shocked to move.

Raiden raised his hand towards her. "Come on Annalee. I'll

keep you safe." He reached in and grabbed Gordon's hand and jerked it off of her. He saw the red marks on her arm.

"What kind of a brute are you?" He, again, grabbed Gordon's arm and twisted it. Gordon yelled out in pain as Raiden dropped his arm. "Next time, beat up on somebody your own size."

Annalee jumped out and ran over to him. She sneered at Gordon and walked off with Raiden and Troy.

"Thank you. You guys are like superheroes. How did you do that, and how did you know where I was, much less know I was in trouble?"

"Look, I'm sorry. We sort of have been following you," Raiden said.

"Well, in this case, that's okay. I did not think he would resort to abuse. That was so scary."

"Pompous jerk." Raiden puckered his lips tightly.

"At least I don't ever have to worry about seeing him again," she affirmed.

"Really?" His face turned bright.

"Yes, really. Hey, we better get out of here. Our ruckus has drawn some attention," Annalee said with urgency.

"Come around this bush and hold our hands," Raiden requested of her.

She looked at him in wonder. Before she knew it, they were standing at her car in the restaurant parking lot.

"Can all of your people do that?" she asked.

"Yes, but we can't decipher where anyone else has gone to unless they give us the coordinates. Sort of a built-in safety precaution for our people. That precaution has saved many a life," Raiden noted.

"Wowwy! Galaxas doesn't even know that. Thanks again, but I need to get home. I have a very interesting evening to describe for Galaxas and Nebulane."

"Yeah, you should. We're finally going to meet her tomorrow," Raiden informed her.

"No kidding," she replied looking at both of them. They both nodded their heads. Troid had kept quiet this whole time, giving them some space.

After Raiden placed a soft, enticing kiss on her lips, she jumped in the car and left. She envisioned in her mind being with him until the sun rose the next day. Her mind kept replaying the scene in the parking lot. She started to wonder if she had some sort of mental condition just like Galaxas felt about her situation. It was just beyond crazy belief.

Chapter Twenty

The door swished open. Annalee clomped into the house. Her eyes were bright, and excitement radiated from her face.

Galaxas paused the movie. "Oh no. You're in love with Gordon."

"Pbbbbbt," and spit rolled from her lips. "Heck no. I'm in love with Raiden, my superhero."

Both she and Nebulane pushed themselves upward, and Galaxas asked, "What's going on? You didn't see Raiden tonight."

With a take-that pitch, Annalee responded. "Oh yes I did."

"Care to elaborate?" Galaxas asked shrugging her neck to her head and hands out, eyes popping wide open.

"He saved me from that jerk," Annalee said excitedly. "Hold on with the questions. I see that I jumped too far ahead. Gordon and I had just parked at the movie theatre. Before we went in, I told him I wanted to talk with him about something. To make a long story short," she held up her arm, "he did this."

"Hhhh! Oh no," Galaxas said tearing up. Memories of her own abuse from Clayton flashed in her mind.

"It's okay Galaxas. Raiden and Troid came to my rescue.

Evidently, they were following me. When Gordon got physical, Raiden LITERALLY tore the driver's door off the hinges. Gordon and I both were shocked. So, I got out and Raiden repaid Gordon with a nice, red hand mark like the one he left on my arm. Then they transported me back to my car.

"You should have seen it. It was like watching a superhero film. It was so freaking amazing."

"Young lady, watch your language," Nebulane demanded with a glare.

"Huh? If I wanted to say the four-letter-word with an 'ing' ending, I would have, but I...I didn't. I used the eight-letter-word."

Galaxas rolled over laughing. Nebulane joined.

"You do seem to forget that we are adults, Mother," Galaxas added for emphasis.

"That has absolutely nothing to do with anything. I will always be a mother to both of you and will always steer you right."

"She has to always win an argument. Have you noticed Annalee?"

"Now that you mention it, yeah." She made the "oops" expression as Nebulane glared at Annalee.

"Girls, get to bed. That's right, I said get to bed. We have a stressful day tomorrow. We all need sleep."

The sun rose with beautiful, brilliant colors. Stomachs inside the house were tied in knots. Galaxas was mostly worried that her mom wouldn't get past thoughts that Troid and Raiden were evil. But what if her mom is right and she was blinded by love?

Annalee strolled into Galaxas' room. The door was open. She moved her hand in a circle around her stomach. "I see you have been delivered a basket of nerves, too."

"Oh, yeah," Galaxas said as she gulped.

"You know what I was wondering? Do you really think Troid and Raiden are gorgeous or are you just saying that to be nice? I mean, you could never hurt my feelings, so I wonder if you're not being honest. Clayton assured me I looked like a freak, and frankly, so did all the people who stared. On the bond of our friendship, please tell me the truth. Do we look like freaks?"

"Do you look different? Yes. A freak? Heck no. You all, including mother, who is striking, are beyond gorgeous. You have to believe me," Annalee pleaded.

"Now, your turn. On our friendship bond, are you just trying to make me feel better about myself by saying I'm beautiful? Maybe your planet sees the inside of a person instead of the outside. I mean, your eyes can probably look right into a person's soul with that much light," Annalee remarked.

"Wouldn't that be a utopia? But to answer your question, I honestly believe you are beautiful. To take it a step further, I'm sick and tired of society acting as if a person who is overweight can't be beautiful. You were beautiful before the transformation. But like me, you fell into the notion that we were the ugly ones because we were different," Galaxas answered honestly.

"True. Very true. Well, I'm going to get ready. Are you?" Annalee asked.

They both crossed their fingers, and both got ready.

The time had come. Dinner dishes were put in the dishwasher and the kitchen cleaned. All three women sat on the couch twiddling their fingers. Nervous. Silent.

The knock at the door caused all three women to jump. "I'll get it, Mom," Galaxas said excitedly, but nervously.

The door slowly creaked open. Her face lit up like the sun. They looked so awesome. They were wearing clothes like you would find on the old TV series of *Beauty and the Beast*, like Vincent, or Jacob, known as father.

Troid looked lovingly into her eyes before stepping inside. Swallowing, Raiden found Annalee and nervously smiled. Nebulane's face was blank.

"Mom, this is Troid and Raiden." They both bowed out of respect for her as queen. Her eyes blinked a few times, forgetting what it felt like to be treated as a real queen. Galaxas was blown away. This was "Mom," and she never required to be treated like a queen.

"Your majesty we have waited what seems to be a lifetime to

meet you. I feel breathless. We know of your courage, integrity, and love for our people. Our people yearn for you to come back," Troid admitted. Galaxas noticed goosebumps appear on his arm that wasn't covered by the shirt.

Nebulane motioned to the two chairs, and they complied. She jerked her head to Galaxas to sit in the middle between her and Annalee.

"I am not at all surprised that you and Galaxas were chosen as a couple. Before the evil ones overtook our planet, I often wondered if you would be the one. Your father was my dearest and most honorable royal guard. Is he still alive?"

"Yes, your majesty. In good health and awaiting your return." Troid bowed every time he answered her.

"On our planet, I know it is a must to show respect to the queen, but here I need you to treat me like anyone else, not the queen. Just in case. We don't want to draw any attention."

"Yes, your majesty," and he bowed his head again. "Sorry, I will keep practicing," Troid offered apologetically.

"And do not refer to me as queen, or your majesty. You can call me Mrs. Gaylord or Nebulane."

Thinking before responding, he answered, "Yes, Mrs. Gaylord," looking over at Raiden with questions. He knew this was not her last name.

"So, Raiden. Who is your family?"

His fingers twiddled. "My father's name is Vesper and my mother's name is Amana."

Her hands went to her mouth and her eyes grew wide. She jumped off the couch and paced.

"Mother, what is it?" Galaxas enquired.

Choking up, through gasps she replied, "She was my dearest, most trusted friend. I cherished our relationship. And your father, he was dear to me as well. All of your parents were my dearest friends. I miss them terribly." Sobs and sniffles followed.

Galaxas and Annalee both clung onto her elbows for support.

"Tell me, Raiden, are your parents well?"

"They are quite well. Both of our parents miss you, too."

"You must tell me, have any of them been corrupted?"

Troid looked at Raiden and answered. "Yes, there were a few of your loyal guards and assistants. Their sun pendants were removed before being thrown out. As you know, very soon after being corrupted, the pendant would poison them anyway. We sketched their initials on the pendant and entered their data into our corruption list so that they couldn't deceive anyone once they were kicked out. The secret living arrangements have worked out well."

"Good to know. Now, what proof do you have that will convince me that you two are not corrupted?"

She stood tall, totally in queen formation. Galaxas watched her feeling proud, emotional, and somewhat confused.

Troid and Raiden reached down their shirts and pulled out the pendant that was made with some kind of stone or mineral that is found only on their planet and shaped, too, like the sun. It started shining like the sun itself when their fingers touched it. Their eyes, along with Nebulane and Galaxas' eyes, formed into suns. They actually looked like miniature suns.

Annalee covered her eyes with an arm. "What's going on, Mom?" Annalee asked confused.

"You can relax and put the stones away before it blinds Annalee," Nebulane ordered with a gentleness.

They did.

"These stones were given to our people at creation from the good Lord Himself. It will only transform and shine for our incorruptible people. These guys are good. We don't have to worry. The stones have a shield of protection around us so that the evil can't detect our whereabouts or whether we are on the side of good or evil. It has saved many a life, just like the serpent's rod Moses held up. ONLY the incorruptible can touch it. If a corrupted one touches it, they dissolve into thin air," Nebulane explained.

"So, why isn't any of that enough to defeat the evil ones?" Galaxas asked.

"I wish I had the answers, but I don't," Nebulane replied. "Before Zareb sent me to Earth, we were actually losing the battle. He couldn't take the chance of me being converted to evil. That would be the final amount of power they would need to destroy our whole planet. I'll explain who they are soon. Also, there is something very special about you, Gal, that I wasn't able to find out. The communication between me and those fighting the evil on our planet is minimal. I get just enough messages from codes in the sky to know that they are getting closer to figuring out how we can defeat them. Something tells me, you're the key to it all." Fear flashed across Galaxas' face. "Right now, I need to speak with these guys in private.

"Don't get mad, girls, but all our people can transport at any given time. Even me. I have to be careful how much information I can tell you right now. It is still for your safety," Nebulane added, feeling the need to explain a little more to them. She could see how fear was taking hold of Galaxas, and she was trying to spare her enough information to keep her safe. She needed to ease her daughter into all the information, because it was a lot. She just didn't have the full story.

Galaxas and Annalee stared at each other.

"We are going to transport to their spacecraft and then we'll return. Please understand and don't worry," Nebulane said.

Both girls nodded their heads, still speechless.

Nebulane and the guys held hands and were gone in a split second. Annalee and Galaxas both plopped on the couch without any energy to hold themselves up.

"This is just wild," Annalee commented with a far-off stare.

Staring at the coffee table, Galaxas just shook her head in agreement. "It just hit me. Our guys are good. We can be together. That is the happiest news I've had in my whole life."

"Me too. I just hope your world will accept me," Annalee responded hesitantly.

"What did I tell you? Queen, remember?" Galaxas responded with a snigger pointing at herself.

She thought longer and a sudden explosion of revelation vaulted Galaxas to attention.

"That's why Mom always got to my house in such a short time. Every time I called her to come treat an animal or any other type of emergency, she was there zippidity zap. That's because she transported. She always claimed to be just down the road heading for my place, like it was a coincidence. That little sneak.

"Annalee, do you feel Mom is holding back on telling me some very important information?"

"Actually, yes. There's a battle going on inside her head. She's being cautious about what she tells you. When the time is right, we'll find out. I mean, the way things are escalating, how much longer can she wait?"

"That's what I thought, too," Galaxas replied.

Annalee's shoulders rose up and down in laughter before she spoke. "Hey, do you think my mom is part of the evil ones?" She fell on the couch in laughter. It was all Galaxas could do but join in on the laugh.

Nebulane appeared in front of them. Alone. Both girls held their breaths for a moment and placed a hand on their heart.

"Forgive me for scaring you. I should have thought that through."

Searching the room, "Where is Troid and Raiden?" Galaxas asked.

"They stayed in the ship, Gal. We thought it best for tonight just in case they were followed. They'll be here first thing in the morning."

"What's your honest opinion of them, Mom?" Annalee asked and smiled as she said 'Mom'. Nebulane and Galaxas both noticed. They formed an affectionate smile.

"As a mother, I couldn't be more pleased. They are topnotch, brave, good and kind, very intelligent and strong. I love them, girls."

Both of them perked up and almost all their teeth showed through their mouths.

"Curious thing, Mom. How come they have superpower strength, and we don't?" Galaxas asked with her index finger pressing on her lips and elbow resting on the coffee table.

"Good question. There is no answer. It has always been that way. It works out, though. After all, I am queen, so it's not some misogynist condition. Women are highly respected."

"When can Troid and I get married?"

"Another good question. It won't be until after we take back our planet."

Galaxas' mouth dropped. "So, then, never."

"Calm down. We are close to going to war and taking back our planet. God is with us."

"Do you think the good army is strong enough to fight and win?" Annalee asked.

"Yes!"

"You seem pretty sure of yourself," Galaxas added.

"You know the Bible stories. If God is with us, who can be against us. I have total faith and confidence," Nebulane answered. For the first time in a while, Nebulane cast real confidence and showed more of a leadership presence. It was all coming back to her and fast.

Chapter Twenty-One

Gray days and heavy rain didn't cause mood swings for Galaxas. Her eyes were sunshine every day, except today. Thunder crashed, lightning bolted through the atmosphere, or was all this commotion happening in her soul only.

Troid put an arm around her and pulled her snug to his body. "Everything is going to be just fine. We'll be back before you know it." He jiggled her in his arm. "Now that I FINALLY found you, you will never get rid of me. I watched that *Terminator* movie last night. "I'll be back," he tried saying in Arnold Schwarzenegger's voice.

That brought a sincere smile.

He was tall, strong and muscular, funny, intelligent, urbane in an alien sort of way, big dimples and a smile that turned her insides into mush. If his skin and hair color, along with eyes that didn't look like the sun were normal, every woman on the planet would be after him.

This is the guy in movies or television shows that is not only gorgeous, but has that sweet, confident, bold and courageous, caring and good personality. It wasn't fake, like when you see an actor you fell in love with on an interview and realize he's nothing like the character he portrayed in the film. He was going to be hers, all hers.

The man took her breath away. But what she couldn't
understand is if he only loved her because it was ordained. If
they were from Earth, would he be interested in her?

While she sat in thought, he stared at her. To him she was
the most beautiful girl in the universe, and he happened to know
quite a lot of women in the universe. Her straight, light green
hair with light gray highlights hung down about three inches
from the shoulder. Features were petite and perfect. Body toned
and thin but not skinny, and her stride had a noble, casual walk,
like a deer taking a stroll.

He loved her wit and charm. A heart of gold and courage. She
had no idea she was beautiful, breathtaking to him, and an
inward beauty that made you feel all warm inside. He didn't want
to leave her either.

With his elbow, he nudged her gently. "Hey, we have three
more days. Three!"

She reacted as though he was saying three years.

"When will I see you again, Troid? A year, three years, what?"

"I wish I knew, Galaxas. There's a whole lot happening up
there. Historical stuff. No matter how long, I will come back and
visit you as often as possible. It would be easier if we could just
transport our bodies but it's too far for that to happen, so it
takes a while to get back here by spacecraft. Although, new technology is almost developed to cut the time in half." He smiled
with lifted eyebrows.

"It's dark outside now. Come out with me and I'll show you
where to look for me in the sky," Troid said lovingly. He grabbed
her hand and kissed it, then escorted her outside.

When they jumped up, they noticed Annalee and Raiden
talking in the kitchen with a plate of chocolate chip cookies.
Annalee was eating carrot sticks. Raiden had a milk mustache
that brought out giggles in her.

Troid pulled Galaxas' hand snug between his elbow and body,
and they walked outside to a clear spot.

"Right up there," he said pointing. "I will send a code to you.
You'll be able to tell it's from me. I promise."

"What do you mean code? And how will yours be different from any star twinkling or any other code?"

He rubbed his jaw staring at the sky. "Let me see if I can explain how we have been in contact with your mother all this time. We have a device that bounces off the stars and makes them flash. You saw that yourself. That flashlight beam. There is a book of codes. We have one and your mother has one.

"A set of codes flash. She can look them up in the book and understand what is going on. Same for us. You watch the stars each night, and you will have no doubt what the code is saying. It is my surprise to you."

"Like a real Sci-Fi show. It's pretty impressive. Any chance we can talk on the phone?" she asked.

"Go ahead and send a text and I'll respond, but it may take a little while for it to get to me or to you."

"How do you feel about ruling our planet?" she asked

"Scared. Happy. Nervous. Excited. It changes back and forth. What about you?"

"I'm terrified," she said with a twitch. "Think about it. I grew up not knowing any of this, feeling like a freak and outcast, and now, hey, you're going to be queen. Imagine that! Oh! And you're an alien from outer space!" She shook her head with an odd expression.

He pretended to wipe sweat from his forehead. "You don't have to draw me a picture. But, from where I'm standing, you have what it takes to rule. From where you're standing, it's understandable to feel the way you do, but there's a whole world out there that believes you are the one for the job."

They walked up and sat on the porch swing. He looked lovingly into her eyes. "I really do love you, Galaxas. So much."

"That's good, because I'm madly in love with you, like the old commercial, "cuckoo for Cocoa Puffs" crazy about you," she confirmed.

His lips met her lips. It was a warm, loving, never-stop kiss. Hot lava streamed through her veins.

~

At the same time on the back porch, Annalee and Raiden sat on lawn furniture gazing at the stars. Excitement flowed through her veins that perhaps she would be going to live on another planet in the solar system. Say what?

Raiden placed a hand on hers. His heart started glowing like a glow bug. This time they both noticed. Annalee slapped a hand to her mouth. He looked at her, but his gaze went right through her as he thought in shock at what his heart was revealing. Invisible fairies walked all over her body sprinkling pixie dust. She just knew it.

"You know what this means, don't you?" Raiden asked her.

"From what Galaxas told me and from what I witnessed myself, I think so," she answered with a swallow.

His hand squeezed hers tighter. He asked, "How do you feel about this? About us?"

She didn't want to jump to conclusions, so she pretended not to understand what he was getting at. "I'm not sure I know what you mean."

"On our planet, when we are in love, and it is ordained, our heart gets a glow around it. I'm in love with you, Annalee. Our ways are different from Earth. When it's time to find our mate, it happens emotionally and physically just like that. Just like us. Since you're not from my planet, I can't tell if you feel the same way about me as I do about you." His heartfelt stare was pleading with her to say yes that she felt the same way.

One solid goose bump engulfed her body. For a moment she couldn't breathe. She wouldn't be able to handle it if he changed his mind later on. "This is happening way too fast. I love being with you, but to say I'm in love with you, it's just too fast." She noticed his disappointment.

"But! I can honestly say it's a safe bet that I'm just scared, and the tingles and warmth I feel being with you is a good indicator that I must be falling in love with you." *Could this incredible hunk of man really love me? Fat ole unpopular me?* Poor thing always resorted to the past not wanting to get her hopes up. She almost stuck her butt up and asked him if it was toned enough, not knowing how to handle sentiment. Almost.

Both of his hands held her one hand. He smiled so wide that she could see his teeth in the dark.

Raiden was tall, like Troid, and built like a dream come true. His light green-gray hair was longer than Troid's and it had bronze highlights, too. It seems all the people on his planet had the same skin and hair colors.

"Are all the men on your planet big and strong? Are there fat or skinny, tall or short men?" she asked humorously.

"Of those not corrupted, yes, all similar."

"Are they all as good and brave, kind and strong like you?"

"Same answer as before," he replied.

"Wow, wow, wow, wow!"

He shook his head. "I have never met a girl who can make me laugh, make me feel things like you do. You know what's cool?"

"Not really," she said with one side of her top lip lifting.

"I'm the only guy from our planet with a woman who looks totally different, and you're so beautiful, kind, intelligent and caring. They will be jealous. Heck, I'm even jealous of me."

She laughed. "That could end up NOT being a good thing, you know. Me looking so different. What if they won't accept me?"

"Wrong. It is a great thing. Who in their right mind wouldn't accept you?" He lifted his hands, palm side up. "Look, even Troid is crazy about you. Not the in-love-with-you kind of crazy, but you're an amazing-kind-of-a-friend crazy. "

Her brows furrowed. "I think I get it. That's really sweet. I wish you didn't have to leave."

"Me too, but we'll be back. Look up at that cluster of stars right there," he said holding her finger and pointing. "That's where we'll be. You can look up there every night to see me. I'll try to make it twinkle to let you know I'm thinking about you."

Her eyes blurred. Never did she expect to have a gorgeous guy, green skin and all, say such romantic things to her; to physically show he loved her. It was almost too much for her to comprehend.

He bent over and saw the glassy eyes, and his lips kissed her forehead, then moved to the cheek, then softly touched her lips.

She literally shivered in the hot temperature outside. The kiss developed into something that could only be part of a fairy tale. Would she always feel this way? Would he?

After the guys left, the girls talked in Annalee's room.

"You know what is hilarious?" Annalee said chuckling.

"Can't say that I do," Galaxas replied.

"We were two misfits, castaways, discarded by our society, but look at us now. We have two gorgeous men madly in love with us. God must be giggling at this outcome.

"You know what else I just thought about?"

Seeing her excitement, Galaxas responded back with excitement. "What!"

"If Raiden and I marry and we have children, what would they look like? How cool is that even?"

"Hhhh! You're right. That is a cool thought," Galaxas responded as her hands in the form of a prayer covered her mouth.

"I mean, you and Troid most likely will have children with light green skin and light green hair with gray and bronze highlights for a boy, and eyes that look like the sun. No shocker there.

"Oh gosh! What kind of eyesight will our children have with me being an Earthling?" Annalee's mouth opened.

"You are getting a little ahead of yourself, but that is a head scratcher."

Chapter Twenty-Two

The guys left early in the morning. The girls moped around until Nebulane found a way to distract them.

"Your father will be home tonight. I'm making lasagna."

"Oh, yum. Can't wait to see him," Galaxas commented.

"Me, too, Gal," Annalee added.

"Something just popped in my head, Galaxas. Care to join me in my office?" Annalee said whimsically.

"Just try and hold me back," Galaxas replied. For fun she transported to her room. Both hands on the hips, Nebulane scowled. That changed quickly to a relaxed smile with a shaking of her head.

"What are those two up to?" Nebulane whispered to herself.

"Close the door," Annalee insisted.

Curious, Galaxas closed it slowly while keeping her eyes on Annalee.

"Wouldn't it be fun to go to the dress shop Prissy Priscilla works at? I mean, dress up to the hills, makeup, the whole bit, and rub it in her face of my transformation? She got a huge laugh out of my crush on Mr. Popular himself. We have pictures that are dark enough to hide the greenish gray skin tones but clear enough to show how gorgeous our guys are. Come on, let's have some fun," Annalee said with a wide smile.

Galaxas tilted her head and thought about it. Even though her skin color was different, after high school she did learn to accentuate those striking features with a minimal amount of makeup. "The way I feel, I could punch someone, and she's got the right stuff to make that happen. Count me in. I'm in the shower first. But, how would you know her?"

With a "duh" expression, Annalee replied, "Uh, we did go to the same school here before we moved to Alaska."

"Geesh. I totally forgot that you went to school here."

Annalee tried to beat her to the shower, but Galaxas transported. The bathroom door was already locked on her arrival. "You cheater, Galaxas!"

Chuckling and banging pipes played through the bottom of the door. The misty sound of the rainforest played a soothing lullaby in the bathroom while blowing out mists under the door made from the heated shower.

❧

They walked into the store with their heads held high. Both dressed in the latest fashion. There she was, Prissy Priscilla, ringing up a purchase. Annalee winked at Galaxas, and they began to shop. The store wasn't very busy at this time, so Priscilla walked over not recognizing them.

"May I help you find something?"

"No, we're just looking. Is this the latest fashion you carry?" Annalee asked in a disappointed tone.

"I'm sure we'll get a new shipment within the month."

"I don't know. Nothing seems like good quality," Annalee said to Galaxas. Galaxas suppressed a laugh.

Priscilla looked at Galaxas for a moment, memories spinning. "Hey, you're that freaky girl from school. Still alive, I see."

"Who are you?" Galaxas asked bewildered not allowing Priscilla the enjoyment of thinking everyone knew who she was.

"The popular girl. Remember?"

"No, can't say that I do. How about you, Annalee?"

Priscilla's face changed from snotty to shock. "You're... you're that fat girl from school who hung out with her?" She pointed to Galaxas.

"Why, yes. We're still best friends," Annalee responded proudly.

A sleek woman with perfect posture, magazine cover perfect skin and unique clothing that made the store's clothing look low quality, stepped up to them. She extended a hand.

"How do you do? You'll have to excuse me. I don't shop in stores like this, but I saw you two walking into this store, and I just couldn't stop myself." Galaxas shook her hand and the lady reached for Annalee, and she shook it as well.

She pulled out a business card and handed it for the two to share. I am a scout for a prestigious modeling agency. Our models are known and sought throughout the world. I have to ask how you have that skin color."

Here we go, Galaxas couldn't help but wonder. "I and my mother were born with a skin, hair and eye condition. It's not a disease. My eyes are too sensitive to be in sunshine or bright lights."

"Oh! Don't take my question as an offense. You are remarkable." Her hand twisted Galaxas' face back and forth. "These features are extraordinary. Fascinating. You are magnificently beautiful. Our agency would pay you the highest wages of any model anywhere in the world.

"And you," she said looking at Annalee, "what a beauty you are. You are very photogenic. Our agency would love to give you a contract also."

Galaxas and Annalee stared at each other's face, speechless.

Priscilla stared in disbelief. None of them noticed that Micah, the most popular guy in school back then, was watching the whole scene. But before either could answer, Priscilla spoke up.

"What about me?"

"What about you?" the woman asked.

"Everyone thinks I'm really beautiful."

"Sorry, but nothing about you stands out. You're one in a million, and you don't have the unique model features like these two beauties have." She turned back to the girls. Priscilla's mouth pulled together tightly, and her eyes glared.

"I'm sorry, but my eyes are too sensitive for camera lights. Plus, I will be moving far, far away soon," Galaxas informed her.

They all heard Priscilla mumble, "Yeah, like moving to outer space where you belong."

Galaxas and Annalee held back a chuckle.

"Me too. I'm moving far, far away with her. We both have a rewarding profession and don't have time for anything else, but we are really grateful for your kindness," Annalee added.

"What a pity. I just found the gold at the end of the rainbow and can't get to it. I wish you two the utmost success. It's rare to have any young women decline our offer. You two have guts and integrity. I admire that."

The lady walked out, and before Priscilla could walk away from this devastating scene, a voice from behind spoke.

"Galaxas? Annalee? Is that really you?"

All three women turned to see still handsome as ever, Micah.

"I just heard that whole conversation. I always thought there was an undiagnosed beauty about you both. I'm sorry I didn't socialize with you in school. You know how peer pressure works in school. Any chance you would like to accompany me for a drink or coffee?"

Priscilla gasped out loud. "You and I can always get a drink," he said to her.

"What professions do you both have?" she asked in a snotty voice, refusing to look at Micah.

"We're both accomplished book illustrators and working on our own children's books," Annalee replied cheerfully.

"That's it?"

They both chuckled.

"You probably wouldn't understand. Probably don't understand the literature world. What is your profession?" Galaxas served back.

"I work here."

"Do you at least own the store?" Annalee asked knowing the answer.

"No. My life's too busy for anything else."

"I see. Too many country club and night clubs to attend."

Annalee made the tennis serving motion to show she just won the match. A gesture she and Galaxas used frequently.

"I think that sounds quite interesting. Do you have a website?" Priscilla's laser eyes tried to disintegrate Micah for asking.

"For now, it is Galaxas' Galaxy. I began it before Annalee and I went into business together. Check it out. It is out of this world and has so many raving reviews. It's time to change the name, Annalee."

"I'll check it out," he replied.

"What about you? What profession did you go into?" Annalee asked sincerely wanting to know.

"High school coach."

Figures, she thought. *Didn't make it in the big leagues.*

"Well, hey, what about that drink?"

"Did you forget we're meeting the gang at the nightclub later?" Priscilla said scornfully.

"Your point?" his annoyed question asked Priscilla.

"Never mind." She turned and huffed off.

"Sorry, but we need to get back to work. Nice seeing you," Galaxas lied.

Inside the car, they broke out in laughter. "Did you see her face? Uh, that felt good," Annalee said fist bumping Galaxas.

"I still wanted to disintegrate her though. I'm so mad about missing our guys. Is it possible physical confrontation is the only cure to relieve such built up anger or anxiety? I mean, nothing else seems to work."

"Hold on, super alien. I don't want to get on your bad side."

"Mom's right. I need to learn how to control this gift. What if I get aggravated and think really bad things and they happen?"

"Good point. Let's get you to Mom before you turn into a villain," Annalee suggested ending with "Yuh-un-un." Her car squealed out of the parking spot.

They walked into the house and Mitchell ambushed them. "Dad, you gave me a scare," Galaxas said breathing faster than normal.

"Me too," Annalee chimed in.

He walked into the dining room with an arm around each of them. Their noses tipped up making a sniffing sound.

"Nebulane, you outdid yourself. Truly this is the best lasagna you ever made," Mitch said.

"And that burnt crust around the edges," squeezing her fingers near the mouth and flinging them out blowing a kiss, "pure perfection," Annalee added.

"Ditto." Galaxas felt the need to be in agreement.

It was going on three weeks since Troid and Raiden left. Each night the girls went to the clearing and stared at the stars. No conversation. Just complete silence.

Galaxas nudged Annalee. "Do you see that?"

She moved her head around. "Where?"

"Right up there," Galaxas replied pointing to the cluster of stars Troid pointed out to her.

The twinkles grew brighter and brighter. They watched until Galaxas realized the special code. "It's from Troid and probably Raiden, too. Watch. Oh, my goodness. The stars are blinking in a heart shape."

Tears streamed down her face. She glanced over at Annalee and her tears were turning into a river. "That is so beautiful. This is the definition of romantic. I love you, Troid," she said softly.

"I love you, Raiden," Annalee said with sniffles.

"Wait! Let me try something." Galaxas made light beams shoot out of her eyes up towards the cluster. Then she stopped. Just like that first day when she saw the light beams from that one star that scared the bejeebies out of her, came into her thoughts. *Isn't life interesting?*

She grabbed Annalee's hand. Bouncing together they cried happy tears. "Maybe there is a way to send a code to them and find out when they're coming back. Let's go ask Mom."

Inside, Mitchell folded his arms and gave an I-know look. "So, you two are in love. Don't know what I think about that."

Each girl cornered him and placed a kiss on each cheek. "You think it's wonderful," Annalee said with a joyous heart.

"Actually, I do. It's a good thing your boyfriend gave that Gordon guy a good butt kicking because I would have had to hunt him down. I'm glad you're okay. And I'm glad you both have very honorable men," he added looking tenderly at Galaxas.

"From what your mother told me, they're both hunks."

"Oh yeah. Real hunks," Annalee answered for her and Galaxas.

"Mom, we just got a message from the guys." She put a hand on her heart and said, "They made the stars twinkle in a heart shape. It was so romantic," Galaxas said holding her balled fist near her heart, squeezing her shoulders inward.

Nebulane held both hands to her heart. "This is so much better than a romantic film or book."

"We need to discuss how to control my gift before I misuse it," Galaxas proposed, "and could you help me figure out a way to send codes?"

"That sounds like a good idea. Let's go sit on the porch swing and discuss it."

Galaxas took one step and stopped, everything and everyone tuned out. She was having a vision. First time anyone other than herself witnessed it. Annalee strolled towards her, but Nebulane quietly said, "No, leave her be. I think she's having a vision."

Galaxas' eyes blinked constantly. In her mind the light bursts were fast and short, but that was it. Nothing else materialized. The light bursts stopped, and she closed her eyes tightly and reopened them. She turned her head and looked at each face.

"You okay?" Annalee asked fast.

"Yes. That was weird. It was like a vision was trying to develop but it couldn't. Truthfully, I have an uneasy feeling about it, like it was going to be bad. Really bad. Something my mind would not allow, maybe even holding it back because I can't bear to see it and what it will mean."

"Don't jump to conclusions. Has this ever happened before?" Nebulane asked.

"No, Mom. It's like something was interfering, perhaps blocking it from happening."

She stopped again. Her eyes stared ahead and Nebulane knew the vision was trying to materialize. It stopped abruptly.

"Anything Galaxas?" Nebulane asked.

"Yes. It was short. All I saw was a black glove with steel blades sticking out over the top of it. In my mind it represented...EVIL."

Galaxas' hand slapped against her mouth, and her eyes, worthy of coming from a horror film actor, gave shivers to Annalee.

"The face was a blur, but those gloves were choking the life out of me." She chewed her lip.

Nebulane turned away from them and stared at the wall. Motionless and speechless.

Chapter Twenty-Three

E diting their books, both girls could not focus for the life of them, each in separate rooms. The thud to the floor of Galaxas' paper tablet caused them both to jump.

Knowing it was hopeless to work, hearing Annalee's frustrated words made Galaxas turn her head.

"I can't seem to work today," Annalee confessed poking her head into the room.

"Me neither," Galaxas replied plopping the tablet back onto the desk. "Let's go get something to drink."

"Good idea. Dad bought some Yoohoos." Annalee licked her lips.

The bag of candy rattling drew Nebulane out of the bedroom. Just as Galaxas stretched the sour worm candy out about six inches from her mouth, Annalee broke out in a chuckle, and it escalated into a cachinnate outburst.

"Okay you two, my extra-sensory skills are telling me that something is bothering you."

"Really, Mom. Like a superpower?"

"No, Gal, like a super mom power."

All three busted up laughing at the remark.

"So, what's wrong?" Annalee asked.

"Truthfully, I can't quit thinking about that partial vision I had. It felt uncomfortable and evil. Not that I can base any truth or proof on my opinion, but there's a question swatting at my mind that asks if I already know who this evil person is. What do you make of that?"

"To not take those thoughts lightly. The good Lord above may just be warning you to stay alert," Annalee interjected.

"I thought so too," Galaxas answered as she stuffed the rest of the sour worm in her mouth.

Annalee looked like Bugs Bunny holding a carrot making a crunch-crunch-crunch sound. Nebulane and Galaxas looked over at her.

"What? Haven't you ever seen a person eat a carrot before?"

"Just wondering if you have anything to add, Bugs." Galaxas choked on a giggle.

"How could I add anything? Human, remember?" she humorously wisecracked, pointing at herself with the carrot.

The other two felt at ease right away. How much laughter and happiness that girl brought to all of their lives.

A loud warning alarm activated from Nebulane's room.

"Mom, what is that? A security alarm?"

"Yes, follow me."

They ran into her room. A door to a secret room was open. Galaxas and Annalee looked back and forth in each other's eyes.

"Step up here. Let me explain what is going on," Nebulane cautiously insisted.

Nebulane explained the code by referring to the code book she had resting on the desk. Computer equipment flashed lights with a variety of buttons. They found the code in question. As Nebulane read it, her body twitched. Not what she was hoping to find. This is bad. Really bad.

"Mom?" Galaxas could not speak any other sensible words at the moment.

"Sorry, girls. I wasn't expecting this news."

"What? What's going on before my heart gives out?" Annalee pleaded.

She stared at Annalee and turned to Galaxas. "Do you want the good or bad news first?"

"Good," Annalee shouted.

"Bad," Galaxas shouted louder. "I'd rather save the good for last, so we have something to overcome the fear I know we will be feeling, Annalee."

"Since you put it that way, bad first," Annalee agreed.

"Someone very evil is on the way to Earth. Can't say how long it will take for this person to arrive. According to sources, this person is very powerful, very evil, and very determined. They don't know for certain who is on the way, but they said we need to be terrified.

"Evidently, our army caught one of the guards from the evil army. Unfortunately, they are starting to question if this guard was caught on purpose so he could find out where our army is hiding. It was just too easy to capture him, and he was willing to be captured."

"You know all those superhero movies? Will this person cause destruction just like in the movies? We can't let that happen," Galaxas said full of emotions.

"Yes and no. This person is powerful. If it comes down to it, I will surrender in order to save Earth."

"Mother! You can't do that. Who is this person?"

She thought hard for a moment, debating in her mind how much to expose. The girls watched the wheels in her mind turn. It saddened them to see the guilt and anguish their mother was feeling.

"They didn't know for sure."

"How any good news could come from this, I'll never know, but what good news could there possibly be?" Galaxas questioned her.

"Troid and Raiden are on their way here."

Both girls held hands and jumped up and down. This news certainly was good news.

Chapter Twenty-Four

Galaxas awoke hearing some type of air transportation engine, except it was different than the sound of a plane or helicopter. With energy like the energizer bunny, she jumped out of bed and ran to Annalee's room. Jumping on her bed, Galaxas dodged Annalee's moving legs. Annalee pulled the blanket down that was covering her sleepy eyes.

"Couldn't you wait until I had a cup of coffee at least?"

"No! I just heard the spaceship. They're here. Like now," Galaxas said not able to control her excitement.

"What? No. First dibs in the shower." But of course, Galaxas teleported leaving Annalee standing alone in the hallway. "This isn't funny anymore. Just sayin'."

Nebulane rounded the corner. "You're right, it's not fair. My shower is free. Mitchell is on a donut run."

"Thank you." She grabbed a bathrobe and ran like the dickens. In forty-five minutes, Mitchell was back and both girls sat eagerly at the kitchen table awaiting the love of their lives.

Mitchell laid the donuts on the table and eyed the girls. They were squirming in the chairs. "A case of the sick-with-love virus hit you, I see."

"Sort of. The guys will be here in minutes. The suspense is too much," Annalee confessed.

"Now it makes sense. I sure hope they get on my good side."

"Dad! Don't you even... "

"Relax, Gal. I won't ruin your time, but I better not see any K-I-S-S-I-N-G." He sang the word in the old children's kissing nursery rhyme.

"Dad!" both girls said at the same time, pink highlighting their cheeks.

"Dig in," Mitchell said.

"I'm going to wait for the guys. They can't get over all the different foods we have here," Galaxas replied. Annalee nodded in agreement.

Small talk went on for the next ten minutes. The girls kept looking around expecting them to appear any moment. A few sighs later, the doorbell rang.

Galaxas and Annalee jumped a mile high. "We'll get the door," Galaxas yelled as Annalee ran behind her. Their hearts pounded and they stopped before opening the door to catch their breath. Hand on the door handle it made a slight squeak. The smiles waiting for them melted their insides. They rushed outside and closed the door.

Mitchell hopped up to see what was going on, but Nebulane gently grabbed his arm.

"Give them a moment, hon."

He frowned and sat back down. Outside, the welcome back kisses were just what the doctor ordered for all of them. Troid held one hand behind his back, Galaxas noticed. She produced a curious look. He pulled his hand out in front and held up a dandelion for her to take. He still had a long way to go in understanding how dating on Earth works. But, not to Galaxas. His adorable face made that dandelion her new favorite flower or weed. She would cherish it the rest of her life.

She had a quick thought. "Don't move. I want to take a picture." She snapped it fast. Now she could refer to it when she needed a memory of his sweet, romantic gesture.

Troid placed his hand on Galaxas' cheek. "I have missed you so much, it physically hurt."

"Me too," Galaxas replied. "Thankfully, the vaccine for this emotional and physical pain has made it just in time. Those kisses are prescribed to make it all better."

Raiden and Annalee held hands and couldn't take their eyes off of each other.

"Ready for some interrogation?" Galaxas said with a chuckle.

Both guys looked at each other. "I prefer to fight the evil army," Troid answered. Raiden agreed.

With laughter, nervousness and anticipation, the front door opened. They walked in.

Troid walked right up to Mitchell. "Mr. Gaylord, my name is Troid. It's a pleasure to meet you."

Before he could respond Raiden stepped in. "I would like to introduce myself, also. I am Raiden. It's nice to meet you. We have heard a lot about you."

After shaking their hands, Mitchell escorted them to the kitchen table. "Ever have donuts before?" he asked them.

"No, sir," they both responded with gleaming eyes.

"Coffee or milk?" Mitchell asked.

"Milk, please," they both said at the same time.

"Girls. Put a move on it," Mitchell ordered in fun.

They hurried to the refrigerator, crossing their fingers.

"Help yourselves," Mitchell said extending his hand towards the donuts.

"And they did. Powdered sugar faces brought laughs. Mitchell couldn't help but notice how the guys kept looking at the girls and vice versa. It looked like sparklers were lit in their eyes. No shocker there for three of them, but is it possible that Annalee could have the eye condition?

After cleanup, they sat around on the couch and talked about a lot of things. All the regular formalities a dad would ask, and they, too, were sincerely interested in his work. The goal post lit up in the girls' eyes. Touchdown!

They had discussed in private how it would tear them up if their father didn't like the guys. How could they ever choose between them and Mitchell? It was looking as though that wasn't going to happen. Annalee was a lot more comfortable calling him Dad and Nebulane Mother.

The girls sat back and stared at the guys. Once again, they were dressed in clothing that looked like it came off the set of the TV series *Beauty and the Beast*. And they loved the look. Their muscles showed through the clothing even though it was loose fitting.

Today was a day of connecting, no business. That would start tomorrow. The couples savored every minute. The guys loved pizza so much that Mitchell brought five large cheese from the neighborhood pizza shop. For a while, the guys did nothing but eat. Forget talking. This was serious food, and they didn't want to be disturbed.

Mitchell and Nebulane, Galaxas and Annalee sat back and watched them be so involved in eating, chuckling how grease covered their chins. Realizing it was extremely quiet, the guys finally took their eyes off the pizza and looked back and forth at each face staring at them.

Grabbing a napkin to wipe his embarrassed and greasy face, Troid confessed. "I'm sorry, but I can't get enough of this. What did you say this was?" He held a slice of pizza up.

"Pizza," Galaxas replied with a grin.

"Do you think we could learn how to make it? We could start a pezza," is how Raiden pronounced it, "shop back home."

"You're in luck. I have a friend who worked in a pizza shop. I'll find out the secret and let you know," Annalee replied.

Each couple sat outside in the front or back of the house.

Mitchell and Nebulane sat on the couch sipping a cup of instant decaffeinated coffee. They needed sleep tonight.

"So...curiosity is getting the best of me," Nebulane began the conversation. Mitchell knew the guys were on her mind.

"They seem pretty great. Talk about big guys! At least we don't have to worry about anyone bothering the girls. They are some pretty handsome dudes."

After giggling at him, she responded. "I never told you this, but the men on our planet have superhero type strength. Not the women, just men."

He pushed his body back against the couch and turned to look at her. "Like *Superman*?"

"Just like that." She winked at him.

"Whoa! I want a demonstration."

"If they feel like it tomorrow, I'll get them to show you. Not tonight. Tonight, they belong to our girls." Nebulane watched his lips pucker and heard him snap his fingers.

"It doesn't matter one bit how strong they are, they better not touch my girls. You know what I mean."

She used a hand to shove him. "Don't be silly. They know better. You forget. I am the queen. 'Off with their heads'!"

A loud guffaw came out of his mouth. He pulled Nebulane over and kissed her.

Chapter Twenty-Five

Waffles, scrambled eggs, hot cocoa and pastries covered the counter. The guys filled a plate and went back for seconds. The girls, being too excited to be with them, could hardly eat a bite.

Dishes were cleared and on to the business at hand.

"Tell me what happened concerning the person who is coming here." Nebulane asked hesitantly. For the sake of their planet, yes, she needed to know. For the sake of her family, she hated the turmoil that plagued their happy family.

"Yes, Ma'am," Troid began. "Raiden and I followed him out for a ways. But, because we came up with a plan to send codes all over the galaxy, they have no idea which planet you are located on. He turned in the opposite direction. Some of the other members of our army are following him.

"With my condition, my heart glowing," he looked warmly at Galaxas, "we thought it would be better for Raiden and me to come here and keep watch. Besides, that's what the good Lord above created us to do, be His shadow."

"That is a strategic plan. It seemed to have worked. And I think you used good judgement by coming here to look out for us, especially since your love for Galaxas will guide you here anyway; and the scary part, who knows if someone else has been following you because of your physical condition.

"Do you happen to know who this person is?" Nebulane ended asking with a serious expression.

Troid looked at Raiden with a worried look and back at Nebulane. She knew exactly what he was hiding. She winked and he understood. For Galaxas' sake, that person needed to remain secret.

Galaxas watched the whole exchange. "Why do I feel you're not telling me something? If you're hiding something, and it is obvious by your expressions you are, then when this secret person finds me, wouldn't it be a good idea for me to know about him or her?"

Troid's face grew disheartened. He didn't like hiding things from her, but Nebulane is the reigning queen. He had to follow instructions. "I won't leave your side, Galaxas."

"We all know that is impossible. You're not even staying here."

Troid's body straightened. That light bulb floated invisibly above his head. Before he could speak, Mitchell jumped in.

"Oh no you don't. You can get that thought right out of your mind."

Galaxas didn't understand. Her eyes squinted almost shut.

"I think it's a marvelous idea. Having them here all the time gives us a much better survival chance. Annalee could share Galaxas' room and they could share her room. It's for a short time," Nebulane replied.

"Why didn't we think of this sooner?" Galaxas asked in total jubilation.

"Hon, our bedroom is on the total opposite side of the house. Get it?"

"We all get it Dad. Way to trust us," Galaxas added perturbed. Annalee crossed her arms and her lips formed to a pout.

"Sir, we would never do anything like what you're suggesting. It's not like that on our planet." Troid informed him.

"Well, haven't you been watching TV? But my girls are not like the girls on those TV shows."

Galaxas and Annalee didn't know if they should feel proud or childish by his remark.

"Oh, good. On our planet it is unacceptable," Troid assured him.

"Is that right?" Mitchell asked relieved.

"Yes, sir."

"Well, in light of this new development, Annalee, move your stuff," Mitchell said in a command voice, and then he winked at her.

"Gladly," she replied.

That evening, the two couples sat out on the front porch.

Galaxas told the guys about her partial vision. "What do you make of it, Troid?"

"He was choking you? All your visions come true?" Troid asked.

Uncomfortable about her answer, she lowered her head and nodded.

"Black gloves with long blades aren't an uncommon thing with that army. It would be difficult to know who it could be. We will stay close to you girls. Two of us to one of them," Raiden pointed out.

"Except, the most powerful of the army has much stronger and many more powers than we have. That does give me a concern," Troid added. Galaxas shivered as though a cold wind blew by. He pulled her tightly against himself.

"I had a sense that this person knew me and that made it easier for me to let my guard down. You know what happened next, him choking the life out of me."

"That is concerning to me, too," Troid interjected.

"Why can't you disintegrate him with your thoughts like you did to Clayton?" Annalee added wondering.

"You have to understand that this is all speculation. Maybe he caught me off guard before I was able to think clearly, instead of gasping for my life. My thoughts came to me before Clayton got to me. I wasn't caught off guard that he was going to kill me. I had time to think.

"That's the only conclusion I can draw right now," Galaxas admitted.

"And that makes a whole lot of sense," Annalee remarked.

"You know what we need?" Annalee asked.

"What's that?" Raiden inquired.

"Fun! We need to have some fun. Why don't we go dancing tomorrow night?"

"Yeah, fun. Except, I don't know how to dance," Galaxas added bending her head down.

"Don't be bummed. We'll show you some of our dances," Troid said with a smile. They demonstrated.

The girls fell over laughing. Their dance was clearly out of this world.

"Come on, Gal. Let's give it a try," Annalee urged. She pulled her by the arm, and they joined in. The dance looked like something from medieval times, and something from outer space with a touch of Earth modernism.

"We will stand out in a crowd even worse than we do now," Galaxas noted.

"I thought about that, too. We will tell people that we belong to a support group for people with rare skin conditions and that it is not a disease or anything they need to freak out over. We'll make up a country for the dance form and explain that.

"Look, we've been recluses far too long. I say we live," Annalee said holding her fist up high.

"Here, here!" Galaxas joined in.

"There is one problem. Your mother and dad," Troid mentioned nervously.

"I'll take care of them. I know just what to say," Galaxas said with a clever smirk.

∾

The next evening, feeling guilty for how she handled her mom and dad, Galaxas informed the guys and Annalee that her mom gave in after showering her with the guilt of having to live like a prisoner. She didn't enjoy doing that to her mother, but they did feel like prisoners and really needed to get out.

The guys looked marvelous in their outdated clothes and the girls looked adorable in their not quite miniskirts. Both girls kissed their parents on the cheek.

"We won't make a habit out of this. Just once in a while. We need freedom. Please understand."

Both parents nodded to Galaxas that they understood. Annalee drove. They walked into the—what else?—the Space39 Art Bar & Martini Lounge, known as one of the best dancing clubs downtown Fort Myers.

It was dark and crowded. Music blasted. At first no one noticed them, until the server took their drink order and couldn't quit staring at the guys. Then, all heads at the bar turned to look at them.

"Here we go," Galaxas remarked dreadfully.

"Maybe the server thought it was strange that we ordered sodas. I'm sure they don't get that order very much. Maybe I'll step up there and find out what she said." Annalee walked off before the rest of them could stop her. They watched her talk with the server. She and the server busted up laughing.

"Well?" Galaxas asked Annalee when she returned.

"She was embarrassed that we noticed her staring at our guys. She thinks they are the hottest thing to ever walk through those doors. I told her, 'Wait until you see them dance. It's right out of this world. She said she couldn't wait'." Annalee was yelling because it was so noisy, and her statement was so ironic.

"Nothing about our skin conditions?" Galaxas asked in a bugged manner, knowing Annalee expected the question.

"Oh, that. I did mention that to her, and she was totally cool with it."

Galaxas raised a hand to Troid indicating, "There you go."

The server came with their sodas. She giggled at Annalee. It was too dark to see her blushing.

"Well, girls. Let's get this party started," Raiden said with excitement.

On the dance floor, to their surprise, a few of the people had on clothing that represented space costumes. That brought a good laugh.

The song was perfect for their style of dancing. They moved to the outside terrace and began their dance while everyone on the dance floor stopped and watched. The place became quiet except for the music. Galaxas looked around, feeling unsure of herself. Troid pulled her close to him as the music turned to a slow dance. Raiden did the same with Annalee.

People joined them for the dance, but they kept looking over at them. At this point, both couples didn't even notice. Maybe it was the love that sparkled around them? Was it the skin condition? They just didn't care.

After they pulled apart when the dance was over, a crowd of people ran up to them asking if they could teach them the dance. Then questions like, is that your real skin color? Cool. Where did you find clothes like that? Cool, all came out.

Of course it looked like a choreographed part of a movie, but it was so much fun. They were having an honest to goodness blast. Prissy Priscilla sat at a table frowning with jealousy. Micah walked up and took Galaxas' hand. He pulled her aside while Troid continued teaching people the dance.

Panic set in as he saw Micah getting really close to her. He kept grabbing her hand asking her to dance with him. Everyone stopped to watch Troid stomp his way to Micah.

Annalee yelled, "Stop, Troid. Don't."

Well whoopee do, like yelling would stop him. He grabbed Micah's shirt and lifted him off the ground with complete ease.

"Troid, we are just talking. He's not trying to hurt me. Put him down," Galaxas ordered, face of fright.

He lowered him to the ground while looking into Galaxas' disappointed eyes. Micah pulled back from his grip with super wide eyes.

"Sorry, man. I thought you were going to hurt her."

"Sorry," Galaxas said in his direction as he walked away.

"Now look at the attention you drew to us. We were having a great time. Did I get all bent out of shape when those girls were flirting with you?"

"What girls?" He didn't even notice. Her face softened.

People formed around him. Question after question. "How'd you do that? Where do you work out? Does your skin condition give you extra strength?" Even the band members jumped off the stage and questioned their skin condition. When they climbed back up, they whispered together in a group.

Troid looked over at Galaxas and her arms were crossed, mouth formed down. He shrugged his shoulders and arched his eyebrows. His hand extended in her direction. Facial muscles softened and she took his hand.

How ironic. The group played a song by The First Edition called, "Just Dropped in to See What Condition My Condition was in." That got both couples laughing with ease. Dancing began again. They were the hit of the night.

As they walked out to their car, Galaxas stopped abruptly. She couldn't talk or move. Troid, Raiden and Annalee formed a circle around her. Her hair blew all around in the wind, the wind that only seemed to affect her. They eyed each other, nervousness transpiring in their faces.

She let out a deep breath, as though she couldn't breathe during the time she was motionless. Her body bent over as she breathed in and out to restore her oxygen levels.

"Gal, talk to me," Troid insisted.

Her hand reached up to find him. When it did, she rested it on his arm. "I'm fine. No, I'm not fine." Teardrops came down like a downpour.

"What did you see?" he asked concerned.

Annalee stood silent, her eyes a blurry mess.

"I could see people's faces as they screamed in complete terror. Then that black leather glove was choking the life out of me again. Same glove."

"I believe God is giving you a warning so that you can stop this evilness from taking over our planet. You must pray and ask for His guidance. Let's get you home and give you the space needed," Troid added.

Raiden stopped them for a moment. "Galaxas, were the people you saw screaming from our planet or from Earth?"

She stared at the ground trying to recapture the vision. Her eyes kept blinking. "I can't remember now. Ugh!"

Troid pulled her in close. "Let's get you home."

They walked in the door and Nebulane was watching television waiting for them. She saw the look on Galaxas' face. It frightened her. "I knew it! I knew something bad would happen."

"No, no, nothing bad happened. We had a wonderful time," Annalee assured her.

"Well, tell that to miss scared out of her wits," Nebulane said almost rising off the couch.

"It has nothing to do with our time out," Troid mentioned. "She had another vision."

Nebulane forced her head forward with pointed lips. She didn't have to say, tell me about it, because her expression said it for her.

"She's pretty upset, so I'll tell you," Troid said. "In one part of the vision, she saw frightened faces of people screaming. The other part was that black leather glove choking her again."

"Thanks, Troid. She needs some rest. I would like you both to leave your doors open. This is getting more and more concerning."

Galaxas laid in bed, tossing and turning. She lied supine, eyes wide open. After a long talk with the Lord, she prayed for an interpretation of her visions. But something was blocking the communication. Her eyes stared at the ceiling. In the Bible there was a time an angel fought with the prince of the kingdom of Persia, found in Daniel chapter ten. Daniels' prayer was detained for twenty-one days as the angel fought the demon. The angel Michael came to his rescue and then the angel was able to speak to Daniel.

Maybe that's why her prayer was being blocked. More of God's divine power, that's what is needed. But while she lay there, a noise got her attention. It sounded like someone was walking on the roof, or could it be acorns rolling down? No, it didn't make that tkk-tkk-tkk-tkk-tkk sound. It almost sounded like footsteps. She jumped up and ran straight into Troid, who heard it too. After getting their wits about them from colliding into each other, Troid placed her next to Raiden. "I'll check it out."

He had teleported to the tree above the house. His eyes scanned the area. To his surprise a huge owl was chasing a squirrel. He transported himself over to the squirrel and saved it.

"Sorry, buddy, but you'll have to hunt elsewhere. Galaxas would never forgive me if I let you eat this critter." He didn't even pay attention to the scared squirrel nibbling at his fingers. The owl flew off and he set the squirrel in a tree. Back inside, Galaxas was trembling, and Raiden was trying to comfort her.

"Everything's okay. I saved a squirrel from the clutches of an owl."

"You did?" she asked in a sweet, grateful voice.

"Yes. I knew you would dwell on it if I let the owl have his dinner."

"Bad ole owl."

"Gal!" he said, tipping his head. "He has to eat, too."

"Why can't he eat birdseed like the other birds? Never mind."

He walked her to the bedroom door and kissed her lips goodnight. She walked to the bed like she was floating on clouds.

Chapter Twenty-Six

The next day, Annalee and Galaxas walked out to the kitchen table where everyone else was seated. Cookies, coffee and milk at each setting. Troid and Raiden were gobbling up the cookies as though they were the Cookie Monster reincarnated. "Man, these are outstanding," Raiden said with excitement. Troid had too big of a mouthful to reply, but he shook his head back and forth in full agreement.

"All done," Galaxas said as she and Annalee wiped their hands back and forth.

"With what?" Troid asked finally able to speak after taking a swig of milk.

"Our books. We submitted them."

"That's wonderful, girls, Nebulane said. "When do you think you'll hear back?"

"There's no way to know that," Annalee answered.

"How exciting it must feel," Raiden thought out loud.

"If you don't write books, there is no way for you to understand how we feel. Rejections will undoubtedly come, but sooner or later someone will see its potential and our writing careers will take off. Then it will feel like the high you get when your car rolls over the Double Ferris Wheel," Annalee added.

Their phones both chimed. Both girls read the texts. "And here is our first rejection," Galaxas said disappointed.

Annalee's mouth turned to a pout.

"It will happen. Rejection is the process in every new author's career. I have total confidence that your books will be published," Nebulane inserted.

"I think we deserve a hot fudge sundae. You in, Annalee?"

"Am I ever. And I will eat the whole dang thing this time."

"Would you mind fixing me one, too?" Raiden asked with a bright smile and pleading eyes.

Was the new love effect wearing off because she almost told him to make it himself. His eyes squinted. "I would be glad to fix you one," she decided after all.

Nebulane cleared her throat. "No, he won't. We are in the middle of a strategic plan. This is a little more important than an ice cream sundae."

"Yes, mother," Annalee answered.

"Troid, would you like one?" Galaxas asked sweetly. His smile was wide. He nodded his head fast looking like a child.

"Mom? Dad?"

"Sure," Nebulane replied. Mitchell kept nodding his head until Galaxas acknowledged she got his message. Faces of pure pleasure, the strategic plan continued.

"If I could add something because a thought just came to my mind. These sun pendants are our saving grace. The evil ones can't fight against them. So, why don't our armies join in a circle, teleport at the same time and shine them on our opponents? They won't suspect us and zippidity zappidity, we got them," Galaxas remarked. "They wouldn't be suspecting it."

Nebulane sniggered. "Being queen all this time, why didn't I think of that?"

"Because there's more to it. The most powerful of them all can probably survive this attack and escape. There must be something more that we're missing. If we don't capture him, this could torment us forever. Don't ask me how I know this, but I keep seeing those screaming faces and someone choking me. We're missing a very big piece of this puzzle," Galaxas cautioned.

"She's right. These pendants won't have the same effect on the leader, and we know he is looking for her. I say we get to our planet, take it back and come back here to find him. With him gone, it should make it easier to win our country back," Troid added.

"It looks like my little girl was born for this role," Nebulane said almost in tears.

Mitchell smiled warmly at Galaxas.

"It's true. I haven't taught her anything and it just comes natural to her. You will make a wise and great queen, Gal."

"Thanks, Mom, but not without my courageous husband," she said looking at Troid. He smiled with genuine love.

"And to take it a step further, where would we be without any of our courageous people, like Raiden, for instance," Galaxas added.

"You took the words right out of my mouth. If I had to choose a mate for my girls, I pray I would have had enough sense to pick these guys.

"Now, let's move on with our plans," Nebulane demanded.

Galaxas and Annalee cleared the plates and sundae cups while the rest of them carried on with business.

"Sorry to interrupt, but Troid, do you have pictures from our planet that we could look at?" Galaxas asked.

He handed her a device. Then he pointed. "You'll find a lot of pictures in this spot."

She and Annalee took off for the bedroom and viewed the pictures. "Annalee, look at this pet. It looks like a cross between a cat and a dog. How adorable. I don't even know what that critter is, but it's pretty cute."

"Whoa, look at that big thing. What the heck is it?" Annalee said staring like she was in a trance.

"Your guess is as good as mine," Galaxas said with humor.

"Hey Gal. They do have trees, mountains, and lakes. It's actually quite beautiful. I don't know why, but I was expecting ugly craters and dirt with pure gray colors," Annalee remarked pleasantly surprised.

"What do we have here?" Galaxas put the device in Annalee's hands so she could view it better.

"Oooh boy, who is she? She is hanging onto Troid with plans

to never let go, it certainly appears." She glanced cautiously at Galaxas.

"When they're done in there, I will get to the bottom of it," Galaxas confirmed.

"Uh, Galaxas. Don't get upset." She handed her back the device.

A hand went to her stomach, and she puffed her mouth out. "He looks like he is in love with her."

"Maybe he was, but maybe she became corrupted, and God released him from that bond," Annalee said trying to console her.

"Yeah, maybe, but it still makes me feel ill. Do you think he could still be in love with her even though the bond was broken?"

"You're asking the wrong person. But the way he looks at you and acts around you, I would say his feelings for this young lady are all over."

"You would think I'd feel better about that, but I don't. Just being honest," Galaxas admitted.

Annalee rubbed her arm. "We'll get to the bottom of this. I'm in the same boat.

"Hey, look at this man. I think he is the most handsome man on my planet and Earth combined. How can anyone be that gorgeous? Of course, I think Troid is, but this man is abnormally gorgeous," Galaxas said handing the device to Annalee.

"Oh, my world! Could he be real? How is that possible?"

Galaxas shrugged her shoulders. For some reason she couldn't quit looking at him. It was like she was a magnet, and he was the metal, magnetically pulling them together.

"Galaxas. Galaxas. GALAXAS," Annalee yelled. She shook her shoulders. Then she waved a hand in front of her face. Finally, Galaxas looked up. "What is going on?" Annalee said in a hyperventilating fashion.

"I don't know. It felt like this picture was pulling me right into it. Like a spell, and I couldn't break it. So strange, I can't even describe what was happening."

She clicked the folder off and dropped the phone from her

hands onto the bed. Annalee stood frozen in time. It was freaky to witness. Scary. Downright frightening. Her spine tingled. Real fear.

"Come on. We're going to find out what is going on." Annalee grabbed her hand and pulled Galaxas' heavy body.

"Sorry to interrupt, but we need some answers." She held the device up for everyone at the table to see. "Who is this guy? Something frightening weird happened when Galaxas looked at his picture."

"Tell me what you were thinking, Galaxas," Nebulane asked worried while looking away fast from the picture and pointedly looking at Troid and Raiden.

Galaxas stared down at the table and just her mouth moved. Everyone remained quiet. "It felt like I was being pulled into the picture. I think a scared feeling came over me. It was just so weird, so hard to explain."

Nebulane, Troid and Raiden kept looking at each other.

Nebulane knew they were waiting for her to respond. This was tough. What should she tell her without telling her everything? Not to mention, complete, one hundred percent fear blanketed her body. "This is one of the most evil and powerful men there is and will ever be." She scrolled through the device looking for more pictures. She found another very evil person and realized that she needed to tell Galaxas a bit at a time who these men were. She decided it best to tell her about the man she stared at in the moment, completely terrified of the man in the picture.

"This very evil and very powerful man is your grandfather."

Galaxas and Annalee stared at the picture with the widest eyes. Galaxas' brows arched and she sucked in her top lip. Her eyes needed relief. They stung her like a hive of hornets were stinging her. Troid jumped up and pulled her in his arms. He squeezed her tight.

"I'm sorry, Galaxas," he said with a strained voice. "I'm so sorry." Annalee and Mitchell watched in horror, tears slipping down their faces. Nebulane had dropped her head. Complete gut-wrenching anguish filled her soul.

Mitchell pulled her close and held her as she cried.

Galaxas pulled away wiping underneath her eyes and using the back of her hand to pat her nose. "He has eyes that look like Satan himself. Is he…Is he your father, Mom?"

Still crying, Nebulane nodded her head.

"How, Mom? Was he ever good?"

She grabbed a napkin. Clearing her throat she finally spoke.

"He was a wonderful, loving father and person. Before he knew what happened, it was like he became an empty shell of pure evil. He killed so many of our people. He and the other man you pointed out. If it wasn't for Zareb, my own father would have killed me. Behind my back even. Zareb saw what he was going to do to me and teleported to me in time to get me out of there. Zareb saved my life."

"I can't even imagine how torn up you have been. Mom, why didn't you confide in us? We could have helped you through this." She ran up to her and embraced her. They cried together.

"This is one of the very reasons I kept it all from you. If you don't convert to the evil side, they just kill you. No questions asked. The other problem with the plans to take back our planet is difficult because their power is too great for us. I don't understand it myself, so how can I explain something I don't understand?"

"Can they convert back to the good side?" Annalee asked concerned.

"It's never happened. I am comparing it to taking the mark of the beast. Once you take that mark, that chip under your skin, you belong to Satan. No turning back. That's what I think is going on with this.

"We have church on our planet and your grandfather never missed going. He knew far too much to let this happen to him, Galaxas." She stopped to catch her breath and compile her thoughts. She held Galaxas' arms and pushed her out to see her eyes as she confessed more. "He killed your grandmother in cold blood."

Nebulane slipped down to the chair, tortured with the memories. Galaxas looked around the room at the morose faces.

"So, he wouldn't blink an eye to kill you or me, Mom."

"Not a blink." She stared hard into Galaxas' eyes. "They are that evil. Beyond help and beyond our comprehension."

"Who is the other man in the picture that caused Galaxas such concern?" Annalee asked.

Nebulane perked up and answered before anyone else could. She wasn't ready to ruin her life, and this could do it. She wasn't about to tell her who the man is to Galaxas. Not yet. "They call him Jagger. It means to chase or hunt. His hunting skills are no match. Whomever he hunts, he finds. He is extremely powerful. I dare say, so far undefeatable."

A blanket of bumps covered Galaxas' body. She didn't see it, but Mitchell, Troid and Raiden kept looking back and forth to each other, shifting their stance several times. Annalee noticed. She could tell they were hiding something, but probably for Galaxas' sake. Therefore, she never brought it up again.

Chapter Twenty-Seven

Days passed. Nothing concerning happened. The young ladies spent a lot of time with the guys. A few more rejection letters ruined the happy moods.

"I have an idea that I think you all will like," Troid said.

"Let's hear it," Raiden said curious.

"Tonight, let's make a picnic basket and go to a private beach. One that isn't prohibited to be on, but one that is pretty much abandoned of people."

"What a perfect idea. I have had to go to the beach myself, since you guys can't be out in the sunlight," Annalee replied.

"Annalee, we can be out in the sunlight. It's just that it blinds our eyes and can get quite painful," Galaxas replied.

With a sneer on her face, Annalee replied, "Like I said, since you can't be out in the sunlight, it will be dark, the stars will be bright, the quietness of the waves rolling up on the beach, and the sea breeze will feel sensational. I'm in."

They all helped with dinner preparations and cleanup. They put together a basket of snacks and drinks.

"Mom, would you and Dad like to join us?" Galaxas asked.

"That would be nice, but maybe next time. We don't want to intrude on your special time together," Nebulane responded.

"No hoochie couchie," Mitchell added.

Embarrassed, Galaxas replied. "Dad! We are adults and you already know that won't happen because of the customs of our planet. Well, maybe not your planet, but ours."

Nobody could have guessed how special the feeling was walking on an almost abandoned beach. It was exactly as Annalee had described. Galaxas was all giddy because it was the first time she walked on the beach. The squishy feel of the sand between her toes caused her to run and laugh, running back and forth playing tag with the waves rolling up on the beach. Annalee joined her.

Then the guys grabbed their hands and each couple walked alone. Troid pulled Galaxas into an intimate embrace before kissing her forehead down to her lips. She became listless. How could his touch do this to her? It was like magic.

Down the beach further, Raiden wrapped his arms around Annalee. He bent down and kissed her lips softly. Then he looked back into her eyes. His heart was blinking with a warm glow.

"Annalee, I know we haven't been together very long, and I know our customs are different from your customs, but I can't help myself. Is it odd to think I'm madly in love with you?"

She gulped and felt sensations screaming through her body. "I couldn't say, but I can say that I feel the same way. It's as though we connect like that missing puzzle piece. We fit so well together. If only my heart could portray it the way yours does."

After a special amount of intimacy and bond building, the couples reunited.

"Hey, let's take a swim," Raiden said enthusiastically.

"I can't swim well," Galaxas admitted.

"You don't have to. I'll hang onto you," Troid said warmly.

The guys stripped down to their swimsuits. The girls stared in disbelief. They couldn't quit staring at the most perfect bodies they had ever seen. Move over *Baywatch*.

"I'm going to take a dip, then I'll come back to the shoreline for you," Troid said.

The pounding of their feet on the sand and having fun laughs gave the girls the courage to join them. Even though they wore a one-piece swimsuit, it still fit perfectly and showed off the benefit of exercising. Annalee had talked Galaxas into joining her in exercises. Those butt-lifter exercises did wonders.

Troid and Raiden stood at the shoreline waiting for them. When they saw them, they looked at each other with a "wowza" expression. The girls stepped into warm water and laid back like they were floating in a tub. They were taking so long that the guys grabbed and pulled them in all the way. Of course, water battles, splashing, and playing went on for an hour.

The breeze filled the girls' skin with goosebumps. They ran to find a towel. The guys stayed in the water until they dried and changed. Annalee held a beach towel up so their eyes couldn't see them changing.

After everyone had changed, they sat on the beach blanket and ate snacks. They talked and talked and talked. The girls looked for their cellphones.

"Yikes! It's 11 o'clock. Dad told us to be back by ten. Yup, texts and phone calls. It's not like we do this very often, if at all! Why can't he give us a break and treat us like adults? I'm getting sick and tired of it," Galaxas admitted.

"Look, Gal, he's just worried for your safety. Nothing else. If the situation were different and we didn't have to fear about the evil ones finding you, he would lighten up. Give him a break. Text him and tell him our phones were in the bag while swimming and we lost track of time. Plain and simple. Tell him we'll be there in five minutes," Troid said.

"Five minutes? We can be there in five seconds."

"Not if I plan to kiss you for four minutes."

She formed a shy smile and mildly nodded her head. "Yes, good point." Her fingers typed and sent the text off. "Now, where were we?"

When they arrived home, Mitchell and Nebulane were already in bed. A note said "Thanks for letting me know. Love, Dad," rested on the kitchen island.

After cleaning up their wet clothes and food basket, they

each took a shower and went to bed. The time on the beach gave them peace of mind and they slept soundly.

In the dead of night and in the near distance, a spacecraft flew around searching. For something. For someone?

Chapter Twenty-Eight

After breakfast, final plans were made to take back their planet. Annalee ran out of the bedroom and collided with Galaxas coming into the bedroom. "Ugh! Oof!" moans followed.

"Why are you so excited?" Galaxas asked.

"Why are you?" Annalee asked back.

"I received a book deal."

"Me, too," Annalee shrieked. They embraced and jumped around. Chairs screeched as Nebulane, and the guys jumped to their feet. "Girls?"

"Yes, Mother," they both responded.

"Something happened. What?"

They looked at each other and smiled big. They both spoke at the same time over each other.

Nebulane pushed her hands out back and forth. "One at a time, please."

"We both got a book deal," Galaxas said gleefully.

Nebulane drew her hands together. "That is simply marvelous. I knew you two would do it. What's next, and my deepest congratulations?"

Annalee pondered before answering. "We need to read the contract over and be certain it is good. Then editing, and all of that begins."

Everyone embraced. It was a happy time.

"Let's go get some ice cream and celebrate," Annalee urged.

"You two go on, but just watch everything going on around you. We have a little more preparation and then," Nebulane swiped her hands over and over, "we end this evil control once and for all."

"Sounds great. We'll be back shortly," Galaxas responded.

Chairs screeched from being pulled out, and they were back in the planning zone. The girls took off in Annalee's car. They drove to Buckingham Community Park to eat the ice cream outside of her car. The shaded spot was perfect. Groans of pure delight were expressed.

"I love these sour candies in my hot fudge sundae," Galaxas said in pure delight.

"Nothing's as good as hot fudge and marshmallow." Annalee was opening and closing her fingers pulling apart the marshmallow. It looked like spider webs.

But from behind them a deep, sexy but scary voice spoke.

"Galaxas. Finally, we meet."

Trembling hands and wide eyes, she turned slowly.

Annalee grabbed her hand and turned with her. He stepped out of the shadows. It was the man in the picture who was too gorgeous to be real. He smiled, white teeth sparkling. His eyes were covered with a thick pair of sunglasses. He wore fabric resembling black leather.

"How did you find me?"

"How else?" He looked at Galaxas, confused by the question.

She pushed her head backwards and scrunched her face. Annalee was shaking visibly. Galaxas' reaction to his picture flashed back in her mind.

"What do you mean?" she countered back.

"I shouldn't have too much trouble finding my own daughter."

Both girls' sundaes splattered on the ground. They didn't even flinch when the melted part splashed on their shoes.

"Wha...t?"

"Don't tell me you didn't know," he said, acting sane and using a gentle tone.

"That's a lie. You're not my father. You can't be. I grew up here my whole life."

"Did you?" His tone was still gentle. He could pour on the charm anytime he wanted, and it always worked. Until now.

She couldn't speak. Her heart pounded an oh-woe-is-me tune

"When Nebulane took you away from me, you were a baby."

"How...how do you know my mother's name?"

"You mean, how do I know my wife's name?"

"Hhhh!" Galaxas' hand quickly hit her mouth. Being in the daylight her eyes hurt from being opened so wide.

"I see. She told you I was evil. She said she would tell you that. You were fooled. Your mother is the evil one and was kicked off of our planet. Why don't you come back with me and see for yourself." He extended a hand and threw her what looked like a genuine smile.

Galaxas reacted by twisting her body away from him. "How can I tell if you're lying or telling the truth?"

He pulled out the sun pendant. It began to shoot out light bursts. His and her eyes shined like the sun. She and Annalee looked at each other dumbfounded.

"If I were evil, there is no way I could hold this pendant, especially around my neck against my heart."

"This is so confusing. Annalee, tell me what to do."

She looked at Annalee's face and found her caught in some kind of trance looking at him, like when she herself was staring at his picture. "I have to think about this. I'll meet you back here tomorrow."

Before he could reply or do anything, she and Annalee disappeared to their front porch. They sat on the swing. "Is it possible he is telling the truth?" Galaxas said with fear stricken over her face, holding a hand on her stomach.

Annalee looked down swinging her head in confusion. "I don't know, Gal. You would think by now your mother would have figured it best to tell you so he didn't find you and corrupt you, like he could have done if you weren't on your "A" game. I am just as confused as you."

Puckering her lips, she jumped up. "Well, it's about time I find out."

The heavy foot stomping caused everyone at the table to look over. "Dear, I didn't hear the car drive in," Nebulane said.

They all took notice of Galaxas' expression. No one knew how to analyze it. Fuming, Galaxas spit it out. "Is Jagger my father?"

Frozen like ice, Nebulane felt she couldn't breathe.

"Mother!"

Mitchell remained quiet and Troid's face produced a guilty expression.

"I will leave and never come back if you don't start talking and telling me the truth." She meant it.

"Okay. I didn't know how you would respond if you knew the truth. The look on your face when I told you about your grandfather was devastating enough. It wasn't the right time to tell you. You were mentally and emotionally drained. Troid convinced me to tell you when you got back tonight. It always bothered him that I kept that from you."

She glanced back and forth at both of them, still a scowl on her face. Looking at Mitchell like she was betrayed, she said, "So, you're not my father?"

"That's where you're wrong. I have always been a father to you. That won't change."

Trying to hold back the tears, some escaping, she replied, "That's where you're wrong. I just met my father. He is the one who gave me life." Mitchell's heart sunk.

"And he is the one who will take your life," Nebulane added.

"It's a little too late to convince me of that, Mom. He said you took me from him, that you are the evil one. He held the sun pendant up and it didn't hurt him. How can that be?" Galaxas screamed the words.

"I don't know, but now that he has found you, he will corrupt or kill you. Zareb saved me from him, too. He was this close," she held her index and thumb together almost touching, "to corrupting me. He is persuasive and very manipulative."

"Galaxas, she's telling you the truth. If she would have stayed, she would have become a powerful and evil ruler. What your grandfather and father have done to our people is so evil you couldn't understand it if you tried," Troid pleaded with her.

"Why did you have to keep it secret? With him being such a great hunter, you had to know he would find me. This isn't making sense."

"I was afraid you would go back to our planet and meet with him. He is so crafty; you would have been turned without even knowing it. He can draw you in with his eyes, sort of like Medusa. I couldn't take that chance. Our planet needs you," Nebulane clarified with genuine mortification.

Galaxas looked at Annalee. "You would think a caring mother would have trust in her child, now adult. Trying to keep such emotional information from me is cruel and unforgiveable. So, I just happen to run into him, like today for instance, and take the chance of being captured not knowing the truth. That doesn't sound very queen-like."

Annalee formed a sympathetic expression. "But maybe it's a mom-like thing."

"I need time to think," Galaxas growled.

"Sorry, Galaxas, but we need to get out of here. We need a new location, one you've never been to," Troid insisted.

"Here's the thing, I don't know right now who is lying and who is telling the truth. I can't be with any of you except Annalee."

"Could I insert an idea, for just a minute," Mitchell asked.

Galaxas looked sorrowfully at him. He was a victim just like she was. "Sure."

"My friend has a huge house and he's not staying there. He said we could use it whenever we wanted. It has plenty of space for you to be alone. Please. I just want you to be safe."

"Thanks, Dad." His eyes blurred when she called him Dad.

Nebulane said, "Let's jump in the car and all join hands, then Mitchell will whisper the location in my ear. We'll need a car, so transporting in the car is necessary." Just in case evil was hiding nearby, their voices were low, almost to a whisper.

Galaxas moved to the backseat between the door and Annalee, only holding Annalee's hand. She just didn't know who to trust right now.

Within half an hour, invisible footsteps walked into their house in Florida. Next a loud crash sound rumbled as appliances crashed to the floor, followed by strong and embarrassing curse words that came out of the invisible person's mouth. He even knocked the refrigerator to the floor. The door opened enough to let the items inside plummet to the floor.

Chapter Twenty-Nine

They hung out at a beautiful, rustic cabin in the forest of Montana. There wasn't a need for an alarm since the owners felt nobody would be walking around this wilderness area. Mitchell and Annalee drove to the grocery store about an hour away and stocked up on food and other supplies.

Galaxas hung out in a bedroom most of the day, except for when she was hungry. Then she brought the food into the bedroom.

"I don't know how to convince her that I'm telling the truth. Why didn't I listen to you when you pointed out how risky and upsetting this would be for her?" Nebulane shook her head back and forth. Troid remained silent for a moment. How could he possibly answer her?

Troid feeling sympathy but a little anger mixed in his emotions replied, "She needs the time to think things through. She has every right to feel angry, hurt, confused and not trust anyone.

"Just stop and think about how her world has been turned upside down. All this emotional information. Who could blame her? I just want to be here for her when she is ready to talk."

Galaxas smiled hesitantly as she stood in the hallway listening. He was sincere and that gave her hope.

"I'm so glad she has you. I feel so much safer with you here.

Maybe soon, she'll forgive me. I just hope she realizes how much Mitchell loves her. He was her father since she was a baby," Nebulane stuttered out. "I handled everything wrong." She broke down in sobs.

"Who could say for certain, but I'm pretty sure she loves him and will always think of him as her dad. Galaxas is amazing. Her response is so justified. In my gut, I feel she'll come around," Troid sympathetically replied.

Gosh, Galaxas loved this guy. He wasn't pushy, but understanding and supportive. Knowing how he felt made her feel so much better. She snuck back into the room and gently closed the door as Mitchell and Annalee walked into the house with grocery bags.

"Go grab groceries, guys," Mitchell insisted. Nebulane began putting them away. Annalee headed straight for Galaxas' room with a small plastic bag.

"Any change in Galaxas?" Mitchell asked.

"No, none," Nebulane replied dropping her head. "I handled this so poorly. My intentions were to keep her safe, including her emotions. How do you tell your daughter that her real father is a stone, cold-blooded killer? How do you get those words out? All the evil he has committed, it's so hard to talk about."

Mitchell rubbed his mouth. "It's all too confusing. She just needs time to process everything." He plopped on the couch and searched for the sports channel. The guys dropped the rest of the grocery bags on the counter and sat down with Mitchell. They were athletic and loved Earth's sporting events.

Tap, tap, tap. "Who's there?" Galaxas asked hesitantly.

"It's Annalee, Gal."

"Come on in."

She handed Galaxas the bag. "Every kind of sweet and sour candy we could find." The sigh of delight was satisfying to Annalee.

Pulling a sour worm out as far as possible, Galaxas took a bite. Her eyes and mouth puckered.

"Any better yet?" Annalee asked.

"I'm trying. You have no idea how hard this is to comprehend."

"You're right, I don't. But I put myself in your tiny shoes and I can see the difficulty of having to deal with all of it. I'd be in a mental institution right now. Actually, there were times when I found out about you and your family that I considered my mind was losing its grip," Annalee confessed.

"The saddest part of all of this is my dad. He doesn't deserve me treating him like a stepfather. I really love him."

"Gal! That man loves you as if he was your real father. Don't allow yourself to think differently. Of everything you found out, he needs to be treated the same. I wish you could have seen his sad eyes. He didn't even buy potato chips. I threw them in the basket anyway.

"Don't hurt him, Galaxas." Annalee choked up at the end of her words.

"I'm so glad I have you. You have always helped me to think clearly. I stood in the hallway and listened to Mom and Troid talk. He really cares how this has affected me. He seems to really love me.

"For Dad and his sake, I'm about ready to discuss this whole thing. You need to be at my side at all times," Galaxas urged Annalee.

She extended her hand. "Let's get to it."

Galaxas took her hand. Annalee could feel the trembles. It caused her eyes to blur. They walked out to the living room and the guys jumped up. She walked right up to Mitchell and kissed his cheek. "Sorry, Dad."

That was all she had to say. He tilted his head down and a few tears dropped. She held his hand and squeezed it. She grabbed both of Troid's hands and said genuinely, "Thanks for understanding and not pressuring me. I really am grateful for you and me really, with all my heart, love you." She pushed herself up and kissed his cheek. He was overwhelmed with emotion.

Then she turned with a scowl and looked at Nebulane. "You, I'm way too angry with to feel any emotion."

"Galaxas, I really wanted to keep you safe, and our planet.

How do you tell your daughter what an evil man your real father is? It tore me up to try and explain it. To this day I picture my father trying to murder me, and how he turned away from all the good we did as a people, and it stuck with me my whole life. How could I do that to you?"

"You know what hurt the most, Mom? How you allowed me to feel like I was a freak all my life. If I had known the truth, things could have been different. Once I knew the truth, and Dad pointed out how beautiful I was, I started feeling beautiful. Did you know a worldwide modeling agency tried to get me and Annalee to sign with them? Once Troid and Dad made me feel good about myself, how I viewed myself changed. That's a big deal."

"Believe me, I think about that all the time," Nebulane confessed looking down. "What a huge mistake. Telling you how sorry I am just doesn't seem adequate enough. I hope in time you will forgive me. For everything."

"And treating me like I'm in high school all the time. I should not have to ask your permission to go somewhere or to date someone. I'm really tired of that, Mother."

"You're absolutely right. I handled all of it wrong."

"And then you keep saying I am too important to our planet that nothing can ever happen to me. You knew my real father would find me eventually, since he is known for his hunting skills. You put me and our planet in danger by not telling me about him."

"There is no doubt you're right about that," Nebulane answered with shame.

"So, I would like to know, why am I so important for our planet? Why? Why? Why?"

"I haven't figured that out yet, Galaxas. I'm trying to figure it all out."

"What's different about me than you or Troid or Raiden? What?"

"There is some power you have that we don't have. It is this power that will save our planet. I just don't know what it is yet. But I realized you have the power not only to disintegrate evil,

174

but to stop a person in their tracks. We don't have that power. But there's more. We just don't know what other powers you have, and now is a good time to find out. How, though?" Nebulane paced as she thought.

"Well, like I asked, and you didn't answer, what is different about me than with you three?"

She pondered deep in thought. "Troid. Raiden. Do you guys have anything?"

"I'm sorry, Galaxas. I don't know yet. All I know is that we can use our eyes just like you to disintegrate evil and see far and wide with our vision."

Raiden just nodded his head and shrugged his shoulders.

"Trying to figure it out is what is holding up this attack," Nebulane added.

"Well, I suggest we all think upon it. This needs to end. Now, I'm hungry. Did you all get any ingredients to make pizza?" Galaxas asked with a relieved smile.

The guys perked up with smiles.

"Gal, we did. Let's go make some pizza," Annalee said with a bright, relieved smile.

"Could we help?" the guys offered.

"We could use some strong hands, so sure," Annalee answered happily.

Annalee snooped around and found some board games. "Look what I found," she said holding one up. "Who wants to play?"

"I don't know," Galaxas replied still a nervous mess.

"Come on. We need to do something to break this tension in the air." Annalee's face lit up. "This was my favorite game as a child."

Seeing the excitement in her face, plus the adorable pigtails making her look younger than she was, the guys and Galaxas gave in. The next thing you heard was "BZZZZZZZZ." Galaxas jumped back not understanding what happened. She looked eagerly at Annalee for clarification, who was laughing.

"Wow, girl. Looks like you have a lawsuit on your hands." Annalee fell over in laughter realizing she was the only one who understood how the game worked.

The guys busted up with laughter. "Go ahead. Let's see you two wise guys try it," Galaxas urged.

Raiden produced a confident expression, took the tweezers in his hand and played. Being very careful he glanced up with a proud look. Bad idea. That caused him to lose his mobility and "BZZZZZZZZZ, BZZZZZZZZZ" rang through the air.

"Hope you have a good lawyer," Annalee mocked and then cracked up.

"Hey, Mom. Why don't you come over here and use your healing powers to help this poor patient," Galaxas suggested in laughter. Then it hit her. "Hey, now I don't have your power of healing. Believe me, I've tried it out many a time over some critter when I lived in the wilderness. So, we can set that one aside."

"That is true. Good. Let's keep checking off one after the other, and soon we'll have it all figured out," Nebulane said with more confidence.

They laughed for a little over an hour. They put together the game *Mousetrap* and then played *Connect 4*. If Annalee had a superpower, it would be her ability to lighten the mood.

Star Wars played on the television screen. Between the crunching of popcorn, the girls were curious to ask questions.

"Is any of this movie true to life?" Galaxas asked Troid.

"Sorry, but no. I've never seen aliens who look like them or anything like it. And as far as the aliens' people on Earth have seen, they are real, just that they are evil. There is no way our government or any country's government should try to communicate with them. Bad idea. We have managed to hold off armies of them from coming to Earth. That is a big part of our shadowing existence. We were never, ever meant to come to Earth. We were never meant to be seen by a human being. Ever. I'm so glad Queen Nebulane thought up the idea that you all have a skin condition. That was a brilliant distraction," Troid explained.

"Drat! How cool would that have been?" Annalee remarked disappointed watching all the crazy alien life on *Star Wars*.

"Aren't we enough?" Raiden asked with hurtful eyes.

"Of course. I'm sorry. That remark wasn't intended to disregard you all. YOU, you gorgeous man, are more than enough. My boyfriend is superman in the flesh, so what do you think?"

He made a get-out-of-here expression that changed to an ah-gee-that's-sweet guise.

Nebulane had tiptoed outside to the front porch. She glided back and forth on the porch glider. A melancholy mood would not go away. Galaxas scanned the room and noticed she had left.

Quietly getting up from the warm embrace of Troid's arm around her, she whispered, "I'll be back in a minute." It felt so good being in his arms. If she could stay that way the rest of her life, she'd be one happy girl.

Finally peeking out the front windows she spotted her mom. Clasping the handle softly, it didn't make a sound as it opened. Her mom looked over as she took a step towards her.

"What are you doing out here?" Galaxas asked.

"Just looking how beautiful it is here. We don't get the changing of seasons on our planet. Right now, everything is so green and luscious," Nebulane exclaimed. She lifted her head and sniffed. "Don't you smell that woodsy, piney smell? I'll never get enough of that."

"I guess I've been too wrapped up in my thoughts to pay attention. What sort of smells do we have on our planet?"

"You won't be disappointed," Nebulane said. Galaxas could see her memory of their planet twirling in Nebulane's eyes. "We have trees and flowers, too. It will bring a smile to your face."

"What is it like there? Do they have cities, farms, excruciating political issues, schools, what?"

"There are similarities to Earth, but we don't have near or close to the population of Earth, so our communities are more like towns. There are farms, stores to shop, even fishing. Of course, our animals and sea life look different than Earths.

"Before the corruption, we never had political issues. Let evil in and hello. Yes, we have schools, but of course different than here. There are a lot of careers and jobs like here, but different. It's so hard to describe, Gal."

"What about fast food and restaurants?"

"That, too, is different, and no, we do not have 'McDonalds' or 'Burger King'."

Galaxas giggled.

"Galaxas, you won't be disappointed."

"Good to know. Oh! What about shopping?"

"No malls, but the stores are unique and wonderful. You will love shopping there."

A relieved smile formed on her face.

"Tell me, Mom. How do I know you are not evil, like my father insinuated?"

"There is no way to show you. I would think if you reviewed your life, there should have been some evidence to prove I am good. I help people and animals. Never have I hurt you, nor will I. If a person had a medical issue, your dad and grandfather would just kill them. No questions asked. If anyone dared to disagree with their commands or philosophy, they're dead. You seem fine with Troid. Doesn't his opinion of me give you enough proof?"

"Yes, you're right. Maybe the anger I felt from finding so much out in such a short period of time was too much for my psyche to handle, Mom. That was a lot of emotional information to learn. And then to find out who my real father was from Satan-man himself, you gotta understand the position I've been dragged into.

"Huh! Do I have a brother or sister?" She just realized that was a question she never thought about until today.

Nebulane's head fell into her hand. She almost couldn't breathe. It was pure torture for her to answer. "No. Your father killed him."

Galaxas mouth opened wide, but the scream wouldn't come out.

"Go ahead. Hate me more. I deserve that," Nebulane said avoiding eye contact.

Shaking her head like she was trying to shake the bad memories off of it, Galaxas asked. "How old was he?"

"Four years old. When you're ready, I'll show you a picture."

She fell back against the chair, too upset to cry or speak. Nebulane glanced shamefully at her.

"Why kill your own son? And, what four-year-old could damage or compromise his plan?"

"Your grandfather demanded that he kill him so he could never take over and rule our planet. That's when I found out Jagger tried to lie and tell me he died of natural causes. But my undercover informants told me the truth. I had a secret autopsy done to find out the truth. He had been smothered to death." By this time gasps came out of Nebulane having to remember the sadness. Galaxas held her hand as she cried.

"Mom, is that why you make a cake the same time each year? Always the same cake?"

Breaking down in tormented cries, she blubbered the word, "Yes."

"Oh Mom. The things you have been through make mine seem small."

After wiping the puddles from her face and sniffles, she looked tenderly at Galaxas. "We both know that's not true. You've been through just as much torment. I just wanted to keep you from the intense pain of what your father did to us and will do to you. How could a mother watch her daughter feel such agonizing pain like that? In my foolishness, I felt I was protecting you. Instead, I treated you like a high schooler, kept you in a lonely prison of a life, and probably more for myself than you. I'm so sorry."

"Not anymore, Mom. If I'm too selfish to understand what you went through and what you hid for my sake, then I deserve to be despised. I'm the one who needs to apologize."

"How about this, Gal: No more secrets, no more treating you like a child and include you in all our plans. We drop the ongoing apologies and move forward. We'll figure it out and conquer our planet. I believe that."

"Me, too, Mom. Let's go inside."

As they stood up and turned, everyone inside ran back to the living room. Galaxas and Nebulane chuckled.

Chapter Thirty

Annalee and Galaxas rushed out of their rooms the next morning. "Mom, we forgot our computers and work. We have to stay in touch with our publisher. We need to go back." Annalee's words were forceful.

"No way. That is too risky."

Raiden cleared his throat. They all looked over at him. "Yes, Raiden, what is it?" Nebulane stood tall, wrapped her arms forcefully around each other, and a foot tapped.

"How about Troid and I go back and pick up your laptops and work?"

"Oh, I see. You guys really want my girls to hate me when they find out Jagger has corrupted you or killed you. As you well know, there is no turning back. Just to look at his eyes is like looking into to the eyes of Medusa. He's that powerful.

"Galaxas, remember the trance you fell into looking at his picture? Just a picture."

"Yes, and so did Annalee when she met him."

"That's all it takes. Zareb was wise enough to not look at him. He pulled me away before it was too late. Nobody is exempt from his power."

"Think of what he could do to this planet?" Mitchell added his two cents.

"I'm not on Jagger's radar. They don't suspect me, so I can go," Annalee offered.

Smashing her hands on her hips Galaxas replied. "Oh really! How soon you forget that you met Jagger. He knows your face."

Without speaking, Annalee's eyes squinted tightly, and her mouth stretched wide. Plan foiled.

"I say we all go back just to pick up their work. All of our power together could be what we need to stop him, for the moment anyway," Troid inserted.

"Now, that makes sense. Let's get to it, but I think Mitchell and Annalee should stay here," Nebulane said with force.

"I'll go nuts wondering for your safety," Mitchell replied.

"It will be quick. We promise. Now, Annalee, tell Raiden where your items are and we'll be off," Nebulane said reverting to queen mode.

Within minutes the four of them teleported to the Florida house. They looked around with cautious eyes for any movement.

"Oh, geez Mom, look at the mess." Troid and Raiden stood the refrigerator up like it was light as a feather.

"See hon, he was furious that you didn't get back to him. You were so smart to leave him as quickly as you did before he figured out your plan. If he had taken his glasses off, you would have probably been drawn to him and had no choice but to convert. You will make a great queen."

"Well, I hope so. Should we clean this mess up?" Galaxas asked.

"No. I have a person to call that will come in and clean it up. Let's just get to the task at hand."

Hands full, Nebulane and the guys walked back to the kitchen. Galaxas needed to grab some clothes and so did Nebulane. She tossed the items on the counter and Raiden accompanied her to the bedroom. Troid waited in the living room.

As Nebulane called for Galaxas, they all stood still, no blinking, no breathing, nothing. They sensed an evil presence. The fear was so great, they all took caution.

Jagger appeared right behind her. He held some type of device at her back. "Hello my dear."

Nebulane froze solid, and the guys began to walk towards him. "Stop or I'll dissolve her right here. She will be nothing but particles and there is no way to bring her back," Jagger informed them. His hand reached to remove the glasses.

"Just hold on for a minute, guys." She had the stance and tone of a queen now. She mouthed to them, "Don't stare into his eyes."

"Now, where's my lovely daughter? I'll take her back with me and let her reign next to her father. How sweet will that be?"

"Except for the fact she's not evil like you," Nebulane said in a mocking tone.

"Such a trivial matter," he said whimsically.

"How is it you don't know where she is?" Nebulane looked curiously at Troid and Raiden.

"That, my beautiful wife, is because she has powers we don't know about. Apparently, neither does she."

Without a sound or notice, his back had laser, strong and powerful light beams starting to go through his body. If it made it to his heart, he would explode, never to exist anymore. He was completely immobile. Nebulane and the guys couldn't move because they were in shock. Galaxas' power in using her eyes was far greater than anything they could have done. Jagger would have escaped in seconds, but not with the power Galaxas had over him.

Thanks to Galaxas' power, they were able to look in his wide and fearful eyes. "Get our things; get behind me and now," Galaxas demanded in a desperate tone. She was invisible.

Jagger fell to the ground, trying to stop the burning pain that flowed through his body by taking short breaths. The pain was excruciating.

Back at the rustic cabin in Montana, they appeared in the living room, causing Mitchell and Annalee to gasp.

"You have no idea how scary it is to have you appear like that," Mitchell said nervously walking up to them.

"Sorry, hon." Nebulane squeezed his hand almost too hard, just wanting to feel it in her hands for comfort.

Galaxas was blowing air out of her mouth, and the guys stood silent. Mitchell looked into each of their eyes. For just a minute, he couldn't move or talk. Once he snapped out of it, he demanded, "Someone needs to start talking and fast."

They all looked over at Mitchell, and Annalee stood behind him leaning around to see their faces. "Jagger appeared out of nowhere and held a weapon against me. Galaxas was in her room unaware. She must have heard the panic in our voices and made herself invisible. She took a stand behind him and used her eyes to scorch through his back, going for his heart. Her power is far greater than ours. But in joining hands to escape, we disappeared before finishing him off." She turned and looked affectionately at Galaxas while Mitchell and Annalee grabbed the stuff from their hands and set it on the counter. "Thank you so much for saving my life."

Galaxas nodded.

"I do have a question, though. Why didn't you finish the job? You could have killed him right there," Nebulane asked bewildered.

Galaxas scratched her head and paced in a slow circle. "I wasn't sure if the beams would go through him and into you, Mom. I still don't know how to use this skill. Maybe, subconsciously, I realized he is still my father." She looked at Mitchell. "Not my dad."

Nebulane relaxed. "That makes a lot of sense from your viewpoint. You know what I just realized? He had no idea you were with us. How can that be?"

"Maybe that's one of her powers," Troid added.

With the thumb and index finger Nebulane rubbed her jaw. "Yes, that is true and to our advantage. If she would have known the outcome, she would have had the chance to end his evil life. But it is probably too soon for her to have to deal with killing her real father. I couldn't imagine. I was taken away before I had to deal with my own father."

"Finally. We have some secrets revealed that can potentially help us conquer their evil army," Raiden said out loud in thought.

"Yes! Yes! Let's convene at the table and discuss it," Nebulane insisted.

"Not without sustenance," Galaxas said rubbing her stomach. The smell of grilled cheese sandwiches caused a whole lot of growls.

"Has anyone figured out what powers Galaxas has that we don't other than what we already witnessed?" Nebulane asked while grabbing a napkin and wiping her hands and face.

"I think I have something," Troid said with a pinch of excitement.

"Let's hear it."

"Haven't you noticed that only Galaxas has the ability to contain someone as powerful and evil as Jagger as she shoots fiery light bursts from her eyes? None of us can do that."

Tilting her head upwards, Nebulane replied in thought. "Mmmm, yes, we already established that. But how can we use that to our advantage?"

"While you were talking, a thought came to my mind. I have an idea," Raiden said confidently.

For hours they sat around drinking coffee, eating snacks, and arranging their attack.

Nebulane pushed her chair out and stretched her back. Mitchell had retired to the couch watching a ballgame. She sat softly on the couch staring into his eyes. It made him feel uncomfortable.

"I'm not going to like this, am I?"

"Probably not," Nebulane said with passionate eyes.

He looked around and they were the only two left in the house.

"They're outside sending codes to our planet."

Mitchell listened nervously.

"With Galaxas' gift from God, we have a plan to take back our planet. Tomorrow evening, we are going to our space vehicles and head back home. All of our people and we four have received inaudible messages. We are certain it is the Lord telling us that now is the time to fight. It takes time to get to our planet and we will keep strategizing with each other to finalize the attacks."

"You're right. I don't like this at all," he commented.

"How many times have you told me to listen to the Lord's instruction? It's as clear as glass," she debated him.

Without looking at her he patted her leg. "I'm being selfish. I just don't want anything to happen to you or Galaxas. Any of you. I care deeply for those two guys."

"We'll be back. Even when Galaxas takes over, we will always come back. You know, did you ever think about staying on our planet for a while? We could go back and forth," Nebulane mentioned with excitement.

His face lit up.

"There is another problem. Jagger knows about Annalee but not you. He will be searching more intently for her and us. Because Galaxas has a way to keep him from knowing where she is, we haven't figured out how to use that skill yet. He won't know we have left Earth. What I'm trying to say is that you will both need to go immediately to a place we haven't been to. This will distract him for quite a while. Just to be safe, whisper to me where you will be."

He thought for a moment. Then he clasped a hand around her ear and whispered his new location. Cellphone pulled out, he made reservations. They pulled Annalee into the house and whispered to her. Silent tears dribbled down her cheeks.

"It will be for a short while," Nebulane whispered. Mitchell, in a tone so low Annalee had to bend her head close to him, provided her the details. She backed away and got together everything she would need.

Feet shuffling and the door slamming shut, she and Mitchell came out of the bedroom. He held luggage and she held boxes of his work tools. Nebulane lifted a finger to her mouth. "Shhh," came out in an undertone. They all joined together in a circle. She didn't know if Jagger had the means to hear their conversation or what all of his powers were at this point.

Galaxas just realized she wouldn't see her dad and Annalee

for a while. There was no stopping the waterfall of tears. Mitchell embraced her and couldn't control the downpour either.

After silent goodbyes, Nebulane accompanied Mitchell and Annalee to the car. They were gone in a flash. Raiden's strong physique grew limp, betraying his emotions. His glow looked like light from a bulb diminishing.

After a sparkling cleanup, Nebulane and Galaxas teleported to her space vehicle and Troid and Raiden teleported to theirs.

Galaxas was so full of emotion. Excitement at the opportunity to see her planet, dread of knowing she may have to kill her own grandfather and many other people, caused her emotions to go haywire. Nebulane was experiencing the same emotions.

It felt like months, but they finally arrived and landed on the secret landing pad.

Galaxas' heart pounded loud enough for her to hear it. She took Nebulane's hand as the door opened.

Their eyes expanded.

Chapter Thirty-One

Nebulane held Galaxas' hand as they stepped down from the spacecraft. Troid and Raiden ran to their side. He held Galaxas' other hand in his. They were all over-whelmed at the reception. As far as the eye could see, armies of people bowed on their knees out of respect and admiration.

Overwhelmed by the sight of her people, trying to catch her breath and swallowing over and over, she finally got up the nerve to speak. "Dear people of Betzalel, please rise. It is such an honor and emotionally overwhelming for me to be back in your presence." She had to stop and squeeze her eyes together, too choked up.

"We have a plan to take back our planet. Please meet my daughter, soon to be queen, Galaxas Anatola Cyrus Regalshade-Gaylord." The cheering was so loud, Galaxas almost covered her ears, but she stood tall and smiled sincerely, waving her hand in all directions. There was so much cheering and weaponry clanging that Galaxas didn't hear her real last name. The people had already stolen her heart. It would be so easy to defend this planet with the heartfelt love they presented.

"After we consult with our generals, we will meet again to discuss strategies. I was told ahead of time that a huge banquet has been set up. Please begin the festivities and we shall join you very soon. You have no idea how long I've waited to be with you." One proud, sentimental tear dropped slowly down her cheek. The crowd applauded with deep affection.

"God's greatest blessings to one and all."

As soon as they left the stage, Zareb, followed by Vesper and Amana, approached them. Nebulane faced them and dropped her head in her hands. The happy sobs were contagious, and the good friends joined in a good cry.

She grabbed Zareb's hands. "I'm so sorry. Seeing you all," her hand went to Vesper and Amana, resting in Amana's hand, "brought back so many good memories. I have missed you all so much. Thank you for protecting our people. Thank you."

"Dear Queen, it has been our utmost honor and desire. We would do anything for you," Zareb informed her.

As all the emotional conversations prolonged, they all settled back at Zareb's place, and emotional outbursts began again as Nebulane and Troid's mother reunited. They had a quick update of the plans and rejoined the people at the festival. Galaxas was in awe at all she saw. The new flavors of food and the love from the people brought out excitement and new emotions. Troid never left her side.

When he did walk away to speak with friends, she stood back and watched how everyone treated Troid with the respect of a king. Raiden was highly received by one and all, too, she couldn't help but notice. Still in conversation, Troid glanced her way and saw that she was watching him. Not only did he smile, but his heart glowed like the morning sun. Man, she loved this guy.

Even though the hiding area was deep inside the planet, there was natural beauty to be seen, Galaxas noted as Troid and Raiden steered them to their quarters. After a welcomed goodnight kiss, Troid and Raiden left them.

"So daughter, tell me what you are thinking."

"So many things, Mom. It feels so wonderful to fit in with people just like me. They are incredible people. I see why this is so important to you to execute this attack so carefully.

"Mom, are you scared about the attack?"

"Terrified. I have yet to go face to face with my father."

"No. You said yourself it would be too dangerous to look at

him or listen to his words. He and Jagger must have some hypnotic powers."

Nebulane put a hand on her shoulder. Tenderly she looked into her eyes, showing without saying, what was on her mind.

"Oh no, Mom. Whatever you are holding back is going to be tragic."

"Very much so. It will be a repeat performance with Jagger, except you will have to finish it this time to the end. Our council members will discuss all the evil and heartbreak these two have done to our people. By the time you are informed of it all, you won't even hesitate. If I could do it myself, I would. I'm so sorry you were chosen for this task."

"Frankly, Mom, so am I. Don't worry, I already love these people. When the time comes, you can count on me."

She rubbed Galaxas' shoulder and they both fell asleep feeling secure and safe. But Galaxas' eyes reopened, and she stared at the ceiling. Even though she has no memory of her father and grandfather, could she destroy them? Nausea claimed her body. Holding an arm around her stomach, she moved in a rocking position begging God to bring some much-needed slumber to her as she rested on the bed.

Thank heavens God knew enough to give their eyes an abundance of lubrication because of the blinding light and heat they produce. But that wasn't the case this time. All the reports, pictures, and testimonies, broke Galaxas' heart in two. Her eyes pulsed with pain. Seeing her emotion, Troid and Raiden couldn't control the tears either.

By the end of the week, Galaxas was filled with rage, looking forward to avenging her people.

It was the evening before the attack. Galaxas walked out to find an alone spot to get some clarity and to speak with the Lord. But instead, she found Raiden staring at the rock wall. Sadness was eminent in his features. She already figured out the reason.

Her gentle hand lay on his shoulder. He jumped.

"Sorry, I almost punched you in the face," he acknowledged.

"Yes, I know. I was just about to teleport as you withdrew your fist. Want to talk about it?" she asked.

He shrugged his shoulders.

"You don't have to be all tough with me. I know you miss Annalee. I miss her and Mitchell so much, my heart feels like a weight is sitting on it."

"Do you find it strange that I am in love with an Earthling?"

"Not in the least. Look at my mother and Mitchell, my dad," she spoke affectionately. "You can't be in love any more than that."

"Wise answer. Who could debate that? I can't stand being away from her. My fear is that this lull in me will compromise my performance on the battleground," he said with a sullen expression. Her face cast a sadness as she eyed him.

She tapped her cheek with her index finger. "How about this? You think about how this evil has put a distance between you and Annalee. Watch the rage flow out of that incredibly strong body. That should build up your determination and create a most powerful foe. Think of Annalee as you fight. I miss how she makes me laugh and has a gift of relieving tension anywhere and anytime."

Raiden patted her hand forcefully. "You are so right for the queen position. Yes, I'll do that. We'll be together before you know it. 'When God is for us, who can be against us'?"

He smacked his fist into his other hand so powerfully, it echoed with a huge thud. He left her so she could gather her thoughts. Everyone knew the severity of what she would endure in the early morning hours.

She sat on a rock and looked up to heaven. "Lord, we fight this battle in Your name and give You the victory. We take back our planet tomorrow and the good people will exalt You on high.

"I seek your wisdom, knowledge and understanding. Please guide every move, every thought, and every strategic battle execution that will give us victory over evil.

"Lord, you put us on this planet to be Your shadow, to watch the universe for the evil armies and their wicked demise. We need Your help to keep them from taking over the Earth.

"All victory, glory and honor belong to You, and in Jesus' name I ask."

The hand on her shoulder caused a heart fluttering like she never experienced before. She turned slowly, ready to teleport.

Seeing her fearful reaction, Troid spoke quickly. "It's me, Troid. Don't be afraid. Raiden told me I could find you here. I just wanted to hold you in my arms before tomorrow."

Her eyes closed slowly, her hand moved to her heart, and she blew out a long and loud breath.

"I'm so sorry I scared you," he said.

"It's okay. I'm fine. Honest," she said as she clicked off the picture of him holding the dandelion.

He pulled her in an embrace and hugged her tightly, resting his head on top of hers. He inhaled her fragrance. Her hair smelled like fresh cotton and spring. Her soft skin gave him sensations like an army of sugar ants crawled up his arm.

She laid her head against his strong, rock-solid chest, eyes closed and body warm with love. They didn't notice the glow that reflected on the rock wall from their hearts.

When they pulled apart it was clear as the sun itself, they were shining. In amazement she asked, "When we get married, will our hearts always glow?"

"From what I have witnessed with all couples, it stops after marriage, but that's because they become as one person. The glow isn't necessary anymore." He noticed her disappointment.

"Don't worry. It certainly doesn't mean they aren't in love. The light that glows from our heart is like a flashlight searching for our true love. Once we find each other and marry, it is complete."

He placed her hand on his heart. "Remember Galaxas, you light up my heart. You're the fire flame in my heart. No one else can cause this warmth to flow through me. I read that play, *Romeo and Juliet*, and it doesn't match up to our love."

His hand tilted her chin up. The kiss was like a warm cup of hot chocolate filling their bodies.

"Troid. I have a wonderful idea. Let's get Mom and Raiden and send a code to Annalee and Dad." Her heart had the glow of a sunset at this point. It reflected off the wall of boulders. They both stared in awe for a moment.

Then his mouth made the clicking sound. "Perfect idea."

The stars above flashed in the shape of a heart.

Troid handed her a dandelion.

"Where did you find that?" she asked with tenderness.

"I grabbed it just before we left Earth. When we get back to Earth, I have something special to show you."

She squeezed her hands tightly and smiled. "I can't wait."

"Can you believe it?" he asked. Sunsets with you forever."

"And dandelion kisses," she added as she pressed it to his lips.

Out at the dig site, Mitchell and Annalee sat around a bonfire. Neither spoke. Her marshmallow burned to a crisp and clumps fell into the fire. Mitchell was lost in thought.

Annalee finally smelled the burning marshmallow and looked up. She pulled the stick out and happened to look up at the stars. Breathless, she watched the anomaly. Realizing it was a message, she yelled to Mitchell.

"Dad! Dad! Look!"

He looked over and followed her gaze. They both broke out in a smile and jumped up next to each other. They placed an arm around each other and began to laugh with joy. It went on for about an hour.

That night, they slept better than all the nights since they have been at the site. She cuddled up with a stuffed alien creature in an attempt to think about Raiden, and he hung onto a photo, warm and snuggly.

Chapter Thirty-Two

Before dawn, the armies of Betzalel gathered. They awaited Queen Nebulane and Galaxas' arrival. Trumpets and drums began to sound, along with instruments Galaxas had never seen or heard in her life on Earth. How long have the good armies anticipated this day of victory? Not one worried or frightened soul in the whole army.

The queen and Galaxas strolled out to the platform. Troid and Raiden stood on each side awaiting their arrival. The four were dressed in royal battle garments and shields. The crowd roared with cheers, fists pushing upward. As ear-piercing as the cheers were, it filled the four of them with a humbled gladness and complete confidence. Adrenaline pumped through their veins.

Queen Nebulane lifted her sword. An instant hush fell over the crowd. Tears spilled from their bright, beaming eyes. This was a proud moment for all.

"My fellow soldiers, raise your arms to the Lord of Hosts, shout victory to His name. Today we take back our planet."

As far as the eye could see, a rush of wind arose as the soldiers swished their swords back and forth. The loud shouts of praise and honor resonated through the air, all the way to heaven itself.

Blinding sunrays burst through the cracks of the rocks. All

eyes and sun pendants glowed like sunrays themselves. Galaxas was humbled and empowered, sentimental and determined at all she saw.

The queen asked everyone to take a knee and bow their heads. Her prayer was heartfelt, full of praise to the Lord, full of submission and strong with confidence. At the end, the soldiers stood in formation. Plans were discussed and everyone was eager and ready. Adrenaline pumped and excitement arose with cheers and laughter.

"My love for all of you humbles my heart." Nebulane patted her heart and a tear dropped. "I pray the good Lord above will use us once again as his shadow, as his eyes in the universe. I pray for each and every one of your safety. Now, place your swords in your scabbard and hold hands. As I finish saying 'for the Lord God,' we shall teleport. She looked around the very front of the army and followed the faces all the way to the last line and ended by looking at the other three of them on the platform.

Looking up to heaven, she repeated the words: "For the Lord God."

Chapter Thirty-Three

The battle was loud and powerful. Voices roaring, screams of anguish echoed through the skies. Smoke was strong and held a bitter, putrid smell as evil was being perished. It went on for weeks. There were so many more people in the good army than in the evil army. They had all teleported in groups around the planet to conquer them. The evil army was caught by surprise and most of them defeated upon impact.

A thought came to Galaxas. She pulled her mother, Troid and Raiden together quickly.

"I think the Lord just gave me a message. He told me to hold hands and think about the power I have with my eyes. But I can't do this for everyone. They would have to stop and hold hands with us, and that's impossible during the battle. It's like a force field protection and it will transfer my powers temporarily to you who hold hands with me. I'm not certain how long my power will last among you all."

"So then, we'll have the same power as you?" Nebulane asked with an excited hope. Galaxas nodded and replied, "Temporarily." They held hands and the transformation was immediate and just in time.

Nebulane's head turned in all directions. Galaxas noticed the concern in her face. "Mom. What is it?"

"Something is not right."

The fighting still continued. It was so bright from all their people shooting scorching rays of light from their eyes and pendants that Annalee and Mitchell would never have survived in the excessive amount of eye-scorching light.

"Galaxas. I need you to disappear and quickly. Stay around me because I have a feeling an ambush is about to happen."

The concern on her mother's face freaked Galaxas out. "Yes, I shall do it now."

This was just way too easy. Troid strolled up with brows almost standing straight up. "This just doesn't feel right. I think you need to inform the armies to be ready for a much stronger fight. There is no sign of Irya."

Just his name chilled Nebulane to the bone.

Galaxas became visible after hearing that name. Her eyes looked forward as though she was looking right through to another dimension. They waited for her to come out of the vision. It was so powerful, she started falling, but Troid was at her side in that moment.

"That vision of the frightened faces came back. Someone with great power is about to arrive. They must depart for their lives, NOW."

"Vanish before he gets here. We need to combine our new power together and destroy him," Nebulane commanded her.

Her fearful eyes looked into Troid's, and she vanished.

Screams were heard. Shrieking and terrifying outcries became louder and louder. Nebulane and the guys looked for the source of it, but so far all they saw were the faces of their beloved people. One hundred percent pure terror as they fell to the ground.

Behind her back a vibrating, powerful voice commanded her to surrender. She turned around as his small army of evil-looking soldiers glared at her. She saw him. His dark purple clothing produced a neon sheen. His hair was a pure gray and green mixture. His gray beard trailed down to the ground. His eyes had a black glow around the bright suns that shot out bursts of light.

The soldiers wore dark silver garments, strong and mighty, to protect them. Nebulane shivered with a fear that engulfed her being as he walked up with such a mortifying evilness, it froze her insides.

"My daughter. I have missed you. Why did you leave? This," he said waving his hands around, "could be all yours. All ours. Why would you give that up? Why would you defy your own FATHER?"

Gaining courage she replied, "You're not my father. My father would never hurt the people of this planet. There wasn't a selfish bone in his body. I thought he loved the Lord."

His powerful eyes widened. He swung his arm out and slapped her so hard she flew across the air and fell to the ground. She propped her hand on the ground and struggled to stand up. Dirt covered her face and garment. She squinted her eyes and puckered her mouth.

"This planet belongs to the Lord God. You betrayed Him. Get out!" she ordered.

His diabolical laugh shot fear through all in hearing range.

"Your GOD is too weak to fight me." He laughed. His voice was so strong and powerful it boomed through the air.

"Father, did you give your soul to Satan? Are you in there somewhere trying to be freed?" she pleaded.

"Daughter, I accepted this role with pride and gratitude. Look what I can do?"

A beam that looked like molten lava shot out of his eyes into a mountainside. It exploded and fell on some of the people in her armies. She witnessed their wide eyes and heard their screams before the ongoing thud of rocks and boulders covered them.

"Stop it! Stop it!"

"I'll stop if you choose to reign with me. Where is my grand-daughter? I must meet her."

"You are not my father. You will never meet your grand-daughter and you will never see me reign with you. EVER. Go ahead and destroy me, but let my people go."

The power in his walk shook the ground below as he came towards her. He stood tall over her and looked stronger than ever. Then he made a fake, hurtful expression. "I will give you one more chance to surrender your armies and reign with me. And my granddaughter."

She straightened her body and stood tall, expression proud and unbending. "No thank you. I'd rather die."

Grasping his big, ultra-strong hand around her neck, he yelled, "Then you shall!"

As she gagged for life, he stiffened and released his hand. Smoke rose in the air above him and a sickening smell developed. He couldn't move, and his eyes widened with a look very similar to fear. How quickly his arrogance faded.

Rubbing her neck and inhaling, Nebulane looked up and pulled the sun pendant out and shined it at his heart. Troid and Raiden joined her, and they used the new power Galaxas gave to them. The rest of her army ran over and shined their sun pendants, too.

While this went on, Troid and Raiden commanded the rest of the army to attack his small coterie and watched them disintegrate into embers that floated off in the wind.

From both directions, the powerful light of their pendants and the power in their eyes shot sizzling holes through his body until it reached his evil heart. He took one last glance at his daughter, turned his head just as Galaxas materialized and exploded with the sound of a volcano erupting.

Exhaustion caused all involved to fall to the ground. But

Nebulane knew she had to keep going. She had a powerful gift of healing and there were a lot of people who needed it. Unfortunately, some of their army were disintegrated and there would be no way for them to come back.

She ran to one after the other, holding her hand above their hearts, eyes shining with God's love. Could she heal the huge number of people? She didn't know but would not quit trying.

Too many fatalities hit the queen hard. After everyone that she could possibly heal were being treated, she sunk in despair. It wasn't supposed to be this devastating. Restoration, consoling, repair, and on and on the weeks went with busy activity.

If only Mitchell was here to comfort her. But would she allow herself the luxury of being comforted after the pain and suffering her planet went through? It's true they won the battle and would pull together as a people, but why so many fatalities? Her mind wouldn't shut off. She felt severe disappointment and sought the Lord for answers.

Zareb knocked at her door. Without getting up from the chair, she invited whoever was at the door to come in.

Worried about her fragile state, he walked over and rested his hand on her shoulder. She didn't look up, but she felt the warmth. "The death toll?"

"Thirty."

"That is way too many." She dropped her head.

"Yes, one is too many, but out of the millions of people standing, you must rejoice for them."

Her hand reached back and patted his hand that was still resting on her shoulder. "I guess I was expecting no fatalities. How did I get that so wrong?"

"Queen, in all the wars throughout the Bible, has there ever been no fatalities?"

"I believe there was a battle or two without fatality on the side of good. I just can't remember right now."

"There is something you are forgetting. We lost count of the innumerable lives you were able to restore."

"Please do not offend me. It was the Lord who restored, not I who did it alone. He gave me the gift as long as I gave Him the glory. You must not forget about that and set that straight with our people."

"Now that is something I agree with. I will set that straight. In time you will see the good done in spite of the undeniable grieving of those we lost. The people understand it is not your fault, and you will see joy and happiness restored likewise. Please do try to seek comfort in these words.

"My dear friend and queen, now is the time that our 'scorched land will become a pool, and the thirsty ground springs of water...grass becomes reeds and rushes, a highway will be there, a roadway, and it will be called the Highway of Holiness. The unclean will not travel on it...no lion will be there, nor will vicious beasts go up on it...but the redeemed will walk there... They will find gladness and joy'."

"Zion. You always did love that passage. Yes, and now our people are free and able to rejoice again, until that day we all hope for: Zion.

"Thank you, Zareb. I am truly grateful for so many things, and that includes your loyal friendship. You have counseled these people with much wisdom in my absence. There are not enough words to express my gratitude to you."

"From the queen I have always admired, those words mean more than you could even imagine."

"Unfortunately, it doesn't end here," Nebulane admonished. "Jagger is hunting us down and I'm pretty sure he is still on Earth. We need to get back and destroy him once and for all. I know the pain of killing your own father. But now, Galaxas will have to help kill her own father after helping to destroy her grandfather. That is too much. What will this do to her?"

"The good Lord above chose her specifically. She is strong and understands what will happen if she doesn't destroy him. We all know how hard this is for her...and you. My evil brother was destroyed in the battle. It was hard to watch. We will all be with you. Do not forget that, Queen."

"My apologies. I am so sorry about your brother. You are correct as usual. Please take the lead in restoration of our planet as we head back to Earth. There is too much urgency for me to call our people together right now. So many injured loved ones and the destruction of our planet. I'll allow you to handle it.

"Now, I must get Galaxas, Troid and Raiden and head back to Earth. Please inform our people that I may be bringing my husband, Mitchell, and our daughter, Annalee, back with us, born on Earth. Raiden and Annalee will most likely wed."

"Yes, Queen, that will be something to celebrate. As far as Jagger, never take his power for granted. He is as powerful as your father was, but more conniving and dangerous. Don't let

Galaxas speak with him. He'll corrupt her before she ever suspects a thing."

"Thank you. We will take heed. Now, we must prepare for liftoff."

Early the next morning, the four of them left for Earth.

Chapter Thirty-Four

Mitchell and Annalee moped around. He was achieving much success and finding valuable artifacts at the dig site, but fear of the unknown and waiting for Nebulane and Galaxas to return took a toll on his thoughts.

Annalee sat around the bonfire that evening staring at the stars. She had been dealing with the publishers for her and Galaxas' books. The only thing left to do was wait for printing.

Mitchell rubbed his eyes. He didn't mean to fall asleep, but sleep made the days go by quicker. He jumped up and walked out to find Annalee. "Why did you let me sleep so long? I'll never fall asleep tonight."

"I'm not your keeper, mister." She cracked a smile.

"When Nebulane is not around, yes you are my keeper. And don't you forget it," he said in jest shaking his finger.

She gently whacked his arm, and he did it back to her. Then they had a hand battle. They were laughing so hard that they didn't realize they had visitors.

"I can't leave you two alone," Nebulane remarked in laughter.

"Hhhh!" They both gasped in surprise and jumped up and ran over to them. Hugs and kisses, and more hugs and kisses.

Holding Nebulane's hand between his, he asked, "Are you all hungry, thirsty, or want some hot chocolate?"

"Hot chocolate sounds yummy." The other three agreed.

"Any chance you have any of my candy hanging around," Galaxas asked with a hopeful face. "They don't have that on our planet. I think we need to find recipes to take back with us."

"As a matter of fact, I do. In my box of stuff there is some, but not much. You got me hooked on it, and him," Annalee said using her head as a pointer towards Mitchell.

They sat down and discussed everything that happened, information about the planet itself and thoughts about the future. Laughs, tears mended, and a happy reunion continued throughout the evening.

"Mitchell, for your and Annalee's safety, you'll need to stay here until we find Jagger. It is just too dangerous," Nebulane said rubbing her neck where visible handprints still remained. Mitchell felt the anguish and pulled her into his arm at his side. She had told him a few minutes ago in private what had occurred. Without asking her, he wondered why the hand marks didn't fade away. Almost like a permanent scar. Was this evil man that powerful? He gulped at his thoughts.

"As hard as it will be for you to leave us again, I will understand. Besides, we'll probably just get in the way and make things worse. Be extra careful my dear," Mitchell responded.

"I have to. How else will we be able to reunite? My planet has heard about you and Annalee and are excited to meet you both."

He rubbed his hands together. "Yippy! New adventure. Right up my alley."

Raiden and Annalee took a walk. Their hands were clutched together since the arrival. "I know you don't like it that we're leaving again, but we have no choice. For the sake of our planet and yours. Jagger could cause a lot of destruction and corruption," Raiden explained.

"Of course, I'm not happy about you leaving and the danger you will be in, but I do understand it has to be done. My only question is, are you all physically capable of this fight right after the battle from your planet?"

"Yes. Besides, there isn't a choice. He needs to be destroyed. Poor Galaxas. She is the one who will feel the pain emotionally and physically. You would have been proud of her. She is true queen material."

Annalee formed an affectionate smile. "I am so proud of my friend, my sister," she added.

The foursome stood together the next morning. "Until we meet again our dearest loved ones," Nebulane said as she waved a hand. Loving smiles were on all their faces as they disappeared.

Back to Florida.

~

So far, no signs of Jagger. Troid never left Galaxas' side.

They slept on the couch so he could be near her. "Troid, you realize one of my visions came true. It tore my heart to see the faces of our people being murdered. The other part of that vision hasn't happened. I'm a little freaked out."

"We are all here together. With our power combined, I'm hopeful, even though it is different from the power Irya and Jagger have, but yet very solid power. We will defeat him."

"If Jagger was your father, would you still fight him to the death?" she asked.

"As hard as it will be for you, it would be the same for me. Galaxas, we all understand the torment of your situation. If there was any other way, we would go that route. You are the only person given these powerful gifts.

"Remember, they chose this destination, as did my beloved uncle. They knew what they were doing at the time. I was involved in destroying my uncle. It's a pretty emotional thing to live with, which is true. The only consolation I have for you is what will happen to the people of this planet and ours if he lives. You saw your own grandfather try to kill his daughter, your mother. They have allowed themselves to turn this evil. Don't make any mistake about it; they all knew what they were doing and what they were doing to us.

"I'm really sorry." He grabbed her hand. "I will be here to help you through it always."

"To be honest, I could never do any of this without you. I

hope the dear people of Betzalel know what a mighty and great king you will be. Without you, I would be of no use. You give me courage and help me to understand why and when action needs to be taken. I am blessed to have you for my husband. I can't wait for that day."

"Galaxas, wait until you see the magic of our wedding. Those in high ranking are given these lavish and out-of-this world weddings. The people will not take no for an answer, no matter how small and simple we may want it. However, we are faithful and serve the people of our planet humbly and proudly. It is not power, fortune or fame we seek. It's all about our people and following the guidelines that made us a great people.

"As you can see by what happened, it is not always easy to stay humble. Some in authority are addicted to fame and power at anyone's cost. We are in charge of preventing such atrocities from happening. Our job is pretty intense at times and time consuming. So, these lavish weddings we accept with much gratitude."

She stared and her face lit up with pleasure. "I am so excited about that. What about Raiden and Annalee?"

"Not to worry. It will be magical, too."

"Did you speak with your father about her and my dad?"

"Yes. No complaints or indifference to them."

"Annalee and I saw the pictures of you and Raiden with some women. Both of you seemed goo-goo eyed over them."

"Before it was time to find you, we dated a lot and really liked many of the women."

"Were you in love with any of them, and Raiden, too?" *Please say no* soared through Galaxas' mind.

"Being silly teenagers, of course we thought we were in love, but obviously we were wrong. They are all married now. How many times do I have to tell you that you are the light and fire of my heart? I plan to live in your sunset until our last breath."

"You don't have to tell me. Your heart is telling me all on its own." She looked down as her and his heart covered them in sunset colors. He pulled out a bouquet of dandelions from inside his shirt and remarked in a serious but tender way, "Sunsets and dandelion kisses forever."

The way he said it brought out so much emotion. Remembering how she felt like a freak, wondering if she would ever find love, seeing and hearing about all the pain her people went through, the words just meant a whole lot more than she anticipated. He pulled her into his strong grip and tightened his grasp. She felt so safe in his arms. And so loved.

After a few moments she spoke up. "You know, I did some research about dandelions. Most people refer to them as weeds. But did you know that they are edible and have many health benefits? Also, according to flowerglossary.com, they are a symbol for healing, whether from emotional or physical pain, and also surviving hard times. Dandelions are the most persistent flower that never gives up. When you give someone a single dandelion or a bouquet, you're giving a message of hope, telling the recipient to not give up and to persevere in sunnier times ahead. I memorized that passage.

"So you see, it wasn't by accident that you chose dandelions."

It was going on a month and still no signs of Jagger. As Nebulane watched a news channel, it was interrupted with breaking news. Detected, but not visible, was an unidentified spacecraft. Sources had nothing to go on except what radar produced. She looked fearfully at the T.V. screen.

"It's possible, but too early to tell if it is him," she mentioned to herself in a quivering voice.

"I should call the gang in and update them with this new information. Lately there has been a lot of UFO breaking news, so hopefully we can keep our heads together," she mumbled fearfully. She yelled out the door for them and inside they all discussed it.

Wrecked nerves weren't getting them anywhere, so Troid came up with an idea. "I challenge you, Galaxas, to a game of ping pong."

"And I accept."

"Raiden and Nebulane will challenge the winners. The one who wins the most games out of three wins the chocolate chunk ice cream," Troid acknowledged, rubbing his already winning hands together, in his mind anyway.

"You're on," the three of them replied.

Pop-pop-pop-pop-pop was the only audible sound. So far Troid was winning, but now that Raiden challenged him, the game became quite aggressive. Shattering glass, a dented cement garage floor, and a lot of ducking continued for forty-five minutes until someone sneezed, distracting Raiden. Troid scored the winning point.

"You know that's cheating. That sneeze caused me to lose focus," Raiden scolded Troid.

"Okay, you're right. It's a tie and you and I will share that yummy ice cream," Troid commented almost hesitantly. He faced the whole ugly truth that he did not want to share.

The garage door to the interior of the house flung open banging against the wall. With wide eyes Galaxas said, "Hurry! Come see this."

Staring at the television, all three were motionless. Two nursing homes in a county close to Lee County were disintegrated into small particles. Eyes blurred. For some reason he couldn't justify, Troid felt a need to run outside and look at the sky. Only people from his planet could read the message in the sky. He yelled loudly. "Get out here!"

All four stood staring at the message in the sky. "There will be more destruction to come. The next lucky winners are daycare facilities. What you did to my army will cost all four of you your lives. I will find my granddaughter's friend. Did you think you could hide from me or hide that girl? Fools! For her sake, turn yourselves in now."

Galaxas slipped to the ground, head down, tears streaming. Raiden paced, running his hand though his hair over and over. Galaxas got on the phone and told Mitchell to hide Annalee in a cave. Now! They had researched the best location, previously, of the perfect spot where it would be hard for Jagger to find them.

It had a lot to do with the minerals found inside it. Everything they needed was already stashed inside the cave for this sole purpose.

"Now we wait, but we watch." The tone was calm and collect, but Nebulane's eyes revealed fright, pure one hundred percent fright. She sat in her room and realized she had to turn herself in for the sake of the people of Earth. How could she sit around and watch him destroy innocent children and adults? She could not live with it.

Chapter Thirty-Five

L ate that evening, Nebulane crawled out her bedroom window and walked to a clearing. She wrote a message to Jagger. "If you hurt any more children or adults, we will not meet with you. That is a promise. Give me time to discuss with Galaxas and I'll send you another message of where and when to meet."

The three of them kept looking back and forth in each other's eyes after seeing the dark circles under Nebulane's eyes. "You didn't sleep at all, did you Mom?" Galaxas asked.

"Couldn't."

"What is the plan?"

"Not a good one." She looked back and forth at each one of them.

"Even so, let's hear it, Mom."

"Jagger won't meet up with just me. He wants to kill all of us. I sent him a message that I had to discuss it with you and will get back to him with the when and where time. It's buying us and the dear people of Earth a little time.

"All we can do is have you stay invisible during our meeting. When I say, "God's victory," we carry out the same attack we used on Irya. It's all I have. If any of you have another idea, I'm all ears," Nebulane said scanning their faces.

"I just have a question," Troid said. "Don't you think he expects us to use this same strategy?"

"You're right. We're dealing with much more power than even Irya had."

"What about this idea?" Galaxas inserted. "What if I stay visible and when you say, 'God's victory,' I disappear, and we continue as planned?"

"We'll all be staged in a square formation, surrounding him," Raiden added.

"Pretty sure he'll see right through that and expect an assault," Nebulane replied.

"Somehow we need to meet him and not look as though we prepared a tactical attack," she added.

"Dealing with such power is an experience beyond my conceptualization. This brain inside is going blank," Galaxas interjected.

"Let's go in without a plan. He was once our ruler and maybe he's had a change of heart," Troid responded.

Wide mouths and wide eyes faced him. He looked sheepishly at them.

"Changed! A man that just destroyed two nursing homes and threatens to destroy child daycare facilities?" Nebulane's voice was stern.

"Maybe he felt that was the only way to get us to come together. If he said, hey, I've repented and want to make things right, would you have met with him?"

"You're not acting like yourself. You have to be kidding," Raiden threw out.

"You're giving me a scare," Nebulane added.

Troid threw his hands up. "Just thinking outside the box. Don't read anything into it." He shook his head and walked away.

Later that evening Troid had walked outside to the clearing. After his remarks earlier, there was little conversation. Galaxas decided they needed to talk. But when she got outside, he wasn't anywhere around. She walked around calling his name. Finally, he walked over to her from down the driveway.

"Where have you been?" she asked.

"Just took a walk."

"I know you're upset, but you have to understand how your statements shook us up. What you said does not sound anything like the person I've been around. Could you explain this sudden change of your heart?"

"There's nothing to explain," Troid huffed. "Is it so wrong to have hope that someone could see the error of his ways and want to make things right? After all the pain and destruction, it was just wishful thinking. That's all and it's not open to interpretation. I don't want to discuss it anymore."

"So, it's okay for you to speak what's on your mind, but I dare not question your reasoning? That's a little offensive."

"You're blowing this whole thing out of proportion," Troid exclaimed with frustration.

"You mean how all three of us are trying to make sense of this change in you?"

"Am I now the enemy because I dare to suggest something hopeful?" He stared at her hard.

"The fact that you're on the defense against us is making me wonder," she replied, backing up nervously.

"Go back in the house. I need some time alone. I wasn't trying to be controlling." He grabbed his hair in a tight grasp. "This whole thing is making me crazy."

She looked at him tenderly. "We're on the same team. We need to discuss our differences without taking it personally. That's all."

"That's true. Just give me a minute to collect my thoughts. I'll be in shortly."

Not totally convinced of his explanation, she walked back into the house disappointed.

Galaxas and Raiden whispered amongst themselves while Troid was outside. "I just don't have any answers, Raiden. It's a little confusing how he shifted gears so quickly. He knows firsthand how evil Jagger is and all the evil he's done."

"He confessed to me the other day how difficult it will be on you to help defeat your own father. After helping to bring down his uncle, the realization of it still haunts Troid today. He just doesn't want to see you suffer for the rest of your life, knowing you killed your own father. His cousins understand what he did had to be done, but it doesn't change the sadness that comes afterwards."

"Maybe that is exactly what is going on with him. He is so brave and so gentle at the same time," Galaxas mentioned. "I believe he'll have no choice but come to reason with the task at hand. If we do nothing, Jagger will work hard to destroy this planet, and then Troid will have to live with the knowledge that it is our fault for not stopping him when we could have." She stood, serious for a moment.

"You're not thinking Jagger converted him, are you?" Galaxas' eyes popped wide open when she made the statement.

"No. We have all been with him each minute of the day, well, except today. He has been by himself most of the day. Maybe we should keep him with us at all times. I'll go get him."

Before Raiden opened the door, Troid walked inside. "I was just coming to make sure you are okay," Raiden admitted.

"Are you sure you weren't checking to see if I was transforming into one of Jagger's evil armies?" His tone was sarcastic.

"Come on. You know me better than that."

"Do I?" Troid asked defensively.

Raiden shook his head and walked off.

"Would you like something to munch on?" Galaxas asked sweetly.

"No thank you. Hopefully, I can fall asleep for a few minutes. I just need to shut down. Would you mind?"

"Not at all. I'll go help Mom with dinner. You get some sleep." She patted his hand affectionately.

After dinner and watching television the rest of the evening, it felt like the evening dragged. Still an uncomfortable feeling between all of them, Nebulane suggested they all get some sleep and start over fresh tomorrow. With total relief, everyone agreed.

The next morning, however, Troid still wore a hangdog look. He couldn't shake it off. They didn't understand the intensity he felt about losing Galaxas. It wasn't something he wanted to share to cause more fear than they already felt, but it was eating him alive. Holding these thoughts in were coming across as warning signs to the rest of them. They didn't know how to interpret his change.

"I'm going to walk around outside. I need some fresh air. If anyone is worried it's a trap, feel free to watch me. I'm a little offended having to even say that, but we're all under a lot of stress, so I will ignore any offensive thoughts."

"Troid," Galaxas said as he walked out unable to complete her thought. "I've never seen this side of him before. Have you, Raiden?"

"Truthfully, no. He is passionate about his beliefs and when it comes to someone he loves dearly, sometimes fear of losing them causes him to act differently, so maybe the battle is catching up with him. He lost a lot of loved ones and friends in that battle, as did all of us, but I think it's much more than that.

"You saw Irya and how evil he became yourself, but what you didn't see was how good of a person he and your father used to be. It's almost like we were living in a nightmare. To see how someone could turn from completely good to evil is a hard thing to grasp. Someone you admired and wanted to emulate.

"Now he has to live with the fact that you could be killed in this confrontation with Jagger. Never feeling this depth of love before, I believe it is scaring him, and he is too worried about compromising his position and how it may affect him when the time comes to fight Jagger.

"Galaxas, he's that good of a man. It's not anything to do with being brave and competent. I'm changing my concern about him after thinking this through. It's all about what he could potentially lose in the process. That loss is you."

She shivered at the realization.

"Galaxas, have you had any other visions?" Nebulane asked.

"No, none. But I'm still worried about it. You know in time they always come true."

"Yes, that is a concern," she replied.

The wind whistled through the trees and the sun beams burst

through the leaves. It felt comforting and warm to Troid. He sat on a stump and watched the squirrels scamper from one tree to the other. He looked over at the birdfeeder and remembered how Nebulane applied Vaseline to the long pole to keep squirrels off. "They get enough corn and peanuts," she had said, "and they aren't going to steal the bird's food from them."

A chuckle escaped. A squirrel attempted to climb the pole but kept sliding back down, to the point it lied on its back with arms and legs sprawled out in exhaustion. It was so funny, he laughed hard.

His bright eyes caught a glimpse of something black and shiny on the other side of the house. He got up and walked over to see what it was. His eyes bulged. He bent down and picked up the shiny glove with metal blades sticking out of it, turning it over and back again. Then he stood staring in thought. This needed to be discussed immediately.

Galaxas saw him walk up through the window and she jumped up to meet him. He walked in with a worried look on his face still walking to the living room. She hugged him and he moved over to the couch next to Raiden.

"Can I talk to you outside?" he whispered.

Raiden noticed the concern in his face. "Certainly."

"We'll be right back. I want to show Raiden something," he said to Galaxas.

"Oh! Okay, I guess."

They walked out to the clearing, but the glove fell from his pocket. Galaxas saw it fall and curiosity got the best of her, so she went out to pick it up.

Out of her view, Raiden asked Troid, "What's going on?"

"I think Jagger is here."

"Why do you think that?"

He pushed his hand in the pocket and felt around for the glove, not realizing it had fallen out. "Oh no. We need to get back in the house before Galaxas finds it."

"Finds what?" but Troid had taken off running before answering.

When he rounded the corner, Galaxas was holding the glove, staring blankly at it like she was bringing up the vision.

"Galaxas, I didn't want you to find that."

"Why not?"

"Because it would frighten you, obviously."

"Too late. What are you doing with it?" Her face looked nervously in his as Raiden walked up.

"Let me explain." As he reached to calm her down, she screamed and moved back, mistaking his intentions.

"Galaxas, what?" Troid's face turned pale quickly.

"In my vision I never saw the face of the person who wore the glove. Is it a coincidence that you started standing up for my father or are you one of them? The one who plans to choke the life out of me. This was all your plan. And you, Raiden, are you in on it?"

"No, of course not," Raiden answered in an offended tone.

"Stay away from me," she said backing up as her mouth dropped.

Troid reached for her. "Galaxas, please let me explain."

But the act of his hand reaching for her brought the vision of being choked right back to her mind. She was gone in a flash.

The guys ran into the house just as Nebulane and Galaxas transported out. "Galaxas! It's not what you think," he yelled, but they were gone.

"Now what?"

"How did you happen to have that glove?" Raiden asked.

"I found it on the ground and that is what I was going to show you. I knew if she found it, there would be no doubt in her mind that I was corrupted, especially after the intense discussion of last night. Raiden, you couldn't possibly think I'm one of them."

"You did have me concerned for a little bit last night, but then I thought it through and realized there is no way that

would ever happen. I understand how worried you must be for Galaxas and the thought of losing her. The love bond you share is so powerful. So inspiring, no wonder it has you all out of sorts," Raiden said to encourage Troid.

"How could I expose those feelings? It made me weak and powerless. She needs me to be strong and confident, but the realization of the power we are dealing with is frightening. Even Queen Nebulane has no idea how much more evil he became. You and I have watched him all these years. The man is terrifying. Downright the scariest evil entity I have witnessed. It's like he is Satan himself. How does one allow himself to turn so evil, where murder is fun and humorous?

"Dad saw him kill their child with a smile on his face. It's so disturbing." Troid's exhaustive body surrendered to the couch.

"We'll get it straightened out. Don't allow yourself to try and figure it out right now. I'm sure they think I am with you. Let's try to come to a sensible conclusion," Raiden suggested.

"No. We need to leave immediately. Jagger is around and he'll be back."

"Then we need to go to our starship and make plans to get to Annalee and Mitchell before they do," Raiden said.

"That's good thinking. Let's go," Troid urged him.

They departed just as Jagger came back. He walked in the house, searched, and with rage, his eyes incinerated the couch. He left with worse plans than the previous threat.

Chapter Thirty-Six

Nebulane and Galaxas sat in the cottage located in North Carolina. Galaxas paced, twirling her hands over and over.

"Gal, come sit. We need to figure out what our next move should be. Since those guys have never been here before, we should be safe for a little while. Plus, they don't know the location of Mitchell and Annalee. That will buy us some time."

"Mom, they have cellphones. I bought them both one from a convenience store. I need to text Dad and Annalee to tell them not to reply to the guys. Let me do that quickly."

~

Raiden had called and spoken with Annalee before Galaxas could alert her. "Annalee, calm down. We're not part of the bad guys. Don't you think by now you all would have figured it out if we were?"

"I don't know. That vision has me creeped out. Galaxas would never have left Troid if she wasn't fearful for her life. How can you expect me to believe you when she doesn't believe you?"

"This is getting way too complicated. Annalee, all I can do is tell you what I know. The rest is up to you."

"Give me some time to think about it. I'm really confused."

"I understand. I love you. So much."

That killed her. Her head dropped and she whispered goodbye.

~

"Mom. Neither one of them is answering. I'm scared," Galaxas confessed.

"Your dad's probably sleeping and maybe Annalee turned her phone off or it went dead. Stop looking for the worse scenario. It won't ease our nerves."

"Mom, does Jagger have the ability to convert Dad and Annalee?"

"Can't say for sure, but I would have to say yes."

"In my opinion, that changes the urgency of the situation. We will have to go to them for their safety. And now."

"Hold on! Just hold on!" Nebulane said pushing her hands out. She thought for a moment. "Keeping them hidden has been the only security I have had through all of this. If we go around them, it compromises their safety posthaste. We have to think this through before responding."

"If Raiden gets in touch with Annalee before we do, then it's too late. They'll find her. Find the coordinates from her phone."

"That's a fair point. I'll try calling them and you try texting," Nebulane agreed.

"Nothing. They must both be in an area that has no service. It's always been hit or miss out there. I can't keep my eyes open. How about we take turns keeping watch through the night? Since you're wide awake, I'll sleep first. Wake me up in two or three hours. Keep trying to get ahold of them," Nebulane requested.

"That works."

Galaxas pushed and shoved things out of the way in the refrigerator trying to find her source of comfort: sour candy in any form. The more puckering, the better she liked it. She balled her hands into fists. No candy. No nothing. Did she want that cup of applesauce? Nope. She slammed the refrigerator door and sat in front of the T.V. Her phone chimed.

"Please let me explain. I found the glove and brought Raiden outside to discuss it before telling you and your mother. I was trying to lighten your burden. It's true," Troid tried convincing her.

The vision popped back into her mind. It always caused her whole body to change temperature. "Dummy. Turn off the phone before he finds us if it's not too late already. How does he expect me to believe him? In my vision I was caught off guard because I must have known the assailant. That makes total sense.

"But what if I'm wrong? What if he's telling the truth?"

She jumped off the couch and paced. Thought and paced. How dangerous it would be if he had been lying to her. It would be so easy to trick her by getting her to fall in love and distract his true intentions. He did, after all, help defeat the evil on their planet. If he were one of them, wouldn't he have fought with them; not against them? She had so many questions.

"I mean," she said still talking to herself, "he did make a complete turnabout in his actions. Maybe that was their plan. Sacrifice their own army because life means nothing to them. So maybe Jagger got to him during these past few days. That would account for the change in him."

A woe-is-me tune played in her subconscious. It's been three hours and boy could she use some sleep. She gently shook her mother. "Mom. Mom!"

"What? What's wrong?"

"Sorry. I'm just really frustrated, but I could use some sleep. Will you be okay, Mom?"

"Yes, yes, I will. Thanks for letting me sleep. Hey, did you get in touch with Mitchell and Annalee?" Nebulane asked frantically.

"Oh, no I didn't, but I turned my phone off because Troid sent me a text. I wasn't sure if he could use the phone, I bought him to find us."

"Wise decision. What did he have to say?"

"You know, he found the glove and wanted to talk with Raiden before telling us about it in order to protect us," Galaxas explained.

"If his attitude hadn't done a complete turnaround, I would believe him. I just can't get over how he was taking up for Jagger. That threw me off," Nebulane admitted.

"I know, Mom. We'll figure it out."

Raiden woke up the next morning and found Troid using advanced searching methods to find Galaxas.

"Any luck?"

Troid, being so discouraged, didn't even flinch when Raiden walked up behind him. "Nope, but I found a small glow. See right here." He pointed to the screen.

"Yes, I do. Do you think it is from Galaxas?"

"If it is, the glow is fading away. Do you think she doesn't love me anymore?"

"Time to have a serious conversation with my best friend." Raiden sat down next to him, and they faced each other.

"You're not looking at any of this from her point of view. She has grown up on Earth, unaware of our customs, and had a vision of someone choking the life out of her wearing the glove you had hidden in your pocket. I'd say she has every right to be uncertain about you, and everything relating to us.

"Nothing you say is going to change her mind right now. She is terrified for herself and her family. It's time you stop and think about her instead of yourself. This moping around stuff doesn't look well on you. I have never seen this side of you before and I don't like it. Let's think this through and do some praying. I suggest the latter first."

"You're absolutely right. That is the one thing I forgot about. The most important thing of all. Will you join me?" Troid hoped.

"Of course."

~

Galaxas sat outside on a porch chair. The air was crisp and clean. It was an overcast day and made it easier on her eyes. She froze. What is the snapping and crunching of ground covering she is hearing? Out of the trees stepped a mother deer and her baby. Not wanting to scare them off, she didn't move. It was adorable the way the mother licked her baby. The fawn was wiggling around and decided to frolic in the field. She could watch this all day. The mother kept eating while keeping an eye on the baby. Every few seconds her head jerked up in search of any predators, obviously, and then she would relax and continue eating.

The mother spotted Galaxas and took off running through the forest with the fawn right behind her. Galaxas decided to open the photo file on her phone and pulled up Troid's picture. Her eyes watered. A finger rubbed his face. She threw her head back and closed her eyes. *I miss him so much. How can I know if he is good or not? Lord above, I don't want to lose him. Please shield him and Raiden with your protection and goodness. And please give me insight.*

The screen door creaked open. Nebulane peeked her head out.

"Follow your heart, even if love takes you to the stars in the heavens or down into the depths of the sea. Reach beyond the stars," Nebulane said, just knowing in her mind Galaxas was daydreaming about Troid. "You okay?"

"What a dumb thing to ask. Why do people ask that question when they already know the answer?" Galaxas twisted her lips and didn't mean to glare.

"That is a stupid thing to ask. I'm at a loss of finding the right words to say to console you, Gal."

"Then don't say anything, Mom."

"Well, I will ask if you would like some waffles. I have pure maple syrup and I know you can't say no to that."

"You're right. How? I don't know, but I am hungry," Galaxas said as her stomach gurgled.

"Step this way, young lady. We need something that will put a smile on your beautiful face."

"I was wondering, Mom, is there a meaning to my name?" while devouring a huge bite of waffles, syrup dripping down her lips.

"Of course, Galaxas Anatola Cyrus Regalshade-Gaylord."

"Regalshade? You never mentioned that name."

"That is your father's surname. It means royal shadow. As you know we are God's eyes watching for evil presences in the stars. Betzalel means God's shadow. Surnames are given according to our status. So being heirs to the throne, Regalshade was fitting."

"Want to hear something funny?" Nebulane added.

"Sure, funny would be a nice touch right about now," Galaxas said with a plate of waffles barely touched.

"I can't wait for you to meet your aunt. She married a jolly good man. It never failed. Every time we got together, he would have us rolling in laughter. His surname is Laughingsnout. It means a long projecting and jolly nose. So, did he have a long, jolly nose you want to ask? Yes, hysterically so."

"Mom, do you have a picture?"

"Yes, I do." She scrolled through the pictures and found one of him and her sister. She passed the phone to Galaxas.

Galaxas snickered, laughed and snorted.

"Before we make too much fun of him, he is an absolute Godsend to our people. If you want to meet someone so good, caring and brave, this is your man. I love that guy."

"That's good to hear. I love that, Mom. Your sister is almost as beautiful as you are."

"Thank you. She is just as good and kind as her husband."

"Maybe on our next visit we will get to meet more of our family. Unfortunately, because of Jagger, we weren't able to visit anyone," Galaxas said disappointedly.

"Yes, that is true. So, what does the rest of my name mean?"

"Galaxas has to do with the galaxy. Anatola means dawn of shining sunset."

Galaxas' eyes blurred.

"Gal, what is it?"

"Troid has a phrase he uses many times. He always says

sunsets and dandelion kisses forever. Our hearts together form a sunset."

"How did I miss that? I have never witnessed anyone's glow looking like a sunset," Nebulane asked in contemplation.

"Guess it happens when we are feeling loads of love around each other."

"Of course it does. Now, back to your name meanings. Cyrus means heir to the throne." Nebulane got up and cleared the breakfast dishes. Galaxas pulled up Troid's picture again. She stared at that romantic dandelion and his sweet, love-filled expression. She stopped abruptly and did a double-take. A sunset appeared in the background of the dandelion picture. She never noticed that before. A tear slipped and a smile appeared. She just wanted to touch him, smell his manly fragrance. The thought sent tingles down her spine.

∾

"Raiden, come here!" Troid insisted.

"Sounds important. What is it?"

"Look at that glow. See the sunset colors?"

"Yes, I do," Raiden said with a hint of excitement.

"Those are the colors that Galaxas and my heart share when we aren't dealing with tension and anxiety. When we focus totally on each other, I have witnessed these colors. This has to be her."

"Truthfully, I've witnessed that being around you two. Are you positive you saw these colors?" Raiden asked.

"Yes, truthfully."

"Maybe we should head that way, Troid."

"I was thinking the same thing, but I don't want to frighten her more."

"You remain hidden and let me speak alone with her."

"I guess that could work, but she probably thinks I converted you to the dark side," Troid admitted in a discouraged voice.

"That may be true, but what do we have to lose?"

"The love of my life, that's what, but you're right. There is no other choice at this point and Jagger is close to finding us." Troid stood.

Making plans to leave, they didn't notice a person hiding behind a cluster of trees. A powerful burst of light came from the person's eyes.

Chapter Thirty-Seven

Troid had the starship on course in no time. The furious person in hiding incinerated the cluster of trees and spouted disturbing words. He was always just a minute too late. Now that he was on his own, this hunt was becoming harder and almost impossible because they moved around so much.

"I did warn Nebulane of the consequences of their actions. Tomorrow morning, she will pay dearly. Poor Earthlings." His diabolical laugh would send shivers up and down any nonhuman or human's spine.

The message in the sky said, "I warned you."

Galaxas and Nebulane looked up in the dark night sky. Always looking for a code or message. Galaxas grabbed her mother's wrist and gasped. "Mother!"

"Oh-my-goodness. I totally forgot about his evil plan. This stuff with Troid distracted me. Galaxas, there isn't a choice. I have to turn myself in before he commits these atrocities."

"No! That won't work and you know it. He wants all of us."

"I'm hoping by turning myself in it will buy us some time for you to make an entrance. You have that special gift."

"Again, no! Besides, I transferred my power to you and the guys. I don't know how long my power will work on you all. I wonder if we should test it. Besides, it's not enough power. We need Troid and Raiden. And you know that, too. It's a suicide mission, and I will not allow it."

"Please, then tell me your solution. We can't trust Troid and now have to question Raiden. I'm all ears."

Galaxas walked around in circles. She prayed silently. Next, she heard something at a fast speed and the sound of hydraulics.

"Mom, I think they're here."

"We can't run any longer. Grab that pendant and disappear. I'll speak with them, but first I'm sending Jagger a message. One way or the other, we are going to meet up with him tomorrow. We'll bring him here to this forest region. It's the safest place."

"Seems like no other choice. I'll be standing near." She was gone in a flash.

Nebulane sat on the porch swing and waited, hoping it would be Troid and Raiden, not Jagger. Nerves getting the best of her, she restlessly scanned the area for signs. Jagger wouldn't be foolish enough to walk out into the opening. That much she knew. With no other choice, she sat bravely waiting for what felt like hours.

Troid and Raiden walked out into the opening. They bowed.

Even though she was not visible, the sight of Troid caused Galaxas to hold her breath. The magnetic attraction was so powerful.

"Queen Nebulane, would you permit us to come closer and speak with you? My good friend here," he said patting the back of Raiden's shoulder, "was kind enough to explain how my mood swing has caused somewhat of a concern. We wish to clear up any confusion. Galaxas, I know you're here. My heart's glow is making that obvious."

"You may walk closer. That's close enough," Nebulane ordered.

"I beg your forgiveness for stirring up these fearful thoughts running through your minds. This has been a side of me that I never saw before. I promise both of you that I will never allow myself to be corrupted or to be alone with Jagger. And this mopey mood of mine is something I will never let empower my thinking again."

"In all honesty, I have never found myself in a situation controlled by fear. Fear that I may lose Galaxas forever, whether because of my stupidity or by death. It was too much to bear and I guess I was trying to create an escape. Never in my wildest imagination did I ever expect to feel this degree of love."

"Galaxas, I can't get you out of my thoughts and I never will. If we cave to this fear, it may destroy our lives together. Think back to the happiness we felt being together. That kind of happiness can't be recaptured with anyone else."

"Queen Nebulane, I would never betray you or our planet. Since you need to protect Galaxas and our planet, I have taken that into consideration. That is why I found a way for you to speak with Zareb. It's the best I can do. So, without further ado, I will lay this device on the porch and back away. Press the button and you will be in direct contact with Zareb. Our technology has superior skills, and this device was created for these very circumstances. Please, speak with him yourself."

Galaxas wanted to run to him, hold him and feel his strong arms around her. Using caution, she waited. A strong ruler takes the necessary precautions for the good of everyone. The wind picked up and his hair blew around his masculine face. A fragrance from wildflowers and trees drifted by with the mild gusts of wind. The butterflies flitting from flower to flower must have been tickling her beforehand, because her heart fluttered whenever their wings fluttered. She squeezed her arms enjoying the sensation.

Nebulane pushed the button. Zareb answered immediately. They spoke for minutes, but then she walked around the corner of the house to speak in private. There was a special secret between them that only they knew about. It was created for this purpose and for when the time came to use it.

She held a hand up to the guys to make sure they didn't follow her. Within minutes she reappeared. Standing silent, looking at the ground in thought, Troid and Raiden stared at each other not knowing what to make of the moment.

"Please come forward. You, too, Galaxas." She appeared at

her mother's side, looking with hope towards Troid. He couldn't take his eyes off of her. As they approached, they bowed.

"Thanks, but living here for so long, I am just not used to the royal treatment. Please, while we are on this planet, I would just like to keep things simple. No more bowing."

"As you wish," Raiden responded. Troid and Galaxas were lost in each other's eyes.

"I feel so much better after speaking with Zareb. I will explain more of it to you, Galaxas, later. But for now, it's pretty obvious you two need some time together. Let's all go inside, and Raiden and I will make some lunch while you two talk things over.

"We have an urgent matter to discuss during lunch." Her stern face drew Galaxas' attention away from Troid momentarily.

"Yes, Mother. It is a discussion that involves all of us and far too important to ignore. I realize that."

"Good." Nebulane and Raiden escaped to the kitchen.

Troid gently took her hand. He closed his eyes and a sigh escaped, savoring the reunion. Still a little uncertain, she walked with him to the couch.

"I don't know how I could say this any plainer. Galaxas, you are the light and fire of my heart." He grabbed her hand and placed it on his heart. Do you feel the fire inside?"

"Oh my. It feels like you are on fire. It is almost too hot to touch. Does it hurt you?"

"What I think is happening is fear of losing you. My heart can't stand the thought. No, it only hurts mentally. You are what causes it to glow. Those sunset colors of your heart," he said pointing to her heart, "are my own personal sunsets. And to add to that, sunsets and dandelion kisses will be forever." His eyes were warm, sincere and pleading.

"Please never doubt that. The fear of losing you caused me mental and physical pain. Love hurts. Who knew? Not a fan of that," he finished saying.

"I guess that's why Nazareth made a song about it."

"Say what?"

She pulled up the song on her phone and played it. The first words were "love hurts."

His mouth dropped. "How about that. I have learned so much from this planet. We need to bring some of this passion back to our planet."

She smiled and shrugged her shoulders. Before long, they were back in each other's arms. Raiden walked out with peanut butter and jelly sandwiches and caught sight of them. "Aww man."

"What? I thought you'd be happy for us," Troid said with arched eyebrows.

"I am. Seeing you two together makes me miss Annalee. Now I see how you felt, Troid. Don't let me get all gloomy and stupid."

"I beg your pardon," he said, rising from the couch.

"Just relax you two. We have much bigger problems to address," Galaxas said holding an arm out in each of their directions.

"You're right, Galaxas. I haven't been able to eat much, and I am starved." Looking at Raiden, he added, "You and me, later," shaking his fist with a smile on his face.

Nebulane looked around and laughed to herself. It seems eating is the topic at hand, and she would need to wait until they were full before getting to the nitty gritty subject. She was always amazed by their appetite. It seemed they could eat five times more than a person from Earth and still not be full.

Galaxas pushed her chair back and leaned against it. "What I wouldn't do to hear one of Annalee's silly stories right about now."

Raiden bit his bottom lip and nodded in agreement.

"I know what you mean. Those silly stories have kept us in bouts of laughter ever since we've known her," Nebulane added.

"Did she tell you the story of her frog prince?" Galaxas asked Raiden.

"Nope. That's one she left out."

"When she was a little girl, she became infatuated with the

fairy tale of the *Princess and the Frog*. Do you know how many times I found her drenched at the creek nearby?"

Raiden cracked a smile and shook his head no.

"Too many to count. She tried to catch so many frogs, certain one of them would be her prince. One day she finally caught one and put it in a container with everything it needed to be happy. She ran right to my house with it and had us close my bedroom door.

"Look Galaxas. I found my 'prince'. I, being too sensible, told her she was crazy. She had said, 'Well, watch this'. She picked it up from the box and stared at it. Next, she kissed the top of its head as it squirmed and slipped out of her hands and down her shirt."

Galaxas fell back in a laughing bout, patting her chest. "Her body made moves that I have never seen before. When I finally stopped laughing, I helped get it out. My window was open without a screen, and it hopped out to freedom. She wouldn't believe me that it was a pretend story. Head lying on her arms, she sat at that window waiting for her frog prince to come to her that night. Truthfully, she didn't move from that spot all night. I found her asleep on the windowsill the next morning.

"Oh, the fun that girl gave me."

"Whatever happened with her belief that the frog would turn into a prince?" Troid asked.

She shook her head. "That silly girl said it wasn't the right frog and she continued hunting frogs for weeks until she finally gave up."

"That is too funny," Raiden interjected. "I just had the best idea. Can you get me a frog costume before we go back to her and Mitchell?" he asked Galaxas.

"Yeah, sure. I know what you're going to do with it."

"Yup, meet her frog prince."

They giggled for a moment.

"I hate to break up this happy occasion, but the sooner we deal with this urgent matter, the faster we can get back to them."

"I sense this may be dangerous what you're about to reveal," Troid responded.

"With a somber face, Nebulane replied. "Yes, I'm afraid so."

Chapter Thirty-Eight

True to their word, they waited deep within the forest for Jagger, hours from their home. It was still daylight and shadows of trees sculpted forest monsters with the ending sunlight. This time of day was less painful on the eyes. Galaxas flashed back to the day she killed Clayton and remembered the forest tree that shook her insides to jello. This setting was giving her the same apprehension as that day.

They all stood motionless, listening. Instead of the melodic sounds the critters of the forest made, the cacophony was adding more tension. Raiden opened his mouth to shush the obvious distressed critters, but Nebulane spoke up.

"He's late. He's never late."

"Mom, he's not late. He's watching us right now and planning his attack."

"Yes, I know. Just trying to ease the tension we all feel. Please, everyone pray silently. If ever we needed the good Lord's power on us, now is that time."

"Hello freak."

Galaxas turned into a statue. Everyone else looked around as Clayton walked out from behind a tree next to her. Troid's eyes were as bright as the sun at its peak time. His breathing was heavy. Raiden placed a hand on his chest to hold him back. "We won't let anything happen to her. Take some deep breaths so you'll be ready for what comes next."

Troid's eyes were so bright that the heat would melt any person or animal of Earth at just a foot away.

"Oh, look at that. More freaks. You're not alone after all."

"You're dead. I don't understand," Galaxas said sneering at him.

"Looks like someone doesn't know how much power your daddy has. Thank him for this miracle."

She made a scowling sound.

"It's impossible. What's going on?"

"We're all going to take a little trip to meet your father. He is waiting in an abandoned building."

The wind whistled through the trees, leaves rattling like a kite caught in a gust of wind. They looked around at the sudden chaos.

"Join hands, gang. We don't have a choice."

"I'm not letting him touch me, Mom."

"Very well. Go stand between Troid and Raiden." Troid looked tenderly in her eyes and gave a nod of comfort.

"Just tell us where we're going and I'll get us there," Nebulane said to Clayton.

"Yeah, no. Jagger gave me specific instructions to stay with you."

"Lead the way then."

In seconds they stood in the abandoned building. The building looked like something found in Greek history, like one of the historical ruins. It had an apteral design, favoring a temple with porticos at each end and no columns along the sides.

"What is this place?" Raiden asked.

"I think if you look around, you'll figure it out," Clayton ended with a freakish laugh.

They all moved around staying close to each other. Clayton stood just feet from Galaxas, not about to let her out of his sight.

In unison they all saw it. Clayton busted up with laughter. Blood stains filled a large platform area.

"How quaint. One of Jagger's sacrifice shrines," Nebulane blurted mockingly.

"Yes, and it's been used a lot lately." Clayton's expression would scare the evilest of people. "And you thought you won, Galaxas. Now it's my turn to repay your kindness."

"Over my dead body," Troid spit out.

"Oh, I think we can accommodate you on that. On all of you, come to think of it. But first, I think Galaxas, and I have unfinished business."

Jagger's voice boomed with power over the ruins. "Hold it! I want to give all of them a chance to repent to me. I am your new lord."

"You're wrong. That, you will never be. You shed the blood of the innocent," Nebulane expelled with hate.

"Silence. I hold the power. Those people died in honor. It may seem tragic to simple beings like yourselves, but for them, they earned a very special place in eternity.

"So, Zareb's son is to be your wedded man. Isn't that sweet? Now, you have one chance to repent to me or you, and your future husband, are first to die. I would love to watch the torture in your mother's face. After all, she did manage to hide you for quite a while. Well done, Neb."

"Don't you ever call me by that name again. That shortened version of my name belongs to my husband and him only, you viper."

"Did I hit a nerve? Just keep your mouth shut. Now, Galaxas, come up here and let's begin this transformation. All you have to do is look into my eyes. It's that easy."

He walked out in an opening. She saw the gloves in her vision just as Clayton walked up. She looked in shock at her mom because Clayton also had on the same gloves. Nebulane offered her a sympathetic smile.

"No thanks. I don't want anything to do with your evil ways. And my father, Mitchell, that's a man I admire. You make the guts of a fish smell like perfume." All of them were wearing extra-strength three-inch sunglasses.

"Clayton, bring that sniveling brat to me."

She glared at Clayton. His hands went around her neck, and he squeezed, harder and harder. She gasped, face turning red, then grayish colors.

"Clayton, stop! Do not disobey my command."

The look in Clayton's eyes was pure evil and pure contentment choking the life out of her. In an instant he was incinerated into tiny particles as Troid, Raiden and Nebulane held their sun pendants at him. This time his scream was final, like the real end of him. His eyes of fear disappeared in seconds. Galaxas covered her nose and mouth and coughed as the putrid odor vanished.

Jagger had transported to them just a little too late in order to save Clayton. It wasn't as though he cared one iota about him, but he was using him for backup.

They quickly glanced at him and Galaxas disappeared. Before his bulging eyes and mouth wide with inaudible screams could get control, she was shining a destructive light through his heart. Galaxas knew the element of surprise was their best defense. Nebulane and the guys gathered on the other three corners and used the sun pendant to help her.

He pleaded with them to stop. He glanced around with pleading, fearful eyes.

Jagger no longer held a proud and haughty expression. His eyes of terror stared at Nebulane, but she fought harder to rid the world of this evil man. Shortly, he was gone forever.

Galaxas appeared and fell onto the ground of cement. Exhausted mentally and physically. The three of them fell down next to her. All she could do was sob. She sobbed and sobbed and sobbed. Troid pulled her listless body into his arms and held her. He knew how hard it was for her to be a part of her father's destruction. He had done the exact thing to friends and family himself. It's not an easy thing to do, much less have the memory haunt you throughout life. But Troid's father always comforted him with scripture to make sense out of the bad times. He would help Galaxas deal with the pain. She could count on him.

"Everyone all right?" Galaxas asked.

No replies, but they did nod their heads.

"How about we take a ride in your starship and get back to the cabin to make plans to bring Mitchell and Annalee back?"

Music to their ears.

"First, I am going to burn that blood off the sacrifice platform. Those dear innocent children and adults deserve that," Galaxas insisted.

Taking a step forward, she froze. The three of them stood silent and waited for her vision to stop. She plopped back down on the ground of cement mixed with grass and weeds poking up through the cracks. She held hands in a praying position over her heavy heart and cried passionately. Troid walked up and bent down, gently placing his hand on her shoulder. She fell over against him.

"Do you want to talk about it?"

With the dorsal side of her hand, she wiped away the tears.

"All the sacrificed faces of the people, children and animals flashed through my mind. I saw each and every one of their faces. I lost track of how many people and animals. Troid, there were so many." Quiet sobs resumed.

He squeezed her shoulder and shed some tears himself. He helped to pull her up and escorted her to the platform. In two minutes, the blood was seared and gone. She just felt better. They rejoined Nebulane and Raiden and left for the cottage. The area gave them all an uneasy vibe. They kept glancing around as if someone would pop up and attack them. Galaxas' hands wouldn't quit shaking. Nebulane looked empty. Exhausted in every form.

Hours and hours of work went into notifying Zareb that Jagger was gone. Their planet rejoiced and prepared a festival of thanks that included an in-memory-of dedication to those who lost their lives.

At the cabin, Nebulane prepared a great dinner. They ate enthusiastically but they were all still on the mellow side. Finally able to think about all of it, it struck Galaxas odd how

Clayton was alive.

"Mom, how is it possible Clayton survived after I disintegrated him into nothing but embers?"

"There is no answer I can give you. None. How Jagger found out about him, I have no idea. I also have no idea how many more powers he received. With him gone, there will be no way to answer your question."

"I suppose you're right. Is it over? Is it all completely over?"

Galaxas' face of uncertainty brought sadness to their thoughts. From thinking she was a freak all this time to finding out she was an alien from another planet, and having to help destroy her father and grandfather, the mental anguish is more than she should have to bear. The only comfort they could provide her was their love. And there was plenty of that.

"Galaxas, I know just how to help cheer you up," Nebulane said with a smile. She waved a hand in front of Galaxas' face.

"I'm listening, Mom."

"Let's transport to Mitchell and Annalee. What a joyous surprise it will be."

"Now that's something that would cheer us all up. Let's go now. We can clean up later."

Troid pulled her up and they faced each other. When their eyes met, the tenderness caused her heart to glow.

"There's my sunset." He kissed her lips gently, then pulled a dandelion from under his shirt.

"And there's my dandelion kisses," she added. He pressed the dandelion all around her face.

After transporting, they stood in the shadows behind Annalee and Mitchell sitting at a bonfire. But they were still mentally and physically exhausted. What they really needed was sleep. Hours and hours of sleep.

Chapter Thirty-Nine

"Annalee, I don't know how much more of them being gone I can take. My heart is so heavy. I know what can ease the pain. Tell me one of your ridiculous stories."

"My heart is matching yours, Dad. But I have plenty of goofy stories to go around." She looked into the bonfire as she thought. Her face lit up. The fire crackled and added a sun kissed look to her cheeks.

"I have just the one." She turned and faced him with a kooky smile. Raiden started to head over to them when Nebulane placed a hand in front of him to hold him back.

"Let's hear her story first."

"When I was about twelve, my dad was at a tavern, as usual, and my mom sat on the couch drinking, as usual. A bottle in one hand and a cigarette in the other. 'Annalee, clean up this mess now! Did you start supper? You're about as worthless as this empty bottle,' she said throwing it against the wall with glass shards shattering around. I had to duck to keep myself safe.

"'Clean up that mess right now or you will be punished.' My mom was a pure delight to be around."

"So far this is not funny at all. You're making me feel worse," Mitchell admitted.

"Pull those britches up, buddy. I'm getting to that part, but I have to set up the scene."

Galaxas cracked up, holding a hand over her mouth so they couldn't hear. The others did likewise.

"How she didn't go deaf, I'll never know, but she turned the volume up so loud watching one of her soap operas, I had to cover my poor, aching ears. So, I cleaned up the mess as I was commanded to do. This stuff was a reoccurring nightmare in my life.

"Next thing I heard was a snorting and buzz saw. I made dinner. I fixed a pot of macaroni and cheese and then I fixed a bowl for myself before spitting in the rest of it. I stirred the saliva in real good.

"Yes, I was *Cinderella* in the flesh, just a plump version of her." Mitchell cracked up even though his insides were hurting for her.

"When my parents were somewhat decent, they allowed me to go to camp in the summer. That is what brought my scheming mind to come up with a plan. My mother was so drunk that she passed out for the night. After filling up a pot with very warm water, I placed her dangling hand in it and turned the T.V. to a station that played calming sounds."

Mitchell and the four of them covered their laughs knowing what was next.

Annalee wrinkled her nose and said, "First I smelled it and then I saw the yellow stain come through her duster."

Annalee's head fell back as she busted out in a laughing attack. Mitchell did the same. They both stopped and turned in the direction of the loud laughter coming from behind them. They jumped up so fast, Mitchell grabbed the bench to stop from falling. Still laughing, hugs and kisses, laughter, hugs and kisses continued.

"You have no idea how good it is to be around you two again. Gosh, I've missed you. You are just what the doctor ordered, Annalee. Thanks, doc," Galaxas said to Nebulane.

"It was my pleasure."

Raiden pulled Annalee aside and grabbed her hands. "I almost turned into Troid's gloomy self from missing you so much."

"Don't worry. I took his job over all by myself. I couldn't stand it anymore," she responded.

The fire was warming, spitting and crackling in harmonic order. The flames reflected in the couple's eyes. The flare dancing, swaying back and forth, making their thoughts match the magic in their eyes.

Troid came out of his trance and sniffed the air. "I don't know what that smell is, but it is divine."

Galaxas broke out in a smile knowing exactly what that smell was about. "Troid, you will just die when you taste a S'more. Prepare for death by chocolate and marshmallow. Two combinations that are a match made in heaven, just like the couples here. Now stick your nose up and take a big whiff, three times."

Galaxas chuckled as they all made the sniffing sound. "Now, put a marshmallow on these sticks and hold them in the fire. You want a mild burnt texture. Good. Here is a graham cracker and pieces of chocolate. Carefully push the marshmallow on it and close it up with another piece of graham cracker."

Raiden looked up with puckered lips. "Here you go. Try it again," she said to him.

"Okay, everyone ready?"

They all shook their heads yes. "Bite and savor the goodness."

With pleasurable faces they all formed their lips in an "O" shape and blew out a few times. Annalee fanning her mouth with her hand.

"Unbelievable!" Troid spoke.

"Never have I ever! Ever tasted something so heavenly," Raiden said almost seductively.

He and Troid gave each other a high five.

After everyone had calmed down and felt comfortable, they described the horrors of what they had to do and what they saw to Mitchell and Annalee. Annalee hugged her body while descriptions of Clayton and Jagger were described. Not understanding how Clayton could come back from the dead had her nerves in a frazzle. She couldn't squeeze the fear away if she tried.

Flames reflecting in her eyes, she asked, "If Clayton became alive again, what is to prevent him or Jagger from returning? How does that happen?"

Nebulane patted her knee. "Obviously, we have no answers, but there is no one left who could do such a thing. I'm ashamed to admit that I had no idea the kind of power Jagger acquired. Listen, all of you. We can't live by fear. That's just no way to live. Now, I think we should head back to North Carolina and then back to Florida."

"I can't leave yet. There's too much to discover in this site. We uncovered an unidentifiable dinosaur fossil. We can't stop now." In the process of finding archeologist finds, a dinosaur fossil laid in the same area.

"You're right, Mitchell. How inconsiderate of me to expect you to just drop everything. This is your profession, and I am so proud of you. How long do you think it will take to complete it?"

"Who knows? Could be years. I at least want to be a part of this before I hand it over to someone else. Can you give me a month?"

"Yes. And then you'll be discovering new things on our planet. We have some unique animals, insects, plants and trees. Our homes are unique as well. Did you know our planet has two moons?"

"I didn't know that, Mom," Galaxas spouted.

"You'll see. It makes for a spectacular view."

"Neb, how could you do this to me?" Mitchell asked.

"Do what?"

"Expose such curiosity in me."

"Sorry. But you won't be able to sleep once you get there. There is so much for you to explore."

"That's a deal. Now, you all go on and get out of here. We'll be together after a month for the rest of our lives," Mitchell urged.

"So, you want to keep Galaxas' house in Alaska and sell the others?" Mitchell asked.

"No. We'll figure it all out in time. That place needs a lot of maintenance."

"All right. I'm going to wrap things up until you return," Mitchell responded with sadness.

Sadness was inevitable. All together and now they had to say goodbye to Mitchell. But they did. Sometimes Nebulane would transport to visit him for a short while.

~

Galaxas ordered a package for Raiden. It came in the mail. Excitedly she handed it to him out of Annalee's sight. He and Annalee planned to sit outside on the porch swing.

"Go ahead. I'll be there in a minute," he assured Annalee.

She swung her legs back and forth like a five-year-old child. The door opened and she almost fell over in laughter. Galaxas, Troid and Nebulane watched from the window.

"Why are you dressed like that?" she asked with chuckles between the words.

He took her hand and got on one knee. "Because I am your Frog Prince. Now, would you be so kind as to kiss my head so I can get out of this ridiculous costume?"

Annalee looked at the window and formed a fist at Galaxas. They both laughed.

"I'm sorry Mr. Frog, but I already found the man of my dreams. You'll just have to remain a frog." She jumped up and acted like she was going back inside.

He grabbed her hand and said, "Oh no you don't. I will be kissed." His adorable smile gave her butterflies. Being Annalee, she acted like she was trying to catch something with a net.

"What in the world are you doing?"

"I'm trying to keep these butterflies all together. They feel so tingly inside of me."

"Save some for me because I feel them too. Now, where were we?"

She caved. She pulled him down and kissed the top of his head. He stripped the costume off quickly.

"You never have to hunt for a frog prince again. He's standing right here in front of you and for the rest of your life."

Her tender smile said all that was needed to say. "I think you guys need to create a blog and show men on Earth what a real macho man is like. You and Troid have all the qualities a girl would ever want in a man. I just can't believe you are mine. Who'd have thunk?"

"What's funny about that is that Troid and I feel the same way about you and Galaxas. I guess we were made for each other," Raiden added.

~

Galaxas and Annalee gave an appearance for their published books. It was a success. But now the most important matter at hand was the weddings. Troid was in contact with his planet to make arrangements. He and Galaxas would take a month and travel the planet for their honeymoon. He had lots to show her.

Raiden was in contact also with wedding preparations. But first, he wanted Annalee to expose more food surprises before they left. She and Mitchell had customized glasses waiting for them on the planet. She wasn't too keen about it.

"Raiden, I know I don't have a choice, but I will look goofy wearing those goggle glasses." He chuckled.

He kissed her forehead and smiled. "You won't have to wear them the whole time. Just when you feel the need to see." He broke out laughing at that remark.

She punched him in the arm. He rubbed it pretending it hurt. "I'm not wearing them at our wedding. No way. But, hey, there is something I need to speak with you about first."

The concerned look in her face almost caused hesitation.

"Will I like what you're going to say?"

"It's nothing to concern you. As much as I hate to, I need to tell my mother goodbye. It's the right thing to do. I set it up so proceeds from my book will go directly to her account."

"You're a special person. Do you know that?"

Pink highlighting her cheekbones she replied, "Who wouldn't care about their mother, even in my circumstances?"

His warm eyes expressed his thoughts. "Do you want me to come with you?"

"She won't be nice to you. Probably offend you because of the unnatural colors of your skin."

"They're natural in my world, but I'm tough enough. I think I can handle it."

"Okay. Let me handle the conversation with her. Just be prepared. It's not pretty. Are you okay with flying?"

His one eye and brow squinted. "Hello. I'm a master of flying."

"Yes, I forgot." She shook her head at him.

"Are you ready right now? Just hold my hand and we'll be there in minutes."

"Oh yeah, I forgot you can do that. Sure, let's get this over with. Raiden, seriously be prepared for the worst."

Chapter Forty

They stood at her mother's door. Annalee inhaled and exhaled several times. "Let me go in first."

The door was never locked. It creaked open making the sound of a haunted house door. The T.V. blasted at high volume. It was a pigsty. Her mother staggered into the living room unaware that Annalee was there, holding a glass of liquor.

"Hi Mom."

She dropped the glass on the stained carpet. One more stain wouldn't matter at this point. She used a few unpleasant words. "You could have given me a heart attack. Is that what you were hoping to do?"

"No. I just wanted to stop in and say hello. I'm moving far away. Far, far away and I wanted to say goodbye."

Her mother made a who-cares wave with her hand and dropped on the couch.

"Do you mind if I turn the T.V. off while we talk?"

Frustrated she answered. "Just get it over with. You look different."

"Yes, I guess I do. Have you been doing okay?"

"Sure. My daughter abandoned me, and I have to do everything by myself. You moving away is a good thing. I won't have to see that pouty face you always had."

Brushing off her ugliness, Annalee responded, "I'm getting

married." Her mom said nothing. Just produced her sour face as usual. "Try to be nice, Mom. Please." Again, her mother sneered.

Annalee opened the door and gave Raiden a here-we-go look. He winked and smiled. When they walked in, her mother pushed back against the couch with her arms pressing back. Her eyes grew wide.

"You're marrying a giant? Is he sick or something? That figures. That's all you could get, someone with a disease."

Her mean words made him want to punch her in the mouth. Being the good man he was, he just extended his hand and said, "I'm glad to meet you." She pushed away and made an even uglier sour face. He stood back up next to Annalee and held her hand.

"It's a skin condition, not a disease. He's as strong and healthy as a horse." Annalee looked tenderly into his eyes and replied, "And I get to marry him." Her mother rolled her eyes.

"Well Mom, I just wanted to drop in and say goodbye. Proceeds from my book will automatically go into your account." Her mom's face lit up. "I can see you're not in the mood for company, so I'll be on my way."

They turned and walked to the door, but Annalee stopped and looked back. "Mom, use some of that money to buy some clothes and go to our church. You need to socialize. The money won't always be there, so use it wisely."

Just before the door closed behind them, her mother remarked quietly, "I'm sorry, Annalee, for being such a bad mother." Tears dribbled down her face.

Annalee threw a hand over her mouth as tears dropped. She looked at Raiden and said, "Just a moment." She ran back to her mother and sat on the couch. She wrapped her arms around her and said, "It's okay, Mom. It's the alcohol talking, not you. Get help. Please. And go to church."

With tears streaming down her face, she said softly as she walked back to Raiden, "I love you, Mom." As the door closed, Annalee dropped her head and cried. Really cried. Raiden held her close, rubbing the hair on the top of her head.

"You couldn't hear it, but I could. She said she loves you, too."

He held her listless body. She cried buckets of tears from years of never hearing those three words. But now, she heard these words from the man she loves deeply. Healing was something she never expected to happen. Ever.

"I will make it a point to bring you back here as often as needed for you to check up on your mother. I promise."

She looked at him quizzically. "Never in my wildest dreams would I have thought about getting married to the most gorgeous alien in the world. An alien?" She shook her head. "I don't ever want to wake up from this dream."

"To show you I understand what you mean by that if you think about it, it's the same for me. I'm marrying an alien."

They both cracked up laughing so hard, they had to catch their breath.

Before leaving Earth, Troid took Galaxas to his special spot. He held hands over her eyes. He pulled them away and with excitement said, "Okay. Look."

Galaxas noticed that she was flanked with dandelions. She pulled her hands together under her chin and exhaled slowly. "This is breathtaking. I feel all warm inside. Thank you for showing me this. How did you find it?"

"I did some research and it led me here. At times when I thought I would lose you, either in death or by my stupid actions, I would transport here in the middle of the night. This place makes me feel all warm, as though you surrounded me. I have visited this spot many times, my little dandelion."

She cuddled up to him. In a few minutes she snapped a picture of them in an embrace surrounded by dandelions. "I wish we could take this to Betzalel."

"I will figure out how to grow them on our planet. They survive everywhere. Just like your life. Dandelions are your life story."

"And sunsets. Can't forget sunsets." She pulled up the picture of the dandelion with a sunset in the background.

Ah, yes. Those two go hand in hand. Sunsets and dandelion kisses."

Chapter Forty-One

The arrival to Betzalel was invigorating. Mitchell and Annalee held their stomachs to contain the butterflies inside. The reception was overwhelming. Mitchell was like a child in a toy store, checking everything out. The moment came that Annalee dreaded.

She held the glasses in her hand. Actually, they were incredibly cute compared to what Galaxas wore at home. Taking a deep breath, she placed them on her head. When she looked up, Raiden smiled ear to ear.

"Be honest."

"My beautiful girlfriend, you look amazing."

"Galaxas, I don't trust him. Tell me the truth."

"Talk about adorable. You look normal compared to what I had to live with."

"See," Annalee scorned Raiden. Then she jabbed Raiden in the stomach.

"Please follow me. It's time to meet my family. They kept out of sight so you wouldn't feel nervous."

"Nothing against them, but too late. I may just throw up. No kidding," she said holding a hand over her stomach.

"They know all about you and Mitchell. You know how confused I was about that movie, *Twilight*, or Moon something and how you characterized imprinting with my planet's customs?" Raiden asked.

She nodded while pressing down harder on her stomach.

"That's exactly what it is for us. Once our heart begins to glow for someone, the only thing that can separate us is death or if they become corrupted. My family has no choice but to accept you, and they are looking forward to meeting you. Please, don't worry so much. It's good. All good."

Annalee glanced back at Galaxas and crossed her fingers behind her back. Galaxas crossed hers as well. Sitting at a table was a huge amount of people. They jumped up when Raiden arrived. Endless hugs. "Everyone, please meet Annalee."

"She's pretty," yelled his eight-year-old brother.

Annalee blushed.

"It is so wonderful to meet you," his mother responded with a hug.

"Ah, yes. I see what you mean, son. My dear, we are so happy to invite you into our family," his dad replied.

A relieved sigh fell. They chatted, ate, laughed and just got to know each other. As normal, she had them laughing continuously. Raiden watched her with love and pride, realizing she was perfect. Absolutely perfect.

"Look Troid." He followed Galaxas' gaze and a happy smile formed. She teared up realizing how well it was going for her friend. They would always be together on the same planet. Her story was just as happy. She loved his family, and they loved her. It was time to turn in for the evening. Galaxas and Troid would be married in three days, and Raiden and Annalee in four.

"I was so nervous about meeting his family, I haven't had time to look at everything. Can you believe that?" Annalee asked Galaxas in the room.

"It was expected. Go look out the window at the sky. I thought I had imagined it when I was last here."

Annalee almost ran to the window, excited about the adventure that awaited her. She gasped.

"Gal. I wasn't expecting this to be so beautiful. Honestly, I was planning to be disappointed. The colors in the sky are breathtaking, and I thought the one moon was a reflection of the other moon, but it is two moons. So lovely. Are we allowed to take pictures? One day I hope to write another book and sketch these scenes in it."

"We have plenty of time for pictures. Besides, I'm quite certain their cameras will be designed for the best exposure."

"Of course. Are you nervous about the wedding?" Annalee asked.

"Do you know the meaning of 'duh'?"

"Behave you," Annalee said to her stomach. "How am I going to get through all of this without vomiting?"

"If you do get sick, I will not forgive you. It's the greatest love stories ever. There is nothing for your stomach to be sick about. Those jitters should be in anticipation of the second greatest day of your life," Galaxas scolded her affectionately.

"Maybe it's spaceship sickness travel. I mean, come on. There were some loopty loops a few times," Annalee expressed.

"You're right on about that. It didn't faze our guys."

"Maybe they're used to it."

"Yeah, that's true," Galaxas replied as she thought.

"Gal, I can't quit thinking about my mother. I did not see that coming. Words I never heard my whole life."

Galaxas smiled tenderly. "I'm so glad it happened. Glad she finally saw how special you are to us.

"Before I forget, come see our wedding gowns."

Annalee's mouth dropped. "Just try and stop me."

"Oh, Annalee. This is beyond any expectations I had. It looks like it is covered with miniature stars. Look how they twinkle."

"I'm officially amazed. We could become billionaires with designs and photographs from your planet."

"It's now our planet."

"Oh, wow! That just hit me," Annalee said with a face that had its own glow.

"Look at your gown," Galaxas said to her.

"Can this be real? Gal, this gown is out of this world." She held it up to her and twirled, stopping at the mirror. Galaxas did the same.

Troid told me that Raiden and you will do the same thing on your honeymoon, touring the planet, except you guys will travel in one direction and us the other way."

Later that day Troid and Galaxas took a walk among the gardens. "Wait until you see the chapel we are to be wed in. It is an architectural masterpiece created out of all the minerals of our planet. Ornate buttresses support the walls. The apse design takes your breath away."

"What is apse?"

"It's the area by the altar inside that is arched with a domed roof. When you walk into the portal, the grand entrance, your thoughts can't help but be overwhelmed by the grandeur. It has two steeples that sparkle like the stars themselves. The people of this planet got together, and we built it with our own hands. Telling you about it doesn't do it justice. This is where we'll be married. It is three magnificent stories, spacious and has even a room for food and gatherings."

"Could you take me there and show it to me?"

"No. We were given instructions to keep it secret until the morning of our wedding while they decorate it. Our custom is to not see each other until the wedding, and that begins now, my love."

"I don't think I can handle being away from you for three whole days." She laid her hand on his wrist.

"Nor I, my dandelion. Until we meet again." He pulled her in slowly to him. They stared for a few seconds into each other's eyes. His lips touched hers softly. She jilted from the sensation. The kiss deepened and she feared he would have to hold her up for a minute.

He backed away, hand slowly leaving her grasp. She hugged herself and went inside. She dug through her things and found the Bible. Lying inside of it was the dandelion he gave her at their first meeting. It was withered. She wanted to carry it as she walked down the aisle.

Galaxas plopped on the bed, mouth turning downward.

"Hey, why the long face?" Nebulane asked strolling in her room.

Galaxas held the dandelion up and it toppled over.

"What's this?"

"It's the first flower Troid gave me. I wanted to carry it down the aisle. He wasn't used to our customs on Earth. It was so darn sweet."

"That is sweet, but don't you fear. I knew all about that weed and potted some to bring here. I knew there was a sentimental meaning behind it. I saw you hold it many times when you thought he had been corrupted. A mother knows these things."

"Oh, Mom, thank you." She leaned over and hugged her.

"A little preparation is needed before you take that walk. This is nothing like weddings on Earth. We need Annalee to hear this too. Do you know where she is?"

"She was sitting outside on the coolest porch swing I have ever seen."

Nebulane rose up and glanced out the window. "I'll go get her. Come here first. Look at some of our birds."

"How utterly adorable. I have never seen anything like them."

"I'll be right back," Nebulane told Galaxas.

Galaxas continued to look outside. A man walked by pulling what looked like a horse, but yet it wasn't. It was magnificent.

A loud ruckus snapped her out of the stare, and she turned to see Annalee and her mother laughing up a storm. "Never mind. Just another one of your sister's crazy stories," Nebulane said before Galaxas had a chance to ask.

"Now, the weddings here are loud and full of laughter, singing, shouting and nonstop hugs and kisses. No princess on Earth has ever had a wedding as spectacular as our weddings. Prepare to be amazed and prepare to hear happy noise, loud instruments blasting and just an absolute joyous day."

"Even as we walk down the aisle?" Galaxas asked.

"Oh, yeah, but it is completely silent as the pastor performs the wedding ritual. Be prepared to be lifted off your feet all day long. The closest thing I can compare it to on Earth is a Jewish wedding, and only from the movies I have seen. But they seem to enjoy the whole occasion. Laughter should fill the day.

"We take this celebration seriously," Nebulane ended with.

"Thank you for telling us. I would have been in complete shock without knowing this," Annalee commented.

"Me, too," Galaxas agreed.

"Annalee, Troid was telling me about the chapel, and it sounds like a description from a fairy tale. I'm so excited."

"Me, too. I can't wait"

"Mom, where will we live?" Galaxas asked. Annalee leaned over interested in Nebulane's reply.

"Your first night as husband and wife will be in the wedding cottage. It is the most romantic setting, and you will not want to leave. It's stocked with everything you'll need. Then, when you come back from the honeymoon, you each have a section of this castle. You will absolutely have privacy."

"I've only seen this section of it, but from what I see here, my imagination would have never dreamed this up.

"On another note, I'm terribly scared about my wedding night," Galaxas added.

"Hhhh! me, too. I'm glad you brought this up," Annalee said rubbing her tummy.

"You poor dear. That nauseous feeling needs to end now. This is all happy. All good. As far as the wedding night, it is only going to be magic. As your mother, I want you to get rid of any fear. It will be the happiest time a husband and wife can share.

"Trust me."

"Thanks, Mom. I will. I just wish our wedding day was now," Annalee admitted.

"And girls, I want you to know what great men God chose for you. If I had to choose, they would have been at the top of my list."

"Do you think Raiden's family really likes me or are they putting up a front for his sake?"

"Rest assured, Annalee, they love you like their own daughter, sister, cousin, and etcetera. You have nothing to worry about," Nebulane reassured her.

"And, Mom, what about Troid's family?" Galaxas questioned.

"They picked you in their minds even before Troid knew you were the one for him."

"That makes me feel all sentimental inside."

"Good, now you both can sleep with peace on your minds."

"One more question, Mom. Was my father ever good?"

"Everyone loved and adored him. He was kind, sweet, strong, confident and the most gorgeous man on the planet. It's kind of like the story of Lucifer. God gave him exquisite beauty, a high-ranking position, great power, wisdom and influence, along with a free spirit.

"And you know the outcome. That's exactly what happened to your father. Your father was admired by one and all. He was a noble and humble ruler. It breaks my heart what became of him. All the horrible murders and crimes he committed; it was hard to tell him to seek God's forgiveness. He was a monster. Why should a monster get a chance of forgiveness? But I realized God doesn't think like us. If we could think like God, why would we need Him? I'm pretty sure he was forgiven in those last seconds as he stared at the sun pendant.

"Remember, all the horrible things we have done, God will wipe away our tears in heaven."

"Believe it or not, that does make me feel better."

Chapter Forty-Two

Galaxas and Annalee were only allowed to explore certain areas. the section of the castle and grounds in which they were staying. Preparations were out of their hands, so all they had left to do was hang around.

Mitchell, on the other hand, was constantly exploring and getting lost. Finally, Nebulane assigned one of her guards to accompany him so he wouldn't get lost.

Searching for her mother, Galaxas found her sitting in a corner crying. "Mother, what's wrong."

"It's nothing. Really. I don't want to upset you in any way during this special time. I'll be just fine. I promise."

But all she heard was sniffle, sniffle, and sniffle. "Mom, I won't move from this spot until you tell me what is going on. You no longer need to carry the weight of the world on your shoulders."

She laid her hand softly on Nebulane's hand. "Please share with me, Mom."

Licking her lips constantly, sniffling between them, she answered in shattered words. "I visited your brother's gravesite. It broke my heart." Her head dropped and like a rainstorm, the droplets fell.

"Oh, Mother. That had to be pure torture."

"After you return from the honeymoon, we'll visit it

together."

Feeling the sadness, Galaxas spoke as tears trailed down her cheeks. "I would like that very much."

"You probably don't know this, and it wouldn't be a good idea to bring it up until Troid does, but Jagger murdered his three-year-old sister, too. It took a lot of prayer and fasting to recover. Since he hasn't said anything about it, I'm guessing it still torments him."

"That makes me so sad. Poor Troid. Poor you. What Jagger put these people through, it's hard not to hate him, except sometimes I really hate him."

"Believe me, I understand. But always keep in mind that it was Satan inside of him. The real Jagger would never have done such things."

"That may be true, but even you said that he accepted the outcome of turning evil. He could have rejected it."

"And that's the part I try to forget. You know what, we need to focus on packing and having you ready for that special day. What do you think of the outfits they wear here?" Nebulane asked changing the subject purposely.

"Super cool, that's what."

Just that moment Annalee walked up wearing one of them.

"Well, does my butt still look toned?" She turned and stuck it up in the air for them to notice.

Like sent right from heaven, they laughed as though someone distributed laughing gas.

Raiden had searched for Troid, but nobody seemed to know where he was. Indirect sunlight beamed on a flower that was lying on the ground. It caught his attention. He bent down and picked it up. *I think I know where he is.*

He walked up quietly and laid a hand on Troid's shoulder.

Troid looked over at him with blurry eyes.

"Something told me you'd be here," Raiden said with sadness.

"I was telling Alula how she would have loved Galaxas."

"She was so intelligent for her age. What a sweet treasure she was to all of us," Raiden commented tearfully.

Troid patted Raiden's shoulder. "Thanks for being here for me, but I'm ready to leave. I want to enjoy my wedding day."

"How do you feel about it?" Raiden asked.

Dodging a few large rocks, Troid answered, "I wish it were today. I literally can't wait. Did you ever suspect love could feel like this?"

"Not on your life. I feel the exact same way."

"Let's make a pact that neither one of us will ever allow corruption to get to us or our planet. We need to do what it takes to make sure our planet and those we watch over will be protected," Troid said with seriousness.

Raiden extended his hand and Troid shook it. "Keep in mind, though, in the end days, we can't prevent it from happening to Earth."

"Well, we certainly have no right to feel proud. We allowed it to sneak onto our planet also," Troid replied disappointed.

"Two days to go and I'll be with Galaxas forever."

"Three days, I'll be with Annalee."

⁓

Music played loudly throughout the air. Laughter was strong and people were happy. After everything they've been through, the weddings and reunions were something to celebrate, and celebrate they did. Two days early.

Hearing the excitement in the air, excitement was building with anticipation for Galaxas and Annalee, also.

"What is this sinful breakfast we are eating," Annalee asked Nebulane?"

Watching Mitchell observing something with a magnifying glass outside of her window, she answered, "It is our version of crepes. The berries are called cerise bibies."

"I like them better than raspberries, and I love raspberries."

"Today, girls, is your spa day, but I get to enjoy it, too."

"So far, there is nothing I am missing from the luxuries of Earth," Annalee commented. "I have no need to go back there."

"I do," Galaxas interjected holding up an empty sour candy bag for them to see.

"Oh no you don't. Wait a second." Annalee scrolled through her phone and pulled up an entry from her note file. She handed the phone to Galaxas.

"You saved my life. Mom, who can we give this recipe to that would be able to make these? Annalee, let's open our own candy and pizza shop."

"Are you forgetting something, daughter?"

"Nope. Nothing is more important than this," Galaxas debated.

"I'm afraid there is. You have a planet to run."

Making an awkward face, Galaxas replied, "Oh, that. What about Annalee? Would you want to open one?"

"Sorry, but I plan on writing. That's my dream and I'm sticking to it."

"What about you, Mom? You'll need something to do."

"That hasn't been my dream, but we can always open a shop and hire people to run it."

"There you have it. The guys will forever be in your debt," Galaxas added.

"I was going to wait until your wedding day, Gal, but I have a gift for you." Annalee pulled a wrapped box out of the closet and handed it to her.

"It's not much, but I think you'll love it."

Galaxas opened it and smiled ear to ear. She grabbed pieces of sour candy and let them drop back into the box as if she were sifting through a treasure box. "You're the best."

"I have something for you, too." She went to the other side of the closet and brought out a wrapped box. "Here. It's not much either."

Annalee opened it and threw her head back and laughed. She copied Galaxas and dropped the chocolates from her hand like they were treasure, too. While she sifted through it, Galaxas walked back over and threw two huge bags of chips at her. Annalee loved sweet and salty and usually ate them together.

"My husband will be happy as well. Thanks, Gal."

～

Troid and Raiden weren't allowed to work or help with preparations either. They rode their all-terrain vehicles for a day of crazy fun. They were built for rugged, mountainous territory, to go on water and even to fly briefly. On the planet, the people learned to make use of the wind gusts that would pick them up and drop them back down blocks away. It was tricky, but once they figured it out, it was considered a thrill-seeker stunt. If not prepared or done right, it could cause bad injuries, and once in a while a fatality.

Technology made it possible for professionals to spot the activity and send out warnings beforehand. Like hurricanes on Earth, surfers would seek out the waves in advance of its arrival and is the same thing thrill seekers on this planet seek to do. They even created well-designed clothing for this activity alone.

Mud, stones and debris shot out behind a trail of dust as the guys drove with speed. Occasionally they would ignite the jet engine and fly over treacherous spots and then prepare the vehicles for a trip over some water.

It was a day of fun, and the best kind of distraction they found to beat the gloominess of not being able to be with the girls.

～

At the spa, eye masks coverings, faces covered in a soft, mild fragrant mud pack, Galaxas had a thought. The mud packs were silky and left a glow on their skin. They had the whole-body works being done. Wearing the eye mask brought about the thought.

"Annalee, you awake over there? I haven't heard a sound out of you, and for you, that's a concern."

"Are you insinuating I talk too much?"

"Yes."

"Just asking."

"Is this wonderful or what?"

"Gal, I almost feel ashamed for partaking in such luxury."

"Me, too. But this is for our special day, so I decided to enjoy the comfort for once in my life."

"Good point. It's not like we do this on a regular basis."

"Did I ever tell you what beautiful eyes Troid has?"

"What do you mean? Your eyes are like looking at the sun. What could be different with his eyes? I can't tell."

"How is it this never came up in discussion? We talk about everything," Galaxas said as eyes closed, body relaxed. "Well, anyway, we have the ability to look past the bright sunlight in each other's eyes. We have colors that you don't have on Earth. Troid's eyes are a mix of emerald and turquoise blue. They are so gorgeous.

"And Raiden's eyes are the color of mint green. So beautiful, too."

"Really! You really see that?"

"Yes, it's true."

"What color are your eyes?"

"A deep golden brown, emphasis on the gold."

"No kidding. I wish there was a way I could see that."

"Believe it or not, we are working on a way to improve your glasses so you can see just what we see."

Annalee clapped her hands. "Yay."

"You know what else?" Galaxas responded.

"I'm dying to know what else."

"Our people were never meant to travel to Earth. Because of what happened, it was necessary to keep Mom and me safe. That is the only reason we came to Earth."

"Not that I'm happy about the circumstances that led you to Earth, but I wouldn't have survived without you, my parents, Raiden and Troid. By the way, I really feel comfortable around Troid. I'm really glad you have someone like him."

"Vice versa. And you know what else?" Galaxas said with a

twinge of excitement. Annalee shrugged her shoulders. "I love how you refer to Mom and Dad as your parents. You have no idea how happy that makes me—makes us."

"Gee, thanks."

"Here we are, twenty-five years old, thinking we were doomed to a life of loneliness. Did you fall into ruination like I did?"

"You know I did," Annalee sighed.

"Annalee, let's let the past be gone and just celebrate the future."

Without looking over at Galaxas, she extended her hand. As it touched Galaxas' hand, they shook in agreement.

"Now, off to sleep land I go. Do not talk or my fist will contact your face," Annalee joked.

"As you wish." They enjoyed the whole day of pampering.

Spending their wedding eve in front of the television, watching the screen with a blank stare, bright and twinkling lights reflected on the screen from the window behind them, and they both followed the reflection with their eyes. Galaxas jumped up, grabbed Annalee's hand and pulled her to the window. In the sky the stars twinkled in two places in the shape of hearts. It was so bright and magical; all they could do was hold their hands over their hearts.

Chapter Forty-Three

The wedding day arrived.

Excitement buzzing in the air. Hymns, love songs and endless laughter could be heard everywhere. The time of the wedding would be when the sunlight was most bright, but always indirect light. This way Annalee wouldn't have to wear glasses.

It was time to put on the wedding dress. Nebulane and Annalee had to have their makeup reapplied a few times. A knock at the door saved the day. A messenger brought a gift for Galaxas. She read the note.

"Today, I will walk in your endless sunsets and dandelion kisses. I love you. Troid."

Galaxas held up the pendant. She had never seen anything like it. It was a small orb with sunset colors swirling around, as if it came from the sun itself. And, she had to squint, but a tiny dandelion rested in the splendor.

"Look at this." She held it up.

Nebulane and Annalee looked with awe.

"Mom, I didn't get him anything."

"And what could you have given him? He knows that. Giving him your love is all that man ever cared about. There is not a gift you could buy that would mean anything more than that."

"Well, he found something for me. I should have at least made an effort."

"When could you have done that?"

"Never fear, the doctor is here," Annalee said standing erect with her hands on her hips, giving the impression a cape blew out in the breeze.

Galaxas looked at Annalee with hope.

"I found some exquisite writing paper. Write him a note expressing how you weren't able to leave your surroundings until after the wedding, but to please accept your gift of love. There is no gift I could buy that would mean as much."

"You missed your calling in life, Annalee. This is a wonderful idea."

She carefully wrote the note in a beautiful calligraphy style. It read:

My husband to be. I wasn't able to leave my surroundings and shop for a gift. So I give you the gift of my undying love. There could never be a store-bought gift that would mean anything compared to my proclamation of love for you.

Troid, I never knew love could feel this fulfilling and this wonderful. I thank God for you and can't wait to spend the rest of my life with you.

I love you. I really love you.

This dandelion is pressing kisses all over your handsome face.

Galaxas

The note was given to a messenger to deliver. While Troid dressed, a knock came to the door. Raiden opened it and gave the note to Troid. He read it slowly. He held it to his heart and stood still for a moment. "She's right. There is no gift better than her proclamation of love. It's funny how I never expected those words to mean so much."

When he looked back over to Raiden, Raiden pointed to his face. He checked in the mirror and cleaned the yellow spots off before the wedding march. Then he attached the dandelion to be used as a boutonniere. He patted it gently.

Raiden patted his shoulder. "You ready? We need to make our entrance."

"I am so ready."

~

Galaxas heard the music change. They had their own wedding march and it built up much anticipation. Mitchell walked into the girl's dressing room. He threw his hand over his mouth embarrassed of the blubbering sounds. "I'm sorry, Gal. You look like a star. Did you fall out of the sky?"

"Oh, Dad, you're so sweet. Before any of this happened, I actually told God I must have fallen out of the sky. I knew I belonged up there with the other stars. There was always a longing to be with them."

"If I ever identify a new star, anomaly or something in the sky, I will name it after you. My own star," he commented with sentiment.

Nebulane was seated. Annalee and Raiden waited outside the entrance. Galaxas put her arm in Mitchell's and they took the walk. Annalee sparkled like her own star. Her dress was a light silver with sparkly gemstones. Raiden couldn't take his eyes off of her. He wore the best man's tux, but in Betzalel style. It was different than something found on Earth.

They were given the signal to walk. As they stepped on the runway of sparkles and flowers, something Annalee had never seen before, the people broke out in a boisterous cheer. It made Annalee and Raiden laugh.

Galaxas shared her final moments with Mitchell. "Dad, have

you ever seen a structure like this chapel? It's like it was modeled from a fairy tale."

"It blows my mind. It must have cost so, so much money."

"Not a dime. All the people built it together with their own hands. This chapel belongs to the people. Not to any one person."

"I love that. And I love you." He squeezed her arm.

"I love you, too, Dad." She smiled at him with tearful eyes of happiness.

"Ready, kiddo?"

"Ready, Dad."

The chapel was created with several openings to allow the air to breeze through it. When they turned the corner and stepped onto the runway, the gasps, the awes and the cheering was mind blowing. She held one dandelion, the stem decorated with gems and ribbons. Troid noticed it and his eyes became blurry. When he had found out that he had given her a weed, he was embarrassed, but couldn't help but notice it was the loveliest weed he'd ever seen.

One of those crazy gusts of wind lifted Galaxas right off the ground. She floated above everyone for a few seconds and mildly descended to the floor. Her dress looked like it was made up with the stars. It twinkled all the way down the train of the gown. It was beyond words or description.

She glanced up and finally made eye contact with Troid. His eyes lit up even more than normal. His smile was eager, proud, sentimental and excited.

With all the happy noises, trumpets blasting and instruments she had never heard or seen before, Galaxas couldn't help but laugh. Everyone was laughing. She stood below the platform of this majestic building. After formalities, Mitchell kissed her forehead for an extended amount of time, staring in her eyes before releasing her.

Troid walked down and took her hand. The electricity was so strong between them. They stood before the pastor. The place had turned completely silent. As the pastor spoke, they stared in each other's eyes. Their hearts were glowing like the sun itself.

"You may now kiss your bride. Please kiss your bride."

Aww oh my, gee whiz and any awe-inspiring gasps there ever were, was heard that very moment. It was as though the people could feel everything Troid and Galaxas were feeling.

The wind picked up again just as Troid and Galaxas walked down the runway, but they were too focused on each other to notice they were ascending above everyone. If they were outside the building, the gust of wind would have taken them through the air, but the structure of the building protected them from the whole force of it.

Annalee and Galaxas couldn't get over the dancing. It was so much more fun than what they were used to.

From the creation of the cake and the sensational flavors of all the food and pastries, it was a heavenly day. But now, it was time for the couple to go to their wedding cottage. Goodbyes, alone, took hours.

Galaxas looked at the vehicles in amazement. It was almost like watching *The Jetsons*. On occasion, the vehicles would fly over tricky areas and land back down on the roadways.

Troid lifted her in his arms and walked her through the cottage. She had never seen anything so enchanting. Her eyes were checking it out as he put her down.

"I gather you're pleased?"

"That doesn't describe my reaction. I have no words."

"Well, I do. I love you. My wife, my friend, my queen, my own sunset."

Her hand caressed his cheek. "You took the words right out of my mouth, except exchange wife for husband and king for queen."

The nervousness she felt had left the minute she walked on that runway. They spent an unforgettable evening of passion and unity. Any emotion there could be, all good and happy, they experienced it. After Raiden and Annalee's wedding tomorrow, they would be on the adventure of a lifetime. A honeymoon of adventure, and everything a person would ever want was at their fingertips.

~

Raiden and Annalee's wedding was almost a repeat performance. Since Troid and Galaxas were to rule, and soon, the people insisted the weddings be separate and the couples should celebrate their special day that way.

The only difference was the wedding gown, different foods and cake, and the excitement was for them and them alone. Galaxas wore the same bridesmaid dress that Annalee wore at her wedding. The laughter, tears, happiness and craziness were a repeat performance, as well.

As Troid and Galaxas walked down the aisle before the wedding couple, the people cheered as though they were at a football game. It was that noisy, but a very welcoming noisy.

Galaxas giggled as they walked down the aisle. Troid looked over feeling the vibration of her body shaking.

"What's so funny?"

"I can't quit thinking about Annalee's question just as I began to walk to the entrance. She turned around, stuck her butt up and asked, 'Can you tell my butt is toned in this gown'?"

Troid cracked up with her.

"I don't know what exercises you girls are doing, but keep them up, is all I can say." His eyebrows moved up and down several times. She punched him in the stomach.

It was a repeat performance for Mitchell as well. He was shocked how emotional he could become looking at Annalee after Galaxas' wedding. He was a blubbering mess.

"Dad," she emphasized slowly and with affectionate eyes, "you're going to make my makeup a mess. Before we make that walk, I just want you to know how special you and Nebulane, Mom, are to me. It's so odd how I really feel like I am your daughter. Thank you. Thank you for everything." Her eyes were a blurry mess, and sniffles were out of control.

He walked her back to the makeup vanity and gave her a moment. "I love you, kiddo, just like my own daughter. For the sake of anything, from now on I refer to you as my daughter, not just like my daughter, and Nebulane and I as your mother and father."

What was taking so long? Raiden, Troid and Galaxas glanced back and forth at each other. She shrugged her shoulders.

"Do you think she's having second thoughts?" Raiden asked twiddling his fingers. My, but he was handsome. "I mean, she is making a complete life change. That has to be overwhelming."

"That can't be it. Just give it a minute," Galaxas encouraged him.

Even the crowd had quieted down.

Raiden's dad peeked inside her dressing room. "Is something wrong?" he asked Mitchell.

"No, No! We just had a tender moment between us, and she needed to touch up her makeup. She's ready."

Raiden's dad had their version of the wedding march start again. The crowd became so loud with cheering and laughter that some of the people covered their ears.

Raiden looked at Troid and exhaled a relieved sigh.

To lighten the mood Annalee told Mitchell a joke before making that turn down the aisle.

"I said to the mirror, 'Mirror, mirror on the wall, who is the fairest of them all?' And you know what it said?"

Mitchell shrugged his shoulders.

"Give up. Just give up, Annalee." They busted up.

How she could be as breathtaking as Galaxas, who knew, but she was.

These two weddings were the most romantic, happy, and fulfilling weddings these people were a part of in so many years. Now that they had their freedom back, the weddings were celebrated for many reasons.

The day was a success, and it was now time for the wedding couple to leave.

Galaxas and Annalee embraced for minutes, tears of happiness slipping from their tender eyes. Same as with Mitchell and Nebulane. They would be separated for a month.

Just before Annalee climbed in a vehicle that looked like some Sci-Fi special effects, she turned around, stuck her butt up in the air and said, "Gal, does my butt still look toned in these loose-fitting clothes?" She was serious this time.

Galaxas responded like any normal person. She shoved her in the car, shaking her head.

As Troid and Galaxas walked to their vehicle, he held the door for her to enter the vehicle. Then he drove her to a special spot. She jumped out of the vehicle and became speechless. Finally, she spoke. "How did you do this?"

"With the help of your mother and some smart botanists here on our planet." They stood in a dandelion meadow. He stopped and turned her around. Her heart was glowing with sunset colors, and his did the same. She looked warmly into her husband's eyes. Eyes that said how blessed she is to have him as her husband, how much she adored and loved him.

He pointed to her heart, she followed it and pointed back to his heart. "When people of Earth stare at the beautiful sunset, they have no idea it comes from true love. I get to live in your sunsets and dandelion kisses forever."

"I feel that way, too," she responded almost too emotional to speak.

Behind them, a sunset appeared, so magnificently. Something their planet had never experienced until now. Something their planet would experience from now on.

Don't miss out on your next favorite book!
Join the Melange Books mailing list at
www.melange-books.com/mail.html

∽

THANK YOU FOR READING

∽

Did you enjoy this book?

We invite you to leave a review at your favorite book site, such as
Goodreads, Amazon, Barnes & Noble, etc.

DID YOU KNOW THAT LEAVING A REVIEW...

- Helps other readers find books they may enjoy.
- Gives you a chance to let your voice be heard.
- Gives authors recognition for their hard work.
- Doesn't have to be long. A sentence or two about why
  you liked the book will do.

About the Author

Linda Phillips lives in S.W. Florida with her two cats, Sprinkle and Skittle. Imagination is an essential component in reading and writing. Life can be hard, but a little imagination can give us wings and determination. Three children and eight grandchildren is a gift from God. Because she loves the color pink, she drives a firefighter pink Mini Cooper that keeps her late husband's thoughts with her everywhere she drives, and plenty of pink accents are found in her house. Writing first began as a way of therapy. Now, God keeps filling her imagination with more stories, and His influence is in each story. So, be on the lookout for other stories in the near future.

lindalouphillips.com

facebook.com/LindaLPhillipsAuthor

linkedin.com/in/linda-phillips-61347270

Also by Linda Phillips
WITH SATIN ROMANCE

Novels

Marry Christmas

Chocolate, Chimpanzees & Court Reporter at Chute Pond

Follow Your Heart
(A Stand Alone Fantasy Romance Series)

Moon Water

Dew of Heaven

Sunsets & Dandelion Kisses